Erle Stanley Gardner and The Murder Room

>>> This title is part of The Murder Room, our series dedicated to making available out-of-print or hard-to-find titles by classic crime writers.

Crime fiction has always held up a mirror to society. The Victorians were fascinated by sensational murder and the emerging science of detection; now we are obsessed with the forensic detail of violent death. And no other genre has so captivated and enthralled readers.

Vast troves of classic crime writing have for a long time been unavailable to all but the most dedicated frequenters of second-hand bookshops. The advent of digital publishing means that we are now able to bring you the backlists of a huge range of titles by classic and contemporary crime writers, some of which have been out of print for decades.

From the genteel amateur private eyes of the Golden Age and the femmes fatales of pulp fiction, to the morally ambiguous hard-boiled detectives of mid twentieth-century America and their descendants who walk our twenty-first century streets, The Murder Room has it all. >>>

The Murder Room
Where Criminal Minds Meet

themurderroom.com

T0352524

Erle Stanley Gardner (1889–1970)

Born in Malden, Massachusetts, Erle Stanley Gardner left school in 1909 and attended Valparaiso University School of Law in Indiana for just one month before he was suspended for focusing more on his hobby of boxing that his academic studies. Soon after, he settled in California, where he taught himself the law and passed the state bar exam in 1911. The practise of law never held much interest for him, however, apart from as it pertained to trial strategy, and in his spare time he began to write for the pulp magazines that gave Dashiell Hammett and Raymond Chandler their start. Not long after the publication of his first novel, *The Case of the Velvet Claws*, featuring Perry Mason, he gave up his legal practice to write full time. He had one daughter, Grace, with his first wife, Natalie, from whom he later separated. In 1968 Gardner married his long-term secretary, Agnes Jean Bethell, whom he professed to be the real 'Della Street', Perry Mason's sole (although unacknowledged) love interest. He was one of the most successful authors of all time and at the time of his death, in Temecula, California in 1970, is said to have had 135 million copies of his books in print in America alone.

By Erle Stanley Gardner
(titles below include only those
published in the Murder Room)

Perry Mason series

The Case of the Sulky Girl
  (1933)
The Case of the Baited Hook
  (1940)
The Case of the Borrowed
  Brunette (1946)
The Case of the Lonely
  Heiress (1948)
The Case of the Negligent
  Nymph (1950)
The Case of the Moth-Eaten
  Mink (1952)
The Case of the Glamorous
  Ghost (1955)
The Case of the Terrified
  Typist (1956)
The Case of the Gilded Lily
  (1956)
The Case of the Lucky Loser
  (1957)
The Case of the Long-Legged
  Models (1958)
The Case of the Deadly Toy
  (1959)
The Case of the Singing Skirt
  (1959)

The Case of the Duplicate
  Daughter (1960)
The Case of the Blonde
  Bonanza (1962)

Cool and Lam series

The Bigger They Come (1939)
Turn on the Heat (1940)
Gold Comes in Bricks (1940)
Spill the Jackpot (1941)
Double or Quits (1941)
Owls Don't Blink (1942)
Bats Fly at Dusk (1942)
Cats Prowl at Night (1943)
Crows Can't Count (1946)
Fools Die on Friday (1947)
Bedrooms Have Windows
  (1949)
Some Women Won't Wait (1953)
Beware the Curves (1956)
You Can Die Laughing (1957)
Some Slips Don't Show (1957)
The Count of Nine (1958)
Pass the Gravy (1959)
Kept Women Can't Quit (1960)
Bachelors Get Lonely (1961)
Shills Can't Count Chips (1961)

Try Anything Once (1962)
Fish or Cut Bait (1963)
Up For Grabs (1964)
Cut Thin to Win (1965)
Widows Wear Weeds (1966)
Traps Need Fresh Bait (1967)

Doug Selby D.A. series

The D.A. Calls it Murder (1937)
The D.A. Holds a Candle (1938)
The D.A. Draws a Circle (1939)
The D.A. Goes to Trial (1940)
The D.A. Cooks a Goose (1942)
The D.A. Calls a Turn (1944)
The D.A. Takes a Chance (1946)
The D.A. Breaks an Egg (1949)

Terry Clane series

Murder Up My Sleeve (1937)
The Case of the Backward
  Mule (1946)

Gramp Wiggins series

The Case of the Turning Tide
  (1941)
The Case of the Smoking
  Chimney (1943)

Two Clues (two novellas) (1947)

Cats Prowl at Night

Erle Stanley Gardner

An Orion book

Copyright © The Erle Stanley Gardner Trust 1943

The right of Erle Stanley Gardner to be identified as the author of this work has been asserted in accordance with the Copyright, Designs and Patents Act 1988.

This edition published by
The Orion Publishing Group Ltd
Orion House
5 Upper St Martin's Lane
London WC2H 9EA

An Hachette UK company
A CIP catalogue record for this book is available from the British Library

ISBN 978 1 4719 0890 3

www.orionbooks.co.uk

1 A DEVILISH PREDICAMENT

BERTHA COOL heaved her hundred and sixty-five pounds up out of the swivel chair and, walking around her desk, jerked open the door of her private office.

The sound of Elsie Brand's typewriter came clattering through the door. Bertha Cool stood in the doorway waiting for Elsie to look up from her work.

Elsie Brand finished the letter with a crescendo of speed, ripped the paper off the platen, laid it to one side, swooped down to the lower drawer of the desk for an envelope to address, then saw Bertha Cool in the doorway.

"Was there something you wanted, Mrs. Cool?"

"What are you writing?"

"Those letters to the lawyers."

"Quit it."

"Do you mean no more letters?"

"That's right. No more letters."

"Why I—I thought—"

"I know you did," Bertha Cool said, "and so did I. That's where we made a mistake. Those lawyers are counsel of record in personal injury cases. I thought we could write to solicit business—that there might be a missing witness or something."

Elsie Brand said, "But why not? I think it's a splendid idea. It gives you a chance to contact future clients who are in the big money, and—"

"That's just it," Bertha interrupted. "I'm tired of big money. Not the *money*," she added hastily, "but the strain and excitement that goes with that high-pressure stuff.

1

"I never used to get those big cases. I ran a quiet, cozy little detective agency specializing in the type of work other agencies wouldn't take. Mostly divorce stuff. Then Donald Lam walked into the office, got me to give him a job, and weaseled his way into a partnership. It wasn't thirty minutes after he'd started working here before the whole business changed. My income went up and my blood pressure went up with it. At the end of the year, the government is going to take away fifty per cent of the income, but nobody's going to take away half of the blood pressure. . . . The hell with it. Now Donald's on vacation, I'm going to run the business my own way."

Bertha glowered belligerently at Elsie Brand as though expecting an argument.

Elsie Brand silently opened a drawer in the desk, dropped the list of lawyers Bertha had culled from the court records into the drawer, scooped up a pile of letters some two inches thick, and said, "How about the letters I've already written? Do you want to send them?"

Bertha said, "Tear 'em up, throw 'em in the wastebasket. . . . No, wait a minute. Damn it, it's cost me money to have those letters written—stationery, time, wear-and-tear on the typewriter. . . . All right, Elsie, we'll use them. Bring 'em in and I'll sign 'em—but we won't send out any more."

Bertha turned, stalked back into her private office, plumped her heavily muscled, competent frame down into the swivel chair, and cleared away a place in front of her on the blotter so she could sign the letters Elsie Brand brought in.

Elsie laid the letters down on the desk, stood beside Mrs. Cool, blotting each letter as Bertha Cool signed it. Bending methodically back and forth, watching the open door, she said suddenly, "A man just came into the reception room."

"What's he like?" Bertha asked. "Damn it, I've spoiled that one. I can't talk and write at the same time."

Elsie said, "Shall I see what he wants?"

"Yes. Close the door."

Elsie closed the door behind her as she entered the reception room. Bertha Cool resumed signing the letters, blotting the signatures carefully, glancing up at intervals toward the door which opened into the reception room.

Bertha was down to the last few letters when Elsie Brand re-entered, carefully closing the door behind her.

"What's his name?" Bertha asked.

"Everett Belder."

"What's he want?"

"Donald Lam."

"Tell him Donald was in Europe?"

"Yes. I told him that you were Donald's partner. I think if I tell him you'll be able to see him right away, he'll talk with you. But he's disappointed about not finding Donald."

"What's he look like?" Bertha asked.

"Around thirty-five, tall, high cheekbones, hair sort of reddish. He has nice eyes, only they look worried. He's a sales engineer."

"Money?"

"I'd say—some. He makes that sort of an impression."

"Much?"

"Medium. He's wearing a very fine overcoat."

"All right," Bertha said. "Get him in. I'll find out what he wants. If he's a friend of Donald Lam, he's probably a wild-eyed gambler. He may be a— What are you standing there staring at me for?"

"I was waiting for you to finish."

"The hell with that polite stuff. When a potential client who looks as if he had money is waiting in the office, don't let politeness interfere with efficiency. Get him in here."

Elsie quickly opened the door, said, "Mrs. Cool, *the senior partner,* will be able to give you a few minutes right away— if you'll step in this way, please."

Bertha once more devoted herself to signing letters. Not until she had finished and blotted the last signature did she look up, then her glance was for Elsie.

"Elsie, get this bunch of letters in the mail."

"Yes, Mrs. Cool."

"Be sure every one of those envelopes is marked: 'Personal and confidential.' "

"Yes, Mrs. Cool."

"See the envelopes are securely sealed."

"Yes, Mrs. Cool."

Bertha swiveled her eyes around to the tall man. "So your

3

name's Belder?"

He widened an expressive mouth into a smile. "That's right, Mrs. Cool." He extended his hand across the desk. "Everett G. Belder."

Bertha gave him an unenthusiastic hand, said, "You wanted to see Donald. He's in Europe, on vacation."

"So your secretary told me. That's indeed a shock."

"Know Donald?"

"Only by reputation. A man for whom Lam once handled a case told me about him. Said he was the nerviest little guy he'd ever seen; that he was fast thinking, quick moving, and courageous. In fact, he summarized his feelings by a colloquialism which, while perhaps coarse, nevertheless conveyed a perfect picture."

"What did he say?"

"It's a bit on the coarse side, Mrs. Cool. I wasn't going to repeat it. I—"

Bertha Cool said irritably, "Do you think *you* know any words I don't? What did he say?"

"He said Donald was a combination of brains and guts."

"Humph!" Bertha said, then after a moment added somewhat irritably, "Well, he isn't here. Do you want to tell me what it's all about?"

"You're his partner?"

"Yes."

Everett Belder studied her as he would a new automobile he contemplated buying.

Bertha said, "You don't have to marry me, you know. If you have something on your mind, spill it; if you haven't, get the hell out of here and let me get caught up on some of this work."

"I had hardly contemplated hiring a female investigator."

"All right, then, don't."

Bertha Cool reached for the telephone.

"On the other hand, you impress me as being just the type to get results."

"Make up your mind."

"Mrs. Cool, do you ever take cases on a contingency basis?"

"No."

Belder moved uneasily in the chair.

4

"Mrs. Cool, I'm a sales engineer. I've been under a lot of expense, and—"

"What's a sales engineer?" Bertha interrupted.

He smiled then. "In my case, just a good salesman with a lot of nerve, and enough dough to see him through until pay day without asking for an advance."

"I get you. What's your trouble?"

Belder became uneasy once more. "Mrs. Cool, I'm in the very devil of a predicament. I don't know what to do, where to turn. Every move I make seems blocked. I've racked my brain over—"

"Don't get steamed up about it," Bertha said reassuringly. "Lots of the people who come in here are like that. Go ahead, open up. Get it off your chest."

"Mrs. Cool, do you ever do any collection work?"

"What sort of collections?"

"Bad bills—judgments—things like that?"

"No."

"May I ask why?"

"There's no money in it."

Belder shifted his position in the chair once more. "Suppose I were to show you where there was a judgment of more than twenty thousand dollars to be collected, guaranteed that you'd be paid for the time you put in, and on top of that gave you a bonus if you did a satisfactory job."

Bertha's eyes showed interest. "Who's the twenty-thousand-dollar judgment against?" she asked.

Belder said, "Let's express it this way. A has a judgment against B. B is judgment-proof, then C gets—"

Bertha held up her hand. "Stop right there. I'm not interested in this ABC stuff. I have too damn many alphabetical headaches right now. If you have something you want to say, say it."

Belder said, "It is very difficult to put into words, Mrs. Cool."

"Then you aren't much of a salesman."

He laughed nervously. "I want you to collect a judgment for twenty thousand dollars. You won't be able to collect all of the judgment. You'll compromise on a percentage basis and—"

"Who's the judgment against?" Bertha interrupted.

"Me."

"Do you mean you want to employ me to collect a judgment from you?"

"Yes."

"I don't get you."

"I'm judgment-proof."

Bertha said, with exasperation in her voice, "So that makes it very simple. You want me to collect a judgment from you because you're judgment-proof. . . . Oh, yes, just an ordinary, routine matter."

Belder's smile was apologetic. "You see, Mrs. Cool, years ago when there was lots of merchandise to be had and not a very brisk market, there was an excellent opportunity for salesmen who were up on their toes to clean up."

"Did you clean up?" Bertha asked curiously.

"I made a small fortune."

"Where is it now?"

"In my wife's name."

Bertha raised and lowered her lids rapidly, a sure sign of interest. Her eyes, hard and intent, held Belder as a moth is held on a collector's pin. "I think," she said with quiet emphasis, "that I'm beginning to see. Now suppose you tell me the whole business. Begin with the things you'd decided not to tell me. We'll save time that way."

Belder said, "I had a partner. A man by the name of Nunnely—George K. Nunnely. We didn't get along very well. I thought Nunnely was taking advantage of me. I still feel that he was, and always will. He was running the inside part of the business. I was on the outside. Unfortunately, I couldn't prove anything, but I decided to get even with him in my own way. Nunnely was smart. He hired lawyers and went to court. *He* could prove his case against *me*. *I* couldn't prove mine against *him*. He got a judgment for twenty thousand dollars.

"By that time the tide had turned and I wasn't making a thin dime. I couldn't have done very much no matter how hard I tried, so not having any current income, I—well, Mrs. Cool, I turned everything over to my wife; put everything in her name."

6

"Did Nunnely try to set the transfer aside?"

"Naturally. He claimed it was a transfer with intent to defraud creditors."

"When did you make it, after he got the judgment?"

"Oh, no. I was too smart for that. I don't think I'd better say very much about that angle, Mrs. Cool, because, of course, if Nunnely could establish even now that the real intent of the transfer was to defraud creditors— Well, let's just let it go as it is, Mrs. Cool. My wife has the property."

"And in court proceedings she had to swear it was her sole and separate property?"

"Yes."

"A gift from you?"

"Yes."

"What did you swear?"

"The same thing."

"What did the judge do?"

"Ruled that because I was engaged in a highly venturesome business, with periods when money came in quickly, followed by long periods when there was no income, that I not only had a right, but that it was my duty, to provide for my family, and that the intent with which I had made this particular transfer was to safeguard my wife from want."

Belder grinned. "It was a nice decision."

Bertha didn't grin. "How much?" she asked.

"Twenty thousand dollars plus interest and—"

"Not the judgment, the property."

"You mean that I turned over to my wife?"

"Yes."

"It was a—a considerable amount."

"I can find out by consulting the court records."

"Over sixty thousand dollars."

"You getting along all right with her?"

Bertha Cool's question evidently probed the end of a raw nerve. Belder jackknifed himself into a new position. "That's one of the things that's bothering me."

"What's the matter?"

"Oh, nothing—too much mother-in-law, I guess."

"Where does her mother live?"

"San Francisco."

"What's her name?"

"Mrs. Theresa Goldring."

"Any other children?"

"A daughter, Carlotta—rather a spoiled brat. She lives here in Los Angeles. She's worked as a secretary, but she doesn't hold jobs long. She's been staying with us the past few weeks."

"Your wife's sister, or half sister?"

"As a matter of fact, Mrs. Cool, she isn't related to my wife at all."

Bertha waited for him to explain that statement.

"She was adopted when she was a child. She never knew she was adopted until just recently—within the last few months."

"Older than your wife, or younger?"

"Quite a bit younger."

"All right, she knows she's adopted, so what?"

"She's trying to find out who her real mother and father are."

"Find out from whom?"

"From Mrs. Goldring and from my wife."

"They know?"

"I guess so—yes."

"And won't tell her?"

"No."

"Why?"

"They think it would—well, they think it's best to have things the way they are."

"How old is Carlotta?"

"Twenty-three."

"Your wife?"

"Thirty. But what I wanted to talk to you about, Mrs. Cool, was that judgment. All of this other stuff just—" Belder laughed apologetically, "well, it just crept in, Mrs. Cool—crept in casually."

"The hell it did," Bertha said. "I brought it in."

"Well, yes, I guess you did."

"And you want to settle Nunnely's judgment?"

"Yes."

"Why?"

"I want to get it off my mind."

"So you can get the money back out of your wife's control?"

"I—I'm not certain that— Well, there's my mother-in-law to consider."

"What's she got to do with it?"

"A lot."

"You mean your wife won't give it back?"

Belder squirmed around uneasily. "Mrs. Cool, you *do* have the most disconcerting habit of boring right in. I hadn't intended to tell you all this."

"What *did* you intend to tell me?"

"Simply this. George Nunnely is in a jam. He's been lifting money from another associate, and this time he wasn't clever enough, or else the other man was smarter than I was. Anyway, he's got Nunnely right where he wants him."

"What does that have to do with you?"

"Nunnely has to have twenty-five hundred dollars or he's going to the penitentiary. He has to have it within the next two or three days."

"And you want me to go to him?" Bertha asked.

"Yes."

"And dangle a sum of cold cash in front of his eyes?"

"That's right."

"To settle the judgment?"

"Yes."

"Do you think that he'll settle a twenty-thousand-dollar judgment for twenty-five hundred dollars?"

"I'm certain of it."

"Then why don't you ring him up and offer to settle?"

"That's the embarrassing part of it, Mrs. Cool."

"What is?"

"I'm not supposed to have any money. Don't you see, if *I* offered to make a settlement, it would be equivalent to an admission that I had money. My lawyer has warned me against that. I'm supposed to be flat broke."

"Are you?"

"Yes."

"Why not have your wife make an offer of settlement?"

Belder rubbed his fingers along the side of his chin. "Well,

9

you see, Mrs. Cool, there's a personal angle."

"I don't see," Bertha said crisply. "But I don't know as I need to. Any particular approach you want me to use?"

"I have the thing all blueprinted for you, Mrs. Cool."

"You don't need to blueprint it for me," Bertha said. "I've forgotten more about these things than you'll ever know. A judgment creditor hates to think the debtor is getting off too easy. If I tell him I can get him twenty-five hundred dollars as a settlement of a twenty-thousand-dollar judgment, no matter how badly he wants to settle, he'll feel you're getting off too easy; but if I tell him that I can get five thousand out of you, that I'm going to keep twenty-five hundred and give him twenty-five hundred, he'll be twice as apt to agree to it. In that way he thinks you'll be getting stuck for five thousand dollars cash."

Belder's eyes sparkled. "That's an excellent point, Mrs. Cool, an excellent point. I can see that you are a woman of experience and discernment."

Bertha brushed his praise to one side. Her chair creaked as she swiveled so that her hard, intense eyes were beating her client into a psychic submission.

"Now, then," she asked, "what's in it for *me?*"

2 SHORT BUT NOT SWEET

GEORGE K. NUNNELY'S SECRETARY had the unsure attitude which characterizes a new employee who is afraid of making a mistake.

"You have an appointment with Mr. Nunnely?" she asked.

Bertha Cool glared just long enough for the other woman's gnawing uncertainty to put her on the defensive. Then she said, "Tell Mr. Nunnely Mrs. Cool wants to see him about turning dubious assets into cold, hard cash. Hand him my card. Tell him I don't work unless I'm paid, but I don't ask pay unless I produce results. Think you've got that?"

The girl looked at the card. "You're—you're Mrs. Cool?"

"That's right."

"A private detective?"

"Yes."

"Just a moment."

The secretary was back within a matter of seconds. "Mr. Nunnely will see you."

Bertha sailed through the door which the secretary held open. The man at the desk didn't even look up. He signed a letter, blotted it, opened a drawer in the desk, dropped the letter into the drawer, took out a daybook, opened it, picked up a desk pen, made a notation. Every motion was calm and unhurried, yet there was no hesitation between separate acts. Each thing that he did flowed into a part of a perfect pattern of continuous work.

Bertha Cool watched him curiously.

It was nearly a minute before he methodically blotted the entry he had made in the daybook, closed it, carefully returned it to the drawer in the desk, closed the drawer with the same tempo which had characterized everything he had done since Bertha had entered the office, then raised his eyes and confronted Mrs. Cool with a perfectly calm expression of poker-faced politeness. "Good morning, Mrs. Cool. The message you gave my secretary was rather unusual. May I ask for an explanation?"

Under the cool, almost impersonal inspection of pale-green eyes, Bertha Cool found it, for a moment, a little difficult to carry out her plan of campaign. Then she twitched angrily as though shaking off the man's influence, and said, "I understand you need money."

"Don't we all?"

"You in particular."

"May I ask the source of your information?"

"A little bird."

"Am I expected to show interest or indignation?"

Bertha Cool's personality broke from its shell to rise superior to the man's cool detachment. "I don't give a damn what *you* do. I'm a sharpshooter. When business gets quiet with me, I go out and make business."

"Very interesting."

"I'll put my cards on the table. You've got a judgment against a man by the name of Belder. You haven't collected. You can't collect. You've had attorneys bleeding you white. They can't get to first base. I can't afford to split my take with a lawyer. I'm not going out and grab the gravy and then hand a percentage on a silver platter to some lawyer. I can't afford to. And when you do business with me, you can't afford to, either. Fire your lawyers, put yourself in a position where you can dèal with me without anybody else butting in, and I can make you some money."

"What's your proposition?"

"You've got a judgment for twenty thousand. You can't collect it. You never will collect it."

"That's a matter that is open to argument."

"Certainly it's open to argument. You and your lawyers argue one way and the other man and his lawyers argue the other. You keep paying your lawyers, he keeps paying his lawyers. What he pays isn't deducted from the twenty thousand he owes you and what you pay is water down the rat hole. You think you have a twenty-thousand-dollar asset, but so far it's simply been an opportunity to pay out lawyer's fees."

"A very interesting way of looking at the situation, Mrs. Cool. May I ask specifically what is your proposition?"

"You can't get the whole twenty thousand. But you could get some of it. I could settle that case if I had a free hand. You'll have to knock off some."

"How much?"

"A lot—and then I'll take my cut."

"I think not, Mrs. Cool."

"Think it over. As it is, it's costing you money. I can make Belder pay a sizable chunk of money. You get yours and the thing's all finished."

"How much can you get?"

"Five thousand."

Nunnely's eyes remained steadily fixed on Bertha Cool but he slowly lowered and raised his eyelids. There was no other trace of emotion or expression on his face. "Net to me?" he asked.

"Gross," Bertha said.

"Your cut?"

"Fifty per cent."

"Leaving me twenty-five hundred net?"

"Yes."

"I'm not interested."

Bertha Cool heaved herself up out of the chair. "You've got my card," she said. "Any time you change your mind, ring me up."

Nunnely said, "Wait a moment, Mrs. Cool. I should like to talk with you."

Bertha waded on past the deep-carpeted luxury of the office to the door, turned in the doorway, and delivered her parting shot. "I've said all I have to say. You could have said either of two things. You said no. There's nothing more to talk about. If you change your mind and want to say yes, call me."

"I want to ask you one question, Mrs. Cool. Did Mr. Belder send you to me? Are you representing him?"

"He wants to ask one question of twenty-five hundred bucks, cash!" Bertha said, and slammed the door behind her.

She sailed across the outer office, conscious of the curious eyes of the new secretary, jerked open the door into the corridor, tried to slam it behind her, and frowned with irritation as her pull on the knob was slowed down by an automatic door check.

3

A FRIEND AND WELL-WISHER

ELSIE BRAND said to Bertha Cool, "Your man's in again."

"Belder?"

"Yes."

"To hell with him. He can't haunt the office. I only made my proposition to Nunnely yesterday. Give the man time. Belder came to get a report yesterday. Then he came back—The hell with him. I'll go out and tell him where he gets off."

Bertha pushed back her swivel chair, strode across the office, jerked open the door to the reception room, and snapped, "Good morning."

Belder jumped to his feet. "Good morning, Mrs. Cool. I want to see you. I—"

"Now, listen," Bertha interrupted. "We've laid an egg. I'm sitting on it. You can't make an egg hatch any faster by sitting on it harder."

"I understand," Belder said, "but—"

"I know," Bertha interrupted angrily. "You're just like nine clients out of ten. You came here in the first place because you were worried. You thought I could help you. Then your go back home, start thinking about things, get worried all over again, and come up here to hang around and keep on talking things over.

"You wouldn't think of going to a doctor's office, getting a prescription, and then going back to haunt the doctor's office waiting for yourself to get well. My time's valuable. I haven't got—"

"But this is something else," Belder interrupted.

"What is?"

"What I want to see you about now."

"You mean something new?"

"Yes."

"What?"

"Trouble."

"More trouble?"

"I'll say it is."

Bertha stood to one side. "That's different. Come in."

Belder was fumbling around in the inside pocket of his coat before Bertha had the door closed. He produce a folded sheet of letter paper, handed it to Bertha. "Take a look at this," he said.

"What is it?"

"A letter."

"Sent to you?"

"To my wife."

Bertha didn't unfold the letter. She held it in her short, stubby fingers while her eyes regarded Belder with glittering concentration.

"Where did this come from?"

"I found it on the floor in the dining-room."

"When?"

"About half an hour ago."

"And why all the excitement?"

"You'll know when you've read it."

"You've read it?"

"Naturally."

"It was addressed to your wife?"

"Don't be silly. Show me any husband outside of the movies who would find a letter on the floor under such cir-cumstances and not open it up to see what it was. Lots of them wouldn't admit it but they'd all do it."

"Come through the mail?" Bertha asked.

"Yes."

"Where's the envelope?"

"I don't know. The envelope wasn't there."

"Then how did you know it came through the mail?"

"Read it and you'll see."

Bertha hesitated a moment, then unfolded the sheet of paper.

The message was typewritten—direct, simple, and to the point:

My dear Mrs. Belder:

Perhaps I shouldn't send you this letter, but I'm going to write it anyway; and then when I go out to dinner, I'll either drop it in the mailbox or the ashcan. Right now, I'm simply writing to get it off my chest.

You probably will never know the reason I am taking this interest in you. I guess you'll have to take me on trust, Mrs. Belder, and consider me an unknown friend.

You won't like what I am going to say to you, but it's better for you to know than to go on living in a fool's paradise.

Has it ever occurred to you that despite the fact domestic help is very difficult to get, you are able to keep a very attractive maid? I wonder if you've ever stopped to think why it is that Sally has been so willing to keep on working for you, despite the higher wages that are being paid in other fields. Why do you suppose she ever came to work for you in the first place? And have you ever noticed that she's a highly competent secretary? Perhaps you didn't know she took a first prize in both typing and shorthand at her business college five years ago. And after that she sold things—got an even better salary as a food demonstrator than as a secretary —and now this very attractive young woman shows up in your house—as a maid!

Why?

Could it be because there are other reasons which make the job so attractive she's willing to stay on, doing menial work?

Perhaps you had better ask Sally these questions—and when you ask her, ask her as though you already knew the answers. Don't ask her as though you were dubious, or merely suspicious; simply tell her to make a clean breast of things.

I think you will be surprised.

And that, Mrs. Belder, is all for this time, but if things turn out well, perhaps I can tell you a lot more.

I might even telephone you around eleven o'clock Wednes-

17

day morning—just to see if you've had your talk with Sally and what you've found out. And in case you have had your talk with Sally, and are willing to place confidence in me, it might be well for you to have your car waiting out in front, all ready to go places.

Doubtless you are surprised that a total stranger is taking such an interest in you, but despite the fact that you have never met me, your interests mean a lot to me.

You'd be very much surprised if you knew just how I fitted into the picture. Perhaps I can tell you sometime. You see, there are reasons why I'm very much interested in you.

The letter was signed simply, *An Anonymous Friend and Well-Wisher.*

Bertha peered up at Belder over the top of her spectacles. "How about it?" she asked.

"Mrs. Cool, I swear to you by all that's holy that—"

"Save that for your wife," Bertha said. "Give *me* the low-down. Never mind that swearing business."

"I tell you, Mrs. Cool, it's a dastardly, lying insinuation, a—"

"What's the insinuation?" Bertha asked.

"That the maid's in love with me, or I'm in love with her, or we're both in love, and that she got the job in order to be near me."

"Good-looking?" Bertha asked.

"Yes."

"Have you spoken to her about this letter?"

"No. I can't get in touch with her."

"Why not?"

"She isn't at the house. I don't know where she is. She was there last night. She's gone now."

"Does your wife know where she is?"

"I didn't ask her. She has her separate room and sleeps late. I thought I'd better talk with you before I said anything to her."

"What's the maid's name?"

"Sally."

"What's her other name?"

"For the life of me, Mrs. Cool, I couldn't tell you. It's something like Beggoner, or Bregner. I've been trying ever since I picked up that letter to think of her last name. I can't."

"How long has she been with you?"

"A couple of months."

"Did you know her before she came there?"

"Of course not."

"What did you do after you found this letter?"

"I read it, then I tiptoed out of the dining-room and went directly to the maid's room."

"Knock on the door?"

"Yes."

"Open it?"

"Yes."

"No one there?"

"No. The bed had been slept in."

"Then what?"

"Then I went down to the kitchen and looked around through the house. I couldn't find her anywhere in the place."

"Her day off?"

"No."

"You think she knows about this letter?"

"I don't know. I'm afraid that my wife got this letter and went directly to her, as the writer of the letter suggested. And Sally blew up and walked out in a rage. A maid doesn't have to put up with that sort of stuff these days, you know."

"Are *you* telling *me!*" Bertha said with feeling.

"What," Belder asked, "are we going to do? We've got to do something."

"For what reason?"

"To straighten this thing out."

"Perhaps Sally straightened it out," Bertha said. "Perhaps your wife took it up with her and found out she'd made a mistake and—"

"I'm afraid you don't know my wife," Belder said. "Once anything instills a suspicion in her mind, it takes days and days and days of explanation to get it out. For a long while, the more you explain the worse it gets. It's only after long repetition she begins to believe. She's a terribly suspicious woman. Just a little thing like this would drive her crazy. We won't be talking about anything else for weeks."

"Even if Sally leaves?"

19

"Of course. It's my guess she's left already."

Bertha looked at her watch. "It's after ten now. Think she'll get this telephone call?"

"Probably. She told me yesterday afternoon that I could have the car until eleven, that I must have it back to the house promptly at eleven, and to see there was plenty of gas in it."

"And you want me to do something in connection with this new matter?"

"Yes."

"What?"

"I want to trap the person who wrote that letter."

Bertha's eyes narrowed. "You want me to get rough?"

"Yes."

"Let's talk about the letter," Bertha said. "Who do you think wrote it?"

"I don't know."

Bertha Cool's quick motion brought a series of squeaks from the swivel chair. "Suppose there's any chance this mother-in-law of yours is it?"

"What do you mean?"

"The one who wrote the letter?"

A spasm of expression twisted Belder's face. "Of *course!* It's Theresa Goldring! How dumb I was not to have tumbled as soon as I picked up the letter. She's always hated me. She's picked on this time to try and hit below the belt. You can see what a sweet predicament I'd be in if she could manage to break things up between Mabel and me now."

Bertha frowningly studied the letter.

Belder went on. "And what a sweet spot it would leave Theresa in, if she could poison Mabel's mind against me. . . . Well, you understand the peculiar situation, Mrs. Cool. I put all of my property in my wife's name. I swore that it was a gift to her, as her sole and separate property. She swore to the same thing. The court found that that was right. Now then, if she pulls out and takes all of the property with her, I'm absolutely powerless."

"But she wouldn't turn it over to her mother, would she?" Bertha asked.

"Not all of it. But—"

"How does your wife get along with Carlotta?" Bertha asked, turning the folded sheet of paper over in her hand.

"Oh, they get along fine, except that of late Carlotta is brooding a lot over the fact that they won't tell her anything about her parents. She says she's old enough now to be free to decide what to do. She is, of course, reconciled to the idea that she probably never will know who her father was. She hopes to find her mother. She's a spoiled, lazy brat, this Carlotta."

"Her mother still living?"

"I think so. That's the rub. As I understand it, the mother has been moving heaven and earth to find out where her daughter is. Theresa doesn't look particularly brilliant, but don't make any mistake—she's a ruthless, savage fighter. She won't stop at anything. I understand she's put every obstacle she could in the woman's way."

"What woman?"

"The mother."

"Theresa Goldring keeps an eye on her, then?"

"I understand so."

"How?"

"I don't know. Through detectives, I think. Theresa is a smooth one."

"Got any money?"

"Some. And believe me, she wants more."

"How did she get her money?"

"Insurance when her husband passed away."

"Much?"

"Around twenty thousand. In place of putting that into sound investments and living on the income, Theresa has been splurging along, spending the money, buying herself everything she wanted, keeping herself well dressed and attractive. She has the idea she's still fascinating to men. She—"

"How old?"

"Around forty-eight."

"A lot of women have their most romantic affairs after they pass forty," Bertha said.

Belder added hastily, "Of course, Mrs. Cool, but they're the women who are genuine; who don't try to be something

21

they aren't. They're the wholehearted, understanding women. . . . Oh, you'd have to see Theresa to understand what I mean. She's around forty-eight and she has hypnotized herself into the belief she looks about thirty-two. She's still got a swell figure—I'll say that for her. She keeps her weight down but— Oh, the hell with her. It makes me sick to talk about her."

Bertha said, "You're going to keep on talking about her just the same. We've got to find out where she's connected with this letter. She has a stooge in it somewhere."

"How do you mean?"

"If your wife is called on the telephone, the voice of the person talking to her must be that of a stranger; and the person she meets must be a total stranger. A friend would simply ring up and say, 'Hello, Mabel. Don't quote me in this, but that husband of yours is on the loose again!' And her own mother could hardly ring her up and try to disguise her voice and say, 'Mrs. Belder, I'm a stranger to you but I—' Do you get me?"

"I get you," Belder said.

"Therefore," Bertha pointed out, "your mother-in-law has a stooge. Someone who's a stranger to your wife. She'll ring up, say, 'Mrs. Belder, I'm the one who wrote you that letter. Would you like to talk with me? . . . Well, I can't come to your house for certain obvious reasons, but if you'll meet me—etcetera, etcetera.' Do you get me?"

"I get you."

Bertha heaved herself wearily out of her chair. "Well, I guess I've got to go follow your wife, find out who she meets, shadow that person to Mrs. Goldring— Hell, it's going to be a chore."

Belder said, "Once you've done it, though, we can go to my wife and show her that her mother has been—"

"Don't be silly," Bertha interrupted. "Mrs. Goldring would say we were all liars and make her daughter believe her. No, we'll go to Mrs. Goldring then."

Belder said dubiously, "Theresa can be awfully hard."

Bertha's jaw pushed forward. "My God, man! If you think your mother-in-law's hard, wait until you see *me* in action. She's an amateur. I get *paid* for being hard."

4
THE VANISHING AUTO

THE FOG WAS LIFTING and the sun was beginning to break through as Everett Belder parked his wife's car in front of his house, glanced surreptitiously back to where Bertha Cool was ensconced in a parked automobile in the middle of the next block. He got out of the car, buttoned his overcoat, and reached up to adjust the brim of his hat, making a furtive signal out of the motion.

Bertha Cool, watching him through the windshield of the agency car, snorted and said disgustedly to herself, *Now what the hell does he think he's gaining by* that?"

Belder looked at his watch, glanced toward the house, reached through the open window in the left front door of the car, pressed his palm on the horn button, then walked briskly down the street.

Bertha Cool, settling herself in the car cushions with philosophic patience, lit a cigarette and waited, her shrewd little eyes taking in everything that went on.

There was but little automobile traffic on the quiet residential street. The main boulevard at which Belder was waiting for a downtown bus had enough activity to give forth a faint hum—not a continuous snarl but nevertheless a faintly audible noise of traffic.

A bus pulled in to the corner, stopped and let Belder aboard, and rolled on. The sun had not yet burned away the high fog clouds that had drifted in from the ocean, but the cloud bank was getting thin, with patches of blue sky beginning to appear.

Bertha Cool finished her cigarette. Her watch said that it

23

was ten minutes past eleven.

Once or twice during the next ten minutes, cars passed along the residential street. None of them seemed to have any business in the immediate locality and none of the drivers paid any attention to Bertha Cool.

At eleven twenty-two the door of the Belder house opened.

Bertha snapped on her ignition switch, pushed on the starter, gunned the motor into life, all the time studying her quarry—a woman who was walking toward the car with the quick steps of a person who is determined to reach some destination in a hurry. Beneath the distinctive plaid coat, Bertha could see that the woman had a good figure. She wore a close-fitting light-green hat, and Bertha had a glimpse of the oval of the smooth, youngish face, dark glasses, and a vivid red mouth. She was carrying a half-grown cat in the crook of her left arm, and the cat's tail was switching nervously back and forth.

The shadowing job was routine.

The other machine proceeded at ordinary driving speed, waited conservatively at crossings, faithfully observed all boulevard stops, but, somewhat to Bertha's surprise, didn't head for the downtown business district. Instead, the machine zigzagged off, hit Crenshaw Boulevard, and turned toward Inglewood. The cat, climbing up to the back of the front seat, made it possible for Bertha to keep the car spotted for a long distance ahead.

Diminished traffic which in one way made it easier to follow the car ahead also made it much more difficult to stay close behind without exciting suspicion. Had the driver ahead given any indication of being aware that she was being shadowed, Bertha would have closed the gap between the cars, preferring discovery to failure. As matters stood, however, Bertha loafed a comfortable distance behind and, for the moment, neglected the axiomatic rules which detectives have worked out for shadowing automobiles.

The signal at an important intersection a full block ahead flashed red. Bertha slowed down so that she could coast along at a relatively low speed, timing the signal so that— Sudden surprise snapped Bertha's left foot back and her right down on the throttle.

Mrs. Belder's car hadn't even paused at that red signal, nor had it speeded up. With the calm courage of sublime ignorance, the driver merely ignored the red signal and blithely continued on her way.

Bertha, charging up to the intersection, was met with a closed signal and a stream of cross traffic.

A quick, searching glance convinced Bertha no traffic cop was in the immediate vicinity. She snapped the car into second gear, watched her opportunity, and after the first rush had subsided, took advantage of an opening to shoot across the street to the accompaniment of screaming brakes, raucous horns, and some verbiage which, while it was intended to be scathing, bounced off Bertha's heedless ears like hailstones from a barn roof.

The car ahead now had a lead of a good hundred and fifty yards but was still dawdling along. Bertha, slamming her gearshift back into high, keeping a heavy foot on the throttle, swiftly shortened the lead to a hundred yards. Then her quarry turned left, making the turn with exasperating slowness, the driver giving a perfect full-arm signal.

Bertha came charging up to the intersection, glanced down a vacant street, lost time with her brakes.

It hardly seemed possible the car could have gained the other corner and disappeared, yet there seemed no other explanation. The driver must then have speeded up the car.

Bertha reached a swift decision. The car had turned either to the left or to the right at the next intersection. A turn to the left would mean that the car was doubling back; that would be the reaction of a driver who was trying to avoid a shadow, hardly compatible with her previously sedate course or the full-armed left-hand signal at the previous intersection. The logical thing, therefore, was a turn to the right.

Bertha, floorboarding the throttle, spun over to the left so that she would have more room for a screaming right turn at the intersection.

She felt the springs of the car sway as she slammed the machine into the turn.

Midway in the turn, Bertha jerked her head for a surprised glance over her shoulder, then she was fighting the brake and the steering wheel.

The car she wanted wasn't on the road ahead, all but precluding Bertha's theory of a right-hand turn, making it now seem possible the driver had discovered she was being followed.

Bertha had too much speed to make the left turn without bringing the car to a complete stop against the curb, backing it part way around, and then charging ahead.

The next intersection offered no more encouraging results than had the first; but the car *could* conceivably have made another left-hand turn. That would have brought it back to the boulevard.

Bertha swore under her breath.

It was an old trick, and a clever trick when you knew you were being followed, just to blunder along at a slow and even pace, give careful full-arm signals, trap the other car into a crowded intersection, and then loop the loop.

Back on the boulevard, driving as though she were a police official headed home for lunch five minutes later than usual, Bertha passed everything on the highway, only to realize, with that sickening feeling of futility that comes to a fisherman when the line suddenly goes dead, that her quarry had escaped her.

Just by way of checking up, Bertha went back to the place where she had first lost the automobile.

It was the seven-hundred block on North Harkington Avenue, a block of bungalows enjoying the luxury of spacious driveways leading to private garages.

Bertha carefully checked all of the driveways. They were deserted. The garage doors were all closed.

Bertha groped for a cigarette, accepted the situation with profane philosophy, and turned her automobile back toward the business district.

5

BELDER HAS VISITORS

EVERETT BELDER'S OFFICE was on the eleventh floor of the Rockaway Building. Bertha went up in the elevator, paused briefly before the door marked: EVERETT G. BELDER, *Sales Engineer—Entrance.* From behind the door came sounds of a typewriter being pounded with rapid rhythm, a speed and tempo that all but matched the expert touch of Elsie Brand herself.

Bertha opened the door.

A straight-backed, slim-waisted woman in the middle twenties looked up from the machine. Her fingers continued to pound at the keyboard as slate-gray eyes silently questioned Bertha Cool.

"Mr. Belder," Bertha said.

The secretary ceased typing. "May I have your name?"

"Mrs. Cool. He's expecting me. That is, he should be."

"Just a moment, please. Be seated, Mrs. Cool."

The secretary pushed back her chair, walked to the door of Belder's private office, went through the motions of a peremptory knocking, and immediately vanished through the door. Bertha Cool remained standing.

The secretary reappeared. "You may go in, Mrs. Cool."

Bertha heard the sound of a chair being pushed back, rapid steps on the floor—and Everett Belder stood beaming at her from the doorway. The lines of worry had been partially erased from his countenance by a shave and massage which left his skin smooth and pink. His nails were lustrous with a fresh manicure.

"Come in, Mrs. Cool. Come in. You're a fast worker. . . .

27

This is Imogene Dearborne—she knows who you are. I have no secrets from her. If you ever have any reports to make or want to get in touch with me when I'm not available, just give whatever information you have to Imogene. . . . But *do* come in."

Bertha Cool nodded and smiled politely at the secretary.

Imogene Dearborne lowered her eyelids. She had long dark lashes which curled up attractively and, when her lids were lowered, showed up to advantage against the smooth contour of her cheeks.

Bertha Cool regarded the demurely downcast eyes, said, "Humph!" and let Belder hold a chair for her.

Imogene Dearborne went out, closing the door behind her. Belder walked around behind the desk and settled himself in a huge polished walnut chair with dark-brown leather upholstery.

"I didn't expect you back so soon, Mrs. Cool."

"I didn't expect to be here myself."

"I understood you were going to follow my wife until she'd made a contact and then shadow that person. I trust nothing has interfered with those plans."

Bertha said, "I lost her."

Belder raised astonished eyebrows. "You *lost* her, Mrs. Cool?"

"That's right."

"But I made certain that you were on the job. That your car—"

"That part of it was all right," Bertha said. "I got on her tail but I couldn't stay there."

"But Mrs. Cool, surely— I should think it would have been absurdly easy. She certainly had no suspicion she was being followed."

"What makes you say that?"

"Because—well, I'm certain she didn't."

"I'm not half that certain, myself," Bertha said. "She either pulled a fast one, so damn fast that I still don't know exactly what it was, or else I'm the victim of a mighty peculiar series of coincidences."

Belder's voice showed distinct irritation. "In either event, Mrs. Cool, the result, I take it, is the same. We have lost all opportunity to bring this poison-pen letter home to Mrs. Goldring."

Bertha said crisply. "Let's see that letter again." Belder hesitated a moment, then took it from his pocket.

"Now, where's your file of personal letters?"

"I'm afraid I don't get the idea," Belder said.

"I want to check over your personal correspondence," Bertha told him. "I think you have a clue there."

"I'm afraid I don't understand."

Bertha said, "Most people don't know it, but typewriting is even more distinctive than handwriting. An expert can tell from the type face just what make and model of a typewriter was used to write any message. I can't go that far, but I'm pretty certain this letter was written on a portable typewriter. I have an idea I'll find a clue either in the personal correspondence you receive, or in some letter that Nunnely wrote you."

"He never wrote me. I'm telling you he made this demand out of a clear sky and then got judgment, and—"

"That judgment is predicated on some business dealings?"

"Yes."

"Dealings he claims were crooked?"

"Well—fraudulent. Just a dirty damn legal technicality which enabled him to claim fraud and that I was an involuntary trustee, or something of the sort for a fund which— However, if you want to see my personal correspondence, Mrs. Cool, we'll get it for you."

Belder pressed a button.

He waited for not more than two seconds, then the door from the reception office opened, and Imogene Dearborne said, with just the proper inflection of polite secretarial efficiency, "Yes, Mr. Belder?"

"Mrs. Cool wants to check over my personal correspondence. Please get the file."

"Yes, Mr. Belder."

Miss Dearborne left the door to the outer office open. Twenty seconds brought her back, a trimly efficient vision of neat lines and slender ankles. She placed a filing jacket well filled with correspondence on Everett Belder's desk with that exaggerated, impersonal efficiency with which some secretaries seek to impress visitors.

"Anything else?" she asked, making the words as close-clipped as the rattle of type bars against the platen of a typewriter.

"I think that will be all, Miss Dearborne."

"Yes, Mr. Belder."

She walked, rigid-hipped, back across the office and closed the door behind her.

Bertha Cool watched her go meditatively. "Puts it on a little too thick," she said.

Belder seemed puzzled. "What's that?"

"Just telling you," Bertha said. "When you've been around as much as I have— Oh, hell, let it go. I'm only getting paid for this letter job. How about the cat your wife had with her?"

"Did she take the cat with her?"

"Yes. Does she usually drag it around?"

"She has lately. He's with her all the time, except at night. You just can't keep him in at night. He loves to ride in automobiles. She's been taking him with her when she goes out."

"What's his name?"

"Whiskers. I wish she thought half as much of me as she does of that damned cat."

"Perhaps *he* thinks more of *her*."

Belder flushed. "After all, Mrs. Cool—"

"The hell with that stuff," Bertha said, puncturing his dignified rebuke before he had it completely formulated. "Let's see that file of personal correspondence."

Bertha helped herself to the file, and started looking through the letters. As she examined each letter, Belder, somewhat mollified, made comments. "This is a chap who wants me to go hunting with him. I was out with him a couple of years ago. He had a good time, I didn't. I did all the cooking and all the dishes. . . . This is a salesman who wants me to get him a job where there's a chance to really work up."

"Who's this?" Bertha asked, pouncing on a letter in feminine handwriting.

Everett Belder cleared his throat. "I didn't know that was in there."

"Who is it?"

"I don't think you'd be interested in that, Mrs. Cool. She really doesn't have anything to do—"

"Who is it?"

"Her name is Rosslyn."

"What's her first name?"

"Mamie."

"What does she mean starting this letter, 'Dear Sindbad'?"

Belder cleared his throat again. "Well, you see, Mrs. Cool, it's this way. Miss Rosslyn was a waitress in a San Francisco restaurant. She impressed me as having a great deal of ability. This, you understand, was two years ago—"

"Go on."

"I thought she could use her talents to better advantage. I was acquainted with some executives in San Francisco, and I got her a job, that's all."

"Still holding it?"

"Heavens, yes! She went right to the top."

"What's this 'Sindbad' stuff?"

He laughed. "I naturally saw something of her—in a business way, you understand, and she laughed at some of the stories I told her of sales technique, and the possibilities of turning buying resistance into enthusiasm. She—she told me I talked like Sindbad, the Sailor. She—"

A businesslike knock sounded on the outer door, which promptly opened. Imogene Dearborne stood on the threshold. "Mrs. Goldring is on the telephone," she said. "I told her you were in conference. She insists that she must speak with you."

"Oh, my God!" Belder said.

Bertha Cool watched him with an air of detached interest. "Going to talk with her?"

Belder looked pleadingly at his secretary. "Tell her that I'll have to call her back. Get a number where I can reach her. Tell her that I'm in a conference where I'm just on the point of signing a contract—a very important contract. . . . Do it up brown, Imogene, put it on thick."

"Yes, Mr. Belder. She asked where Mrs. Belder was."

Belder put his head in his hands and groaned. For a moment there was silence in the office, then Belder raised his head. "Hell, I don't know. Tell her I haven't been home since— Tell her to go jump in the lake, tell her to go fly a kite."

"Yes, Mr. Belder." She quietly closed the door.

Belder hesitated for a moment, then pushed back his chair, strode across the office, jerked open the door to the reception office. "Fix the telephone so I can listen in, Imogene."

"Yes, Mr. Belder."

Everett Belder leaned across Bertha Cool's chair. His long arm snatched up the telephone. He left the door to the reception office wide open.

Bertha could hear Imogene Dearborne's voice fairly oozing sweetness, saying, "He's *so* sorry that he can't talk with you right *now*, Mrs. Goldring. If you'll leave your number, he'll get in touch with you at the *first* available opportunity. . . . No, Mrs. Goldring, not at all. . . . No, it's a *most* important conference. He's *just* on the point of signing a contract with a manufacturer covering the distribution of a product in all of the territory west of the Rockies. . . . Yes, Mrs. Goldring. . . . Yes, I'll take the number. . . . *Thank* you, Mrs. Goldring. . . . Oh, yes. I'm to tell him Carlotta is with you. Thank you *very* much, Mrs. Goldring. Good-by. . . . What's that? . . . Why, he said he didn't know, in case she wasn't home. He hasn't been there since leaving for the office. . . . Yes, Mrs. Goldring. I'll tell him, yes. Thank you. *Good*-by."

The receiver clicked in the outer office. Belder dropped the desk telephone back into place and said, *"That's* a complication."

"Your mother-in-law?"

"Yes. I gather from what she said over the phone that she came in on the train just now. Mabel evidently knew she was coming, but said nothing to me about it. The train was late. Carlotta was there and waited. Mabel either wasn't there or else didn't wait. Her mother is sore—trying to find some way of blaming the whole thing on me."

Bertha said, "Your wife considered this eleven-o'clock telephone call a lot more important than meeting her mother."

"So it seems."

Bertha said almost meditatively, "I'm not so certain but what I'll have to revise my opinion of your mother-in-law," and then turned her attention once more to the file of correspondence.

"What's this?" Bertha asked abruptly.

Belder grinned as Bertha Cool picked up some dozen letters all clipped together with a big wire clip. On the top was a typewritten memo reading: *Looks as though you were on a sucker list. I.D.*

Belder laughed. "Miss Dearborne told me I was going to get into trouble on that. You know, you get a certain number of solicitations from charitable organizations. Starving foreigners, underprivileged children, all that sort of thing. A few months ago I got one that was so personal in its appeal, so touching, that I sent twenty-five dollars, and this deluge is the result."

Bertha Cool ran through the letters.

"They seem to be from different organizations."

"They are. But you can see Miss Dearborne's note at the top. Evidently they exchanged addresses. If you answer solicitations by mail from the Society for the Relief of the Starving Whosis, they evidently turn your name and address, as a likely prospect, over to the Association for the Underprivileged Daughters of Pre-Revolutionary Generals, and so on down the line. Once you make a remittance you're positively deluged."

Once more there was a peremptory knock on the door of Belder's office. Imogene Dearborne opened the door, said, "Mrs. Cool's secretary is on the line. Says that it is very important that she get in touch with Mrs. Cool immediately. She wanted to know if Mrs. Cool was here."

"What did you tell her?" Belder asked.

There was just a trace of a smile on Miss Dearborne's lips. "The woman on the telephone said she was Mrs. Cool's secretary. I told her that I personally didn't know of any Mrs. Cool, but if she'd hold the phone I'd make inquiries."

"She's on the line now?" Belder asked.

"Yes."

Belder glanced inquiringly at Bertha Cool.

Bertha said, "Fix it so I can listen in. Talk with her a minute. If it's Elsie Brand, I'll recognize her voice. Stall her along."

Without a word, Imogene turned back to the outer office. Belder silently handed Bertha Cool the desk telephone. Bertha sat there waiting until she heard a metallic click, then Imogene Dearborne saying, "I'm afraid I didn't get that name correctly. Did I understand you to say that you wanted a Mrs. Pool. P-o-o-l—that's *P* as in *private?*"

Elsie Brand's voice, sharp with impatience, said, "No, it's Mrs. Cool. C-o-o-l. *C* as in *confidential.*"

Bertha said promptly, "Hello, Elsie. I'm on the line. What do you want?"

"Oh." Elsie's voice showed relief. "I've been trying to get you every place I could think of."

"What's the trouble?"

"A Mr. Nunnely called up."

"How long ago?" Bertha asked.

"It must have been a good half hour now."

"What did he want?"

"He said he had to reach you at once upon a matter of the greatest importance. He said that it was about something you had taken up with him yesterday and that you'd want to have me make every effort to get in touch with you on it."

"What did you tell him?"

"I told him I'd *try* to get in touch with you and have you call him."

Bertha thought that over for a moment, then said, "All right, Elsie. I'll call him from here. I don't want him to know where I am. If I'm not able to get him and he should telephone again to ask if you delivered the message, tell him that I came in about ten minutes ago; that I was in very much of a hurry; that you gave me the message but that I didn't have time to call him. Assume the attitude that I didn't seem to think that it was so terribly damned important. Get it?"

"I understand," Elsie said.

"Okay."

Bertha dropped the receiver into place, said to Belder, "Nunnely's been telephoning my office, very anxious to get in touch with me; says it's about a proposition I made him yesterday; told my secretary to rush that message through to me."

Belder became excited. "That means he's going to accept, Mrs. Cool. I knew he would. I knew that—"

"Don't count your chickens before they're hatched," Bertha said. "He's a poker-faced gambler. He's probably going to make me some counter proposition. You heard what I told my secretary, not to seem too eager, in case he called up before I could get him. What's his number? I'll give him a ring."

Belder pushed back his chair, walked to the door which led to the outer office, said, "Imogene, get the number of Nunnely's office right away, dial that number and then put Mrs. Cool on the line just as soon as you have dialed. Don't let them hear *your* voice over the telephone." He came back to his desk. "Cigarette?" he asked Bertha, reaching nervously for a package.

"Not now," Bertha said. "Not if I'm going to telephone. . . . Suppose he wants to boost the ante, what do I tell him?"

"Tell him—tell him you'll call him back but that you don't think it's any use to come back with any counter proposal, that you've offered all you can afford to pay."

Belder scraped a match into flame and his hand shook as he conveyed the match to the cigarette. "I can't begin to tell you what it will mean to get that matter off my mind, Mrs. Cool. I made the most awful, the most ghastly mistake a man ever made. I—"

The short, sharp ring of the telephone interrupted him.

Bertha picked up the combination receiver and mouthpiece, said, "Hello."

There was only a faint singing sound on the wire.

Bertha said parenthetically to Belder, "Evidently she's just dialed the number. I can hear it ringing. I—"

A feminine voice said, "Hello, Nunnely Sales Products."

"Mr. Nunnely, please," Bertha Cool said in a calm, methodical voice which barely missed being a drawl.

"Who is this talking, please?"

"Mrs. Cool."

The feminine voice at the other end of the line flashed into quick response. "Yes, Mrs. Cool. Hold the line just a moment, please. He's been trying to get you."

Another click, and Nunnely's voice, much more rapid in its tempo than when Bertha had talked with him last, said,

"Hello, Mrs. Cool?"

"Yes."

"I left word at your office for you to call me. Did you get my message?"

"Yes."

Nunnely cleared his throat. "Mrs. Cool, I'm not going to try beating around the bush. I'm going to come right out and put my cards on the table."

"Go ahead," Bertha said. "Beating around the bush won't get you anywhere with me."

"When you called on me with your proposition, I thought it was a joke. I intended to tell you to go jump in the lake."

"Uh huh," Bertha said, and then added, "I know."

"But the situation has changed somewhat. I happen to know of an investment I can make where I can quadruple my money."

"I see."

"Of course, you may be just what you said—a speculator who buys up judgments and sits on them, and then again you *may* be just a stooge for Everett Belder."

"Haven't we been all over that before?" Bertha asked.

"Yes, I suppose we have, Mrs. Cool. I'm coming directly to the point. If you get two thousand five hundred dollars in the form of a cashier's check or a certified check in my hands not later than four o'clock this afternoon, I'll sign over the judgment to you lock, stock, and barrel."

"I see."

"But it has to be by four o'clock this afternoon, understand?"

"Yes."

"Naturally the incentive which has caused me to accept this ridiculously low offer of yours is in the nature of an emergency; that's the *only* reason I'm accepting the offer. If the money isn't in my hands by four o'clock this afternoon, it won't do me a bit of good."

"I see."

"Now, can I count on having that money by four o'clock?"

Bertha Cool hesitated for a swift flicker of an eyelash. She glanced at Everett Belder's anxious face and said into the telephone, "That's moving pretty fast. Can't you give me

36

just a little more time?"

"Mrs. Cool, you represented yourself to me as having ready cash. You dangled that offer in front of my face. I want that money by four o'clock this afternoon or the deal is all off. After four o'clock I won't discount that judgment by so much as one red cent. Four o'clock this afternoon is the absolute deadline. One minute past four is going to be too late. Now, do I get the money or don't I?"

"You get it," Bertha said. "Where will I find you?"

"At my office."

Bertha said, "I'll have *my* lawyer draw up the assignment of the judgment. I don't want any quibbling over it."

"What's going to be in it?" Nunnely asked suspiciously.

"Everything," Bertha said.

Nunnely laughed. "Well, I guess that's all right, Mrs. Cool. Now, get this: I want the money as soon as you can get it. If you can get it here in half an hour, that will be marvelous, but four o'clock is the deadline."

"I understand," Bertha said.

"Very well. I'm glad that you do. Now, what's the earliest possible moment that you can have the money here?"

"Three fifty-nine," Bertha said, and hung up.

"Is he going to take it?" Belder asked eagerly.

"He's falling for it. He's in a jam, all right. Tried at first to pretend there was some investment he could make. Old stuff. He's going to take twenty-five hundred dollars in the form of a certified or cashier's check, he doesn't care which."

Belder jumped up out of his chair and brought his hand down hard on Bertha Cool's solid shoulder. "Mrs. Cool, you're a brick! You've put it across! Somehow I had an idea you could. My gosh, if you could realize—"

"Wait a minute," Bertha Cool said. "There's a deadline on it, an absolute deadline—four o'clock this afternoon. One minute past four is too late. That's what he says, anyhow."

Belder sobered. "That's probably true. He's been dipping into funds and they must have given him an absolute deadline of his own; something that he's got to meet before five or six o'clock in order to keep from going to jail. . . . Well, that means I've got to work fast."

Bertha Cool said, "I presume a cashier's check will be the

best way of handling it. That will save you putting money in my account and then having my check certified."

Belder was looking at his watch. "I've got to get in touch with my wife," he said.

"You can't handle this without her?"

"Certainly not."

"She may be a little difficult to handle after that letter business," Bertha pointed out.

Belder laughed. "Not on a business deal like this. She'll nag me for weeks about my supposed affair with the maid, but she'll write a check within five minutes after I tell her about this. After all, Mrs. Cool, it's really *my* money, you know."

"It used to be," Bertha said dryly.

Belder's smile was all but condescending. "Even if she's sore as a sprained ankle, she'll get rid of a twenty-thousand-dollar judgment for twenty-five hundred."

"You're cutting things awfully fine," Bertha said.

"I know that," Belder said, frowning at his watch. "She'll be back home pretty soon, even if she's meeting the writer of that letter. That's the worst of it, though. They'll chatter and chatter and perhaps go to lunch. When two women get at lunch— Good Lord, Mrs. Cool, if you'd *only* kept her in sight!"

"Can't you go to your banker," Bertha asked, "explain the circumstances to him, tell him that you were judgment-proof in order to get rid of this—"

"Not a chance in the world," Belder interrupted. "In order to beat this judgment I had to put everything in my wife's name, and I mean everything; and it's in there so tight I can't even get carfare unless she gives it to me. Remember this, Mrs. Cool, I haven't enough income to pay the expenses of maintaining my office. I made mine while the making was good, and then, when the going got tough, I crawled in a hole and pulled the hole in after me. It's an ideal setup to beat a judgment, but it's an awful fix to be in when you want to raise money. . . . No, I've got to get hold of Mabel. One thing's certain. If Mabel's out to lunch, she'll have gone to one of four or five places. I guess the only thing for me to do is to cover them all."

"Want me to go with you?"

"Yes. When we get the check it will save time. . . . No, wait a minute, there's that damned poison-pen letter to be considered. If I find my wife and you're along— Oh, damn! Why did they have to pick *this* time to write that dirty letter?"

Bertha Cool got to her feet. "I'll be waiting in my office. You can telephone as soon as things are fixed up."

Belder's face lit up once more. "Gosh, Mrs. Cool, that's simply swell. It was a lucky hunch I had, coming to you." He walked across and pulled open the door to the outer office. "I feel that I can never repay you—"

The door from the corridor opened. Two women came sweeping regally into the office.

The vociferous cordiality of Everett Belder's greeting carried its own stigma of insincerity.

"Theresa!" he exclaimed, "and Carlotta! I'm certainly glad you were where you could drop in! I couldn't interrupt a conference to talk with you on the phone— Excuse me, please," he said parenthetically to Bertha Cool.

"Certainly," Bertha retorted with frigid formality.

Mrs. Goldring looked Bertha over from head to toe, her eyes hesitating slightly on Bertha's waistline.

Belder said hurriedly, "Theresa, you're looking simply marvelous! You look like Carlotta's sister," and he added with the haste of a person trying to rectify a *faux pas*, "Carlotta herself is looking marvelously well. Better than I've ever seen her. I've been saying so all week, haven't I, Carlotta?"

Carlotta looked bored. Mrs. Goldring, despite herself, favored Belder with a simpering smile. "Do you think so, Everett, or are you just saying so?"

"No, Theresa, really I mean it. A person seeing you on the street would certainly take you for—I mean wouldn't think— that is, would never suspect you and Carlotta were mother and daughter."

"We aren't, you know," Carlotta said acidly.

"Well, you know what I mean," Belder said. "Just go into my private office. I'm finishing up here."

"Oh, I do so hope we're not intruding," Mrs. Goldring said.

"No, no. Not at all. Just go on into my office and make yourselves at home."

Mrs. Goldring didn't move. "Everett," she asked, "*where* is Mabel?"

Belder said desperately, "I don't know. I want to see her. I— You're sure she isn't home?"

"Of course I'm sure. We just came from there."

"Well, go on into my office and sit down. I'll be with you in just a moment."

"Have you any idea where she was going?" Mrs. Goldring asked.

"She had an appointment somewhere. I had her tires checked and the car serviced. I'll— Just go on in, please."

"But Everett, I *must* find Mabel. I came down from San Francisco especially to see her. She certainly must have received my message. I know she did. She told Carlotta I was coming."

"Your message?" Belder repeated mechanically, sparring for time.

"I sent her a wire after I'd— Didn't she tell you I was coming?"

"Why, no. I— She must have gone to the train to meet you, then."

"The train was hours late. Carlotta left early. Mabel said she'd see her at the depot. How long since you've seen Mabel?"

"Why, I don't know. I can't turn my mind on it right now. I have a business matter. Won't you *please* go in and sit down?"

Mrs. Goldring turned once more to look Bertha over. "Oh, yes," she said, "I remember. You were signing a contract with a business executive, weren't you, Everett? I'm *so* sorry. I hope we haven't bothered you."

"Not at all. Not at all. I'll be right with you. Just make yourselves comfortable."

Mrs. Goldring said to Carlotta, "Come on, dear," and to Bertha Cool, smiling acidly, "And I trust we haven't inconvenienced you, or interfered with your *sales contract*."

Bertha said, "Not at all. I never let myself be inconvenienced by *minor* interruptions."

Mrs. Goldring's chin came up. She half turned, locked eyes for a moment with Bertha, thought better of it, and

40

swept on into the private office.

Bertha said in a low voice, "You going to let her know anything about the settlement?"

Belder glanced with concern at the door which Carlotta had very pointedly failed to close. "No, no," he said, in almost a whisper.

"Okay, then," Bertha announced. "You'd better get rid of them as soon as you can."

Belder said, "You're not telling me anything. I can't even go out to look for Mabel while *they're* here."

"And why do you suppose your wife didn't tell you anything about the telegram saying her mother was coming?"

"I don't know," Belder said, his voice showing how worried he was. "It's not at all like her."

"The only reason," Bertha went on, "is that your wife didn't want you to know she was coming. Evidently she was anticipating some sort of a domestic crisis and wanted to have her mother here for moral support. I'll bet you she wired or telephoned for her mother to come on account of that letter."

"I know. I know," Belder said. "It's that letter. As soon as she got it, she telephoned her mother. What a mess it is!"

"Take my advice," Bertha said, "and call for a showdown. Tell her where to get off. Don't start flattering her and toadying to her. You overdo that stuff, anyway. And it's no good. You can't appease a woman of that type. You—"

"Sh-h-h, not so loud, *please*," Belder pleaded in a whisper. "I—"

"Everett," Mrs. Goldring called, "can't you spare us just a moment of your valuable time? We're worried about Mabel. She didn't meet the train and we know she planned to."

"Yes, yes—coming," Belder said.

His eyes pleaded with Bertha to leave.

"Go on in," Bertha said, "and assert yourself."

"You'd better leave," Belder whispered, his eyes on the open door to his private office. *"Please."*

"Oh, all right," Bertha said and crossed the office, opened the door to the corridor, went out, and then stood for about four or five seconds just to the left of the closed door; then she turned and abruptly opened the door.

The door to Belder's private office was closed. Imogene Dearborne, halfway across the office, caught herself in mid-stride and returned to her typewriter.

Bertha said, "It's just occurred to me that I want some information. Can you put a piece of paper in the typewriter and take a note to Mr. Belder? I'll dictate it directly to the machine."

Imogene Dearborne fed a sheet of paper into the machine. Bertha dictated: "Suppose you should report your wife's automobile as having been stolen. You could claim afterward it was a mistake. The police would pick up the machine if—"

Imogene Dearborne's hands flew over the keyboard, paused as Bertha hesitated.

Bertha Cool frowned down at the note in the typewriter, said, "On the other hand, that may not be the best way in the world to go about it. I'll think it over. Perhaps I'd better telephone him." She pinched a thumb and forefinger against the top edge of the paper, jerked it out of the machine, folded it, and casually dropped it into her purse. "I'll see that he gets this note later if I decide it is the way to handle it."

Imogene Dearborne's slate-gray eyes regarded Mrs. Cool enigmatically.

"You certainly do play a wicked tune on that keyboard," Bertha said.

"Thank you."

"Do a lot of practicing?"

"I'm kept fairly busy."

"Have a typewriter at home, I suppose?"

"Yes."

"Portable?"

"Yes."

Bertha Cool smiled. "Thank you very much."

Imogene Dearborne was watching her with steady, expressionless eyes as Bertha Cool pulled open the door and marched out of the office.

42

6

THE SECOND LETTER

ABOUT THREE-FIFTEEN Belder rang Bertha Cool in her office.

"Everything all set?" Bertha asked when she heard his voice on the line.

"Mrs. Cool, I'm afraid this is more complicated than I'd suspected."

"What's the matter?"

"Mrs. Goldring is down here for some specific purpose. I'm afraid that letter did more damage than I had anticipated. Sally seems to have left, and my wife *may* have decided to leave, also. She may have met the person who wrote those letters, and— I can't explain in detail—"

"And your mother-in-law doesn't know where Mabel is?"

"No. And she's sticking with me every minute of the time so that *I* can't do a thing. My hands are completely tied."

"Where are you now?"

"Out at my house."

"Your mother-in-law there?"

"Is she here! She's been with me every blessed minute."

"Why didn't you stay in your office and kick her out?"

"You can't kick her out—not when she's determined not to let you out of her sight."

"Bosh." Bertha snorted. "*I* think she knows where your wife is, and is giving you a run-around. Kick her down the front steps and then go find your wife."

"You don't understand, Mrs. Cool. Suppose Mabel met the writer of that letter and heard some more lies. Suppose she decided to leave me. Can't you see? I had to come to the

43

house to wait. If she *did* decide to do something drastic, she'd have to come back here to get her clothes. . . . Now you've simply *got* to get Nunnely to give us a little more time. This thing is one of those processions of unfortunate coincidences that have been hounding me lately. . . . Ring up Nunnely, or better yet, go to his office, tell him that you simply have to have another twenty-four hours. He probably won't give you that—may not give you anything—but you can try for—"

Abruptly Belder's voice changed. Bertha heard him say in the unctuous tones he reserved for his mother-in-law, "Oh *there* you are, Theresa! I was wondering where you were. . . . Just telephoning the office, that's all. . . . No, she hasn't communicated with the office. They haven't heard anything from her. . . . Don't be so worked up about it. Nothing's happened to her. She's gone to lunch and a bridge party or something—"

Then Belder's voice became louder and crisp with authority. "Put all the mail in the box. If anyone rings up, tell him I may not be back to the office this afternoon. If Mrs. Belder should call, ask her if she's forgotten about her mother coming, and tell her we're all waiting here at the house. . . . Good-by, Imogene."

The phone slammed in Bertha's ear.

Bertha pressed the button which brought Elsie Brand in on the line.

"Get me George K. Nunnely on the phone, Elsie."

Bertha sat back in her chair thinking, until the bell rang and she heard Nunnely's cold, well-modulated voice saying, "Hello, Mrs. Cool. What is it, please?"

Bertha said, "You're rushing me a little."

"Just what do you mean by that, Mrs. Cool?"

"I mean that I'm not certain I can get the money ready by four o'clock this afternoon. I may need another twenty-four hours."

"Impossible."

"I'm putting an outside limit on it," Bertha said, encouragingly, "I'm *hoping* to get the cash *before* four o'clock this afternoon, but I *may* need another twenty-four hours."

"Mrs. Cool, your proposition was spot cash."

"It still is."

"That's not my definition of spot cash."

"It's mine."

Nunnely said coldly, "I'm going to expect you to have the money here by four o'clock this afternoon; otherwise the deal's off."

Bertha started to make some answer, but the click of the receiver at the other end of the line stilled the words on her lips.

She glowered at the telephone. "Hang up on *me*, will you," she stormed. "Wait until we get this deal cleaned up, my fine friend, and I'll give *you* a piece of *my* mind."

Bertha stamped out to her reception office to deliver a message to Elsie Brand personally. "If that man rings up again, I don't want to talk with him."

"Nunnely?"

"Yes."

"Do I tell him in those words?"

"No. Tell him I'm busy and left word I wasn't to be disturbed. Then, if he insists I'll want to talk with him, ask him if he is the Mr. Nunnely who hung up on me the last time we talked. Keep *your* voice very sweet, as thought you were asking merely as a way of identifying him."

Elsie made a few rapid strokes of her pen in a notebook, nodded her head.

"I have an idea that's going to be the best way to handle him," Bertha went on. "If he didn't need the money damn badly, he'd have told me to go to hell long ago. This way, he'll start sweating, and a little sweat will crack that hard-boiled exterior. I'm going to do some work, and I don't want to be disturbed."

Bertha returned to her office, locked the door, cleared her desk, took out the letter Belder had given her and went to work on it, studying each separate character with a magnifying glass, making notes of various characteristics, breaking off from time to time to consult a chart showing the different type faces of all makes and models of typewriters.

It took Bertha something over an hour to decide that the message had been written on an early model Remington portable typewriter. It had taken her only a few minutes to convince herself that the memo she had found attached to the letters in Belder's office had been written on the same typewriter that wrote the letter.

Bertha went down to the lunch counter on the ground floor of the building for a quick cup of coffee and a sandwich, was back within a matter of ten minutes.

"Anything new, Elsie?"

"Mr. Nunnely called up."

An expression of serene satisfaction settled on Bertha's countenance. "What did you tell him?"

"Exactly what you told me to."

"Did you tell him I was out?"

"No. Just told him that you had left word you were busy and didn't want to talk with anyone. He said he thought you'd want to make an exception in his case. I asked him if he was the Mr. Nunnely who had hung up on you earlier in the day."

"What did he say?"

"Well, he sort of cleared his throat and finally said, 'Oh, wasn't she finished? I'm sorry.'"

"Then what? Did he start begging?"

"No. He just said 'Thank you,' and hung up."

Bertha scowled. "That doesn't fit," she said. "He should be getting anxious."

"But he called up," Elsie Brand pointed out. "That means something."

"I mean *damned* anxious," Bertha said. "How was his voice —did he sound worried?"

"No. Just the same well-modulated voice."

"Oh, well, the hell with him. I—"

The door of the office pushed open and Everett Belder, rushing in, said, "My God, Mrs. Cool, I don't know *what* we're going to do."

"Keep your shirt on," Bertha said. "Has something else happened?"

"Has something *else* happened! Great heavens, there's been a procession of things. Do you know what the latest is? My wife's left me—and she's got every cent I have in the world. Every dime, every receivable contract. She even owns the office furniture!"

Bertha studied him for a moment, then turned toward her

private office. "Well, I suppose I've got to hear the lurid details. Come in."

Belder was talking even before Bertha had closed the door to her sanctum.

"She's had her mind poisoned against me, and now she's simply walked out on me."

"Without taking her clothes?" Bertha asked.

"She went back and got her clothes, Mrs. Cool."

"Oh, oh," Bertha said significantly.

"I didn't find it out until half an hour ago," Belder said. "I had looked in her closet just to be certain. I saw her clothes hanging up and didn't notice anything was missing, but when Mrs. Goldring got alarmed and started making a search, she and Carlotta discovered several things that had been taken out. The blue suit, a plaid skirt and blouse, two pairs of shoes, and—"

"Toothbrush?" Bertha asked.

"Yes, she had taken a toothbrush out of the medicine cabinet."

"Cold creams?"

"That's what fooled me, Mrs. Cool. Her jars of cream and bottles of lotion were on the dresser just as she usually left them."

"Humph," Bertha grunted. "She didn't have a suitcase when I saw her leaving the place. She must have gone back for that stuff."

"Undoubtedly, that's what happened. She went out to meet the person who telephoned her. She was intending to have her interview and then go meet her mother at the depot. But something this person said changed all that. Mabel went right back home, threw just a few things into a suitcase and beat it—either forgetting all about her mother or else thinking this other thing was more important—and until I can reach her my hands are tied. Could you get Nunnely to wait until tomorrow?"

Bertha said, "Now, listen, you're all worked up about this. There's absolutely nothing you can do. The probabilities are your wife hasn't really left you. She's simply been told a lot of stuff about you and has decided to walk out on you for a while, *just to teach you a lesson.*"

"What makes you say that?"

"Lots of things. You mark my words, your wife has set the stage to give you a good scare, and her mother is in on the play. Your wife will be back as soon as she thinks she's accomplished her purpose. She's keeping in touch with her mother and knows everything that's happening. That's why she had her mother come down here.

"Now you go on back and start adopting the attitude that if your wife wants to leave you, that's her privilege. You hate to see her go, but if she really *has* gone and it's all over, there are lots of other women in the world. Don't carry it *too* far, but get that idea across to your mother-in-law and then go out for half an hour. That will give your mother-in-law a chance to get in touch with your wife on the telephone. The minute your wife hears that you've recovered from the shock and are starting to think in terms of other women, you'll find your little wife will come back so fast—"

Belder said suddenly, "That's not all. There's been another one."

"Another what?"

"Another letter."

"Let's see it."

Belder passed over a sealed envelope addressed to Mrs. Everett Belder.

Bertha studied the envelope, turning it over in her fingers, examining the stamp, the somewhat smeared cancellation mark. "How did you get it?" she asked.

"It was in the afternoon mail."

"You took it from the postman?"

"No, confound it, my mother-in-law did."

"What did she do with it?"

"Put it on a little table, together with some of the other mail. But she looked this over pretty carefully. She looked them all over, as far as that was concerned, but this was the only one that really attracted her attention. You see, it's marked: 'Personal, private, and confidential.' "

"How do you know this is another poison-pen letter?" Bertha asked.

"Well, it looks like the other one, the way the type looked."

Bertha examined the typewriting with a magnifying glass,

nodded her head in a gesture of slow, deliberate affirmation. "What are you going to do about it?"

"I don't know. That's what I wanted to see you about."

"Any idea what's in it?"

"No."

"Could you simply ditch it? Throw it in the fire?"

"No. My mother-in-law's seen it. If Mabel comes back, Mrs. Goldring will make it a point to be on hand for the opening of the mail. She seemed to be particularly interested in *this* letter."

"And if she can't find it?"

"Then, of course, I'll be accused of taking it, and that, coupled with the other stuff—even if Mabel *should* come back—well, you can see what it would do."

"She'll come back, all right," Bertha said. "We could steam it open."

"Isn't that a Federal offense?"

Bertha said, "I suppose so," pushed back her swivel chair, walked to the door of the outer office, and said to Elsie Brand, "Elsie, dear, connect up the electric plate and put on the teakettle. Bertha wants to steam open a letter."

Elsie Brand brought in a portable electric plate, plugged it into a wall socket, put on a little kettle of water.

"Anything else?"

"No. That'll be all for the present."

Bertha made certain the plate was getting hot, then moved over to sit down in the chair across from Belder, ignoring, for the moment, her swivel chair. "You're all churned up about this thing, aren't you?"

"I'll say I am. I can't help it. It's too much—Mabel leaving, this business with Nunnely, then Mrs. Goldring and Carlotta swooping down on me— If I only knew whether Mabel had walked out. It's the uncertainty on that point that's such a strain. If she's left me and would come right out and say so that would at least relieve the uncertainty."

Bertha walked over to her wastebasket, bent down, and started rummaging through the contents; abruptly she straightened, holding a somewhat crumpled piece of printed paper in her hand.

"What's that?" Belder asked.

"Advertisement from a furrier—a circular about putting furs in storage for the warm weather. It may come in handy."

"I'm afraid I don't get you."

Bertha grinned. "Don't try to."

They sat in silence for several minutes, Belder restless, fidgeting, Bertha calmly placid.

The teakettle started singing. Steam which had been curling up in little wisps from the spout gradually became a full-throated stream.

Bertha gently held the envelope over the spout.

"Can't they tell the envelope has been steamed open?" Belder asked.

"Not when I get done with it."

"You're more optimistic than I am."

Bertha gently inserted the point of a lead pencil between the flap and the envelope. "I should certainly hope I was."

Two more applications of steam and the flap curled back. Bertha took out the letter.

"All in typewriting, same as the other," she said. "Signed on the typewriter: 'A Friend and Well-Wisher.' Want to read this privately, or shall I read it out loud?"

"I'd better just glance at it," Belder said, extending his hand. As his fingers closed on the sheet of paper, his hand began to shake with a series of tremors; the letter slipped from his nervous thumb and forefinger and volplaned back and forth to the floor in a series of swinging zigzags.

"You read it," he said to Bertha.

Bertha cleared her throat and read:

" 'Dear Mrs. Belder:

Who was the woman who came to your husband's office Monday afternoon—a woman who threw her arms around him and kissed him as soon as the office door had closed? Perhaps you'll be willing to meet me and talk with me; perhaps you prefer to live in a fool's paradise. In any event, please believe that I am your sincere friend and well-wisher.' "

Bertha raised her eyes over bifocal glasses to regard Everett Belder's startled countenance. "Who," she asked, "was the girl?"

"Good heavens! No one knows about her."

"Who was she?"

"Dolly Cornish."

"And who's Dolly Cornish?"

"An old flame. I almost married her. We had a fight and—well, I got married. I guess perhaps to show her that I could be independent; and very shortly afterward *she* got married."

"Where is she now?"

"She's—somewhere in the city."

"Got her address?"

"I—er—"

"Yes or no."

"Yes, I have it."

"Where?"

"The Locklear Apartments, apartment Fifteen B."

"What happened Monday?"

"She came to call on me."

"Does she do that often?"

"Don't be silly. It was the first time I'd seen her since my marriage."

"She's been living here in Los Angeles?"

"No, New York."

"And what happened?"

"She came to Los Angeles and wondered about me. She'd found her marriage was unhappy, and gone ahead and secured a divorce. She didn't know whether I was still living with Mabel. She wanted to find out. She looked up my office and simply walked in."

"Did you put on the clinch in front of your secretary?"

"No. I was so surprised I was all but speechless. Then Miss Dearborne closed the door and Dolly—well, Dolly *was* glad to see me."

"That was after the door to the outer office had been closed?"

"Yes."

"And you tried to turn back the clock a little?"

"No, not exactly."

"Did a little necking?"

"No, no! Not that! Heavens, no!"

"Seen her since?"

"Well—"

"Yes or no?"

"Yes."

"How many times?"

"Twice."

"Been out with her?"

"Dinner once, yes."

"What did you tell your wife?"

"That I was working at the office."

"Well," Bertha said, "don't be so goddamned apologetic about it. The way I see things, you're just an average husband."

Bertha folded the letter, slipped it into her purse, picked up the circular from the furrier and carefully fitted it into the envelope, added a bit of adhesive to the flap of the envelope, pasted it shut, and tossed it over to Belder. "All right," she said, "watch for your opportunity. Put this back on the table with the other mail."

Belder's face showed relief. "Mrs. Cool, you're a veritable lifesaver. I—"

A quick, nervous knock sounded at the door of the outer office.

"What is it?" Bertha asked.

"May I come in, Mrs. Cool?" Elsie Brand asked.

Bertha moved toward the door. "What is it, Elsie?"

Elsie slid the door open a few inches, slipped through the opening, pulled the door tightly closed behind her.

"Nunnely's out there," she said in a low voice.

Belder twisted the fingers of his hands nervously. "Oh, my God!"

Bertha pushed back her chair. "You leave this baby to me," she said to Belder. "He's my meat."

"Don't let him know I'm here," Belder said in a half-whisper. "If he thinks we're working together he—"

"I tell you to leave it to me," Bertha said. She turned to Elsie Brand. "Tell him I'm busy, that I can't see him at all today. If he wants to see me, he'll have to make an appointment, and the earliest available moment I have open is at ten-thirty tomorrow morning."

Elsie nodded, slipped quietly out through the door.

Bertha turned to Belder. "Now you," she charged, "get the hell out of here as soon as he leaves the office, and go give that mother-in-law of yours something to think about."

7 A BODY IN THE CELLAR

BERTHA COOL made a habit of stretching out in bed when she wakened in the morning, flexing her muscles, stretching her arms, reaching as far as she could with her extended fingers, pushing her feet down against the foot of the bed. Following which, she would reach for the package of cigarettes which was always on the stand by the side of the bed, light up, and relax in the enjoyment of the first smoke of the morning.

The alarm clock said eight-ten as Bertha awakened and began her muscle-stretching exercises.

She had her first cigarette, then lay back against the doubled pillows, her eyes half closed, relaxing in the warmth of the bed.

Outside, the morning was drab and cold, with a low, thin fog obscuring surroundings. A faint damp wind billowed the curtains back from the open window. The screen was glistening with particles of fog moisture.

Bertha knew it would be clammy cold in the apartment. She was glad she had individual gas heat and didn't need to rely on a central heating plant. . . . Eight-thirty—the buildings that had steam heat would have turned on the heat just enough to break the chill, and would have been turning the steam off by this time.

Bertha stretched her shoulder muscles, yawned, kicked back the covers, and found it was even colder than she had anticipated. She pulled down the windows, lit the gas, and then popped back into bed, snuggling down into the warmth of the covers.

54

The clock seemed to tick more loudly in garrulous accusation.

Bertha reached for another cigarette. Her eyes, glittering with malevolence, regarded the face of the clock. "You're a damned liar," she snapped angrily. "It isn't eight forty-five. It's only seven forty-five. You can't move the sun ahead an hour just by saying so, so shut up your damned tick-tick-ticking and quit leering at me or I'll throw you out of the window."

Bertha scraped a match into flame and lit her second cigarette.

The telephone rang. She started to reach for the instrument, then thought better of it and said, "Go ahead. Ring, and be damned. I'm not going to get up until it's warm."

The telephone rang intermittently for almost two minutes, then quit. Bertha finished her cigarette, tried the temperature of the floor once more with her bare toes, wriggled them into bedroom slippers, and went across to the apartment door. She opened it, took in a quart of milk, a half-pint of coffee cream, and the rolled-up morning newspaper. She slammed the door shut and retired to bed with the morning paper.

She glanced through the paper, keeping up a running fire of devastating comments. "Baloney. . . . Sugar-coated. . . . The hell it is! Oh, bunk! . . . You'd think we were a—" Her last comment was interrupted by the insistent buzzing of the front doorbell.

"Hell of a time for callers," she grumbled to herself.

The metallic ticking of the alarm clock advised her that it was ten minutes past nine, Pacific Time.

The apartment was getting warm. Bertha threw back most of the covers.

The buzzing signal from the lower front door continued at intermittent intervals. Bertha calmly ignored it. She put on a robe, went to the bathroom, and turned on the shower. She was in the middle of her shower when peremptory knuckles sounded on the door of her apartment.

Bertha grunted annoyance and stepped out of the shower. She dried her legs and feet, wrapped a big bathtowel around her torso, thrust her head out of the bathroom door, and yelled, "Who is it?"

A man's voice said, "Is that Bertha Cool?"

"Who did you think it was?" Bertha demanded truculently.

"This is Sergeant Sellers. Let me in."

Bertha stood for a few seconds blinking angrily at the door, then she said, "I'm taking a shower. I'll see you at the office at—" she glanced hastily at the clock—"at quarter past ten."

"I'm sorry," Sergeant Sellers said, "but you'll see me now."

"Stand there until I get some clothes on," Bertha snapped. She retired to her dressing-room, rubbing herself into a glow with the coarse towel.

Sergeant Sellers kept up a steady, monotonous pounding on the door.

Bertha stood it as long as she could, then she flung a robe around her, went to the door, and jerked it open. "Just because you're the law," she stormed, "you think you can bust in on anybody at any time. Go right ahead, wake people up in the middle of the night."

"It's quarter past nine," Sellers said, grinning at Bertha and walking nonchalantly into the apartment.

Bertha kicked the door shut and regarded him sourly. "You might just as well leave your badge at home," she said. "Anybody can tell you're a cop, walking into a woman's apartment while she's dressing, keeping your hat on, smoking a soggy cigar, stinking up the the apartment before I've had my breakfast."

Sergeant Sellers grinned again. "You'd get my goat, Bertha, if it weren't for the fact that I know you have a heart of gold under that hard-boiled exterior. When I think of what you did in that blind man's case, I feel that I should buy you a drink every time I see you."

"Oh, hell," Bertha snorted. "What's the use. I can't even get under your damned thick hide. Sit down and read the newspaper, but, for Christ's sake, throw that stinking stogie out of the window. I'll brush my teeth and—"

Sergeant Sellers held a match to the cold, soggy cigar, tilted his hat back, said, "I've seen the newspaper, and never mind your teeth. What do you know about Mrs. Everett Belder?"

"What's it to you?" Bertha demanded, instantly alert with suspicion.

"Seems to be a sloppy housekeeper," Sellers said.

"Yes?"

"That's right. Goes away and leaves bodies in her basement and forgets to come back."

"What *are* you talking about?

"A body in Mrs. Everett Belder's cellar."

Bertha Cool became as wary as a veteran trout in a deep mountain pool watching a fly being flicked over the surface of the water. "Who did she kill, her husband?"

"I didn't say she killed anyone. I said she left bodies in her basement."

"Oh," Bertha said. "I thought you meant she killed someone."

"No. I haven't said that—not yet."

"Then there's nothing for me to get concerned about."

"I take it you want to be of every assistance to the police."

"Why should I?"

"Because you'd like to stay in business."

"Sure," Bertha said, her eyes watching Sellers's face for any telltale flicker of expression. "I'll help the police clean up a *murder* case, but I see no reason to get steamed up over the fact that the woman's a sloppy housekeeper. How many bodies?"

"Only one."

"Give her a chance. You shouldn't accuse her of being a sloppy housekeeper on the strength of *one* body. I've read of cases where people have had as many as a dozen; and then again, if it hadn't been there too long, it might mean she merely—"

Sellers chuckled. "You aren't kidding anybody, least of all, me."

"Perhaps I'm kidding me."

"Go ahead, then."

"Then quit interrupting."

"When you quit stalling around, we'll get down to brass tacks."

"Who's stalling?"

"You are."

"Why should I stall?"

"Damned if I know," Sellers said cheerfully. "It's just a

habit you have. Whenever the going gets tough and someone tries to pin you down, you get as elusive as the cherry in a cocktail."

"You're the one that's stalling. Who's the corpse?"

"The name's Sally Brentner, a young woman of twenty-six or so."

"How did she die?"

"We don't know yet."

"Natural death?"

"Well, it *might* have been an accident."

"And then again?" Bertha said.

"And then again, it might not."

"*You're* a big help, aren't you?"

"It's mutual."

"Just who is this Sally Brentner?"

"A maid in the place."

"How long has the body been there?"

"A day or so."

"In the cellar?"

"That's right."

Bertha made her voice sound elaborately casual. "What does Mrs. Belder have to say about all this?"

"Nothing."

"You mean she won't answer questions?"

"She doesn't seem to be available for questioning. She seems to have left. That's where *you* come in."

"What do you mean?"

"I understand that when she was last seen, you were the one that was doing the looking."

"Who told you that?"

"A little bird."

The telephone started ringing again. Bertha welcomed the interruption.

"Just a minute," she said to Sergeant Sellers, and then, picking up the telephone, said, "Hello."

Everett Belder's voice showed that he was under great emotional stress. "Thank heavens I've located you! I've been calling you everywhere. I called your apartment before and you didn't answer. Your secretary gave me the number—"

"All right," Bertha interrupted, "get it off your chest."

"Something terrible has happened."

"I know."

"No, no. This is in addition to all my other troubles. They've found Sally's body in the basement. She's been——"

"I know," Bertha said. "The police are here."

There was dismay in Belder's voice. "I wanted to get you before they got there. What have you told them?"

"Nothing."

"They're there with you now?"

"Yes."

"And you've told them nothing?"

"That's right."

"Can you get away with that?"

"I don't think so. Not for long. Is your wife home?"

"No, she didn't show up all night. My mother-in-law was frantic. That's how it happened the body was discovered. She swore she was going to search every room in the house. She said she'd start with the cellar. I heard her going down the cellar stairs, then she screamed and fainted. I rushed down after her, and Sally was lying all sprawled out——"

Sergeant Sellers interrupted good-naturedly. "I'm giving you a lot of rope, Bertha. Don't try to tie any fancy knots or you might get tangled up."

"Was that the law saying something?" Belder asked.

"Yes," Bertha commented tersely, and stopped there.

Belder said, "I told the officers someone had written a poison-pen letter to my wife. I told them I couldn't show it to them because you had it. I didn't tell them specifically why I'd employed you. Just gave them the general picture and skirted around the whole situation very lightly."

"I see."

"Now I think we've got to show the officers that first letter, Mrs. Cool. It *may* be connected with Sally's death. It's just possible it *might* have something to do with the case; but that second letter, the one we opened last night, that doesn't have *anything at all* to do with the case, and I don't want the police to know anything about it."

"Why?"

"Because I don't want Dolly Cornish dragged into this."

"Why?"

"I tell you I don't want Dolly dragged into it. I don't want a lot of notoriety for her. That letter makes things sound pretty bad."

"Why?"

"Can't you understand? There are a lot of angles to this thing. The police might make things unpleasant for Mrs. Cornish."

"Why?"

"My God, can't you get the picture? My wife probably— We'll have to protect Dolly."

"Why?"

"Damn it, can't you say anything except 'why'?"

"Not now."

Belder thought that over.

Bertha, expecting Frank Sellers to interrupt the conversation, asked, "What about Sally? How did she die? Was it an accident? Was she killed, or—"

"It may have been an accident."

"Shoot," Bertha said, bracing herself for an interruption from Sellers.

"Apparently Sally had been peeling potatoes. She'd gone down to the cellar to get some onions to mix with them. She was carrying a dishpan with some peeled and some unpeeled potatoes in it. She was also carrying a big carving knife in her right hand. She evidently stubbed her toe and tripped on the top of the stairs and fell all the way down, running the knife through her chest."

Bertha became absorbed in the telephone conversation. "Anything that makes it appear death *wasn't* accidental?"

"Well, yes."

"What?"

"The color of the body."

"What's that got to do with it?"

"The police say it indicates carbon monoxide poisoning."

"Go on."

"I gather they think the knife may have been pushed into her body immediately after her death, instead of being the instrument which caused that death."

"I see."

"I want you to try and clear things up."

"In what way?"

"Well, my wife is naturally under a cloud. I want you to explain to the police all about the poison-pen letter, and why *you* think my wife disappeared; that it was simply because she was leaving me, and not because she was running away from a murder she'd committed."

"I see."

"And there's another reason I'm concerned about that second letter. Dolly is rather a striking-looking young woman. If she were dragged into it, the newspapermen would play her up big. She photographs well. . . . You know the sort of pictures newsmen take."

"Leg?" Bertha asked.

"Yes. I don't want that sort of newspaper notoriety for Dolly."

"Why?"

"Because it's inadvisable."

"Why?"

"Damn it, my wife was jealous of Sally. Sally's dead. Why advertise another potential victim? Leave Dolly out of it, I tell you."

Alarmed by Sergeant Sellers's continued silence, Bertha glanced apprehensively over her shoulder to find that the sergeant, his soggy cigar propped up at an aggressive angle, had appropriated her purse which had been lying on the dresser, zipped it open, and was now completely engrossed in reading the two letters which Belder had given her.

Bertha said angrily, "Why, damn you! You—you—"

Belder's voice said over the wire, "Why, Mrs. Cool! I haven't done—"

Bertha said hastily into the telephone, "Not you, I'm talking to the dick."

Sergeant Sellers didn't even look up. He was completely absorbed in the letters.

"What's he doing?" Belder asked.

Bertha said wearily, "Oh, hell! What's the use? While you've been keeping me occupied telling me how *you* wanted me to handle things, Sergeant Sellers has taken the liberty of opening my purse and reading *two* letters that he's taken from it."

"Oh, Lord!" Belder groaned.

"Next time," Bertha said, "let me run things my own way."

She didn't even wait to say good-by, but slammed the receiver into place with a jar that all but broke the instrument.

Sergeant Sellers folded the two letters, dropped them into his pocket, zipped Bertha Cool's purse shut. He either hadn't found, or hadn't considered important, the memo that Bertha had filched from Belder's office.

"What the hell gave you the idea you could do that and get away with it?" Bertha demanded, her face dark with anger.

Sellers looked smug. "Because I knew you wouldn't mind, old pal."

"Mind!" Bertha screamed. "Goddamn you, I could beat your brains out—if I thought you had any! Of all the nerve! Of all the consummate, high-handed, dastardly—"

"Save it, Bertha," he said. "It isn't getting you anywhere."

Bertha stood glowering in indignant silence.

Sellers said, "What the hell, Bertha. You wouldn't have held out on me, anyway. I asked Belder where the letter was he told me about, and he said that you'd taken it. The last he saw of it, you had put it in your purse. So I thought I'd take a look at it."

"Then why didn't you ask me for it?"

Sellers grinned. "You know, Bertha, I had an idea that Belder might be holding out. He was just a little too anxious to tell me about that one letter, and talked fast every time I asked him about it. You take a man of that type, and when he begins to talk real fast, you know he's trying to keep you from asking a question about some particular thing. So I began to wonder if there hadn't been a *second* letter."

"And you knew he was going to ring up, to tell me to ditch it," Bertha said, "and made up your mind you'd go for my purse as soon as the phone rang. . . . I could make a squawk about that and make trouble for you."

"Sure you could," Sellers said soothingly. "But after all, Bertha, you aren't going to do it. Too many times *I* could make a squawk about *you*. In this world it's a question of live and let live. You pull your fast ones, and I pull mine. When you hit me below the belt and hurt, I don't start yelling for the referee and claiming a foul. . . . Come on, now, tell me about the girl who threw her arms around Belder's neck."

"What about her?"

"Who is she?"

"I don't know."

Sellers, clucking his tongue against the roof of his mouth, made noises of chiding disapproval. "Come come, Bertha. You should be able to do better than that."

"What makes you think I know her?"

"You know damn well you wouldn't let Belder flash a letter like that on you without finding out all about the jane."

"There wasn't any," Bertha said.

"What do you mean?"

"It's just poison-pen stuff. I tell you there wasn't anyone."

"How do you know?"

"Belder told me so."

Sellers sighed. "Well, I guess I'll have to let it go at that for the time being."

"How about Mrs. Belder's mother?" Bertha asked.

"In a state of collapse. Mother and sister both had been having fits all night. They'd been calling headquarters at intervals, trying to find out if Mrs. Belder had been in an automobile accident. Finally I guess the mother-in-law got the idea Belder might have knocked her on the head and hidden the body some place in the house, so she started prowling. Declared she was going to search the house from cellar to attic. She started with the cellar. . . . That was along about eight o'clock this morning. What she found knocked her for a loop. She thought it was Mabel's body at first, then it turned out to be a total stranger to her. Belder made the identification of the body."

"Didn't Mrs. Goldring know the maid?"

"Apparently not. Mrs. Goldring lived in San Francisco. She hadn't been down since Mabel had employed that particular maid."

"Well," Bertha said, "I don't see how all this concerns me."

Sellers scraped a match on the sole of his shoe, made an attempt to get his cigar burning again.

Bertha said, "I don't suppose it makes any difference to

you, but that damn cigar makes me sick to my stomach."

"Too bad. You haven't had breakfast?"

"Not with restaurants serving their sort of coffee."

"Okay, make it good and black, and give me a big cup."

Bertha Cool flounced indignantly into her dressing-room, dressed hurriedly, returned to make up the wall bed and wheel it out of the way. Then she went out into the kitchenette, put on a big pot of coffee, and said to Sergeant Sellers, "I suppose you'll insist on having an egg, too?"

"That's right, two."

"Damn it, I said t-o-o."

"I know. I said t-w-o."

"And toast?"

"Oh, certainly. And plenty of bacon."

Bertha said nothing, busied herself at the gas stove. Her mouth set in a tight line of indignation.

Sergeant Sellers, his hat pushed back on his head, the cigar now giving forth puffs of light-colored blue smoke, lounged easily in the doorway. "First rattle out of the box," he said, "we'll run over to see Belder, and we'll all three have a little talk."

"Why drag me in on it?" Bertha asked.

"I thought I might get farther," Sellers admitted cheerfully. "If Belder starts lying, you'll tell him he can't get away with it, so he'd better tell the truth."

"Oh, *I'll* tell him that, will I?" Bertha demanded sarcastically, standing poised with a frying pan, which she had been about to put on the stove, held at an angle of forty-five degrees.

"That's right," Sellers said. "You have your intellectual blind spots, Bertha, but you aren't exactly dumb."

Sellers watched the color mount in Bertha's face, grinned at her, said affably, "Well, I guess I'll go telephone Belder and arrange for a conference."

He left the kitchenette. Bertha heard him in the other room dialing a number on the telephone, heard low-voiced conversation, then he was back standing in the kitchen door.

"Okay, Bertha. He'll see us at his office; doesn't want to meet us at the house; says his sister-in-law will horn in on the conversation if we meet there."

Bertha said nothing.

Sellers yawned loudly and obviously, left his position in the kitchen doorway to move over to the most comfortable chair in the living-room. He settled down, opened the morning newspaper to the sporting page, and started reading.

Bertha Cool placed plates, cups and saucers, knives, forks, and spoons on the little table in the breakfast nook.

"Tell me something about detectives," she called in to Frank Sellers.

"What is it?"

"Do they take their hats off when they eat breakfast?"

"Hell, no. They'd lose caste if they did. They only take their hats off when they take a bath."

"How do you like your egg?"

"Three minutes and fifteen seconds—and it isn't egg, it's eggzzz—the plural of egg—meaning two or more."

Bertha Cool banged a plate down on the table so hard she almost broke it. "There's one thing about giving you breakfast," she said. "You can't drink coffee with that stale cigar in your mouth."

Sergeant Sellers didn't answer. He was interested in reading an account of a prize fight which he had seen the night before, checking the reported facts against his own impressions.

"All right," Bertha Cool said. "Come and get it."

Sergeant Sellers, minus his hat and his cigar, with his thick, wavy hair combed back with a pocket comb, entered the breakfast nook, waited for Bertha Cool to seat herself, then sat down opposite her.

"Okay, Bertha, have your coffee and then give me the lowdown. You've had time to make up your mind now."

Bertha Cool poured the coffee, sipped the hot, fragrant beverage, said, "All right, here it is—all of it. I was supposed to tail Mrs. Belder. I lost her. She was going to keep a rendezvous with the person who wrote those letters. I went to Belder's office, looked through his file of personal correspondence to see if I could find anything that tallied with what I was looking for."

"*What* were you looking for?" Sergeant Sellers asked.

"An expert typist who had her own portable typewriter

65

at home," Bertha said.

"I don't get you."

"You can tell a lot about a typewritten letter by studying it. The even touch and uniform spacing show that these letters had been written by a first-rate typist. That sort of typist commands a good salary, which means she has good equipment at her office. It was written on a portable typewriter that was badly out of alignment. That meant it was a private portable machine she had at home. . . . Quite by accident, I stumbled on the answer."

"What's the answer?" Sergeant Sellers asked.

"Imogene Dearborne, the slate-eyed little siren who sits up in Everett Belder's office and looks as though she didn't have a thought in the world except to get her duties discharged with secretarial efficiency."

Frank Sellers cracked an egg open and judicially inspected the contents.

"Now then, how does *that* look to you?" Bertha asked, awaiting praise for her powers of deduction.

"Just a little bit too well done," Sergeant Sellers said, "but what the hell, I can eat it."

8

WHO SAW WHAT?

SERGEANT SELLERS pushed open the door marked EVERETT G. BELDER, *Sales Engineer*, and stood to one side for Bertha Cool to enter.

"Don't say we aren't polite on occasion," he muttered.

"You slay me," Bertha said, marching into the office.

Imogene Dearborne glanced up from her typewriter. Bertha saw that she had been crying. The girl hastily averted her eyes, said, "Go right on in. He's expecting you."

Sergeant Sellers raised a questioning eyebrow at Bertha, and at Bertha's almost imperceptible nod the sergeant sized up the girl at the typewriter.

Imogene Dearborne seemed to be aware of his scrutiny. Her back stiffened, but she didn't look up. She continued flinging her fingers at the keyboard of the typewriter, beating out a staccato tune of business efficiency.

The door from the private office opened. Everett Belder said, "I thought I heard you come in. Good morning. Good morning! Step right this way, please."

They entered Belder's private office.

Sergeant Sellers settled himself in a chair, pulled a cigar from his waistcoat pocket, bit off the end, and groped for a match. Bertha Cool sat down with the grim formality of an executioner calling on the condemned man.

Everett Belder adjusted himself nervously in the big chair behind the desk.

Sellers got his cigar going, shook out the match, tossed it into a small fireplace where some papers were burning, looked at Belder, and said, "Well?"

Belder said, "I presume Mrs. Cool has told you every-thing."

Sellers grinned at Belder through blue cigar smoke. "I don't think she's told me everything, but she told me more than you intended her to tell."

"I'm afraid I don't understand," Belder said trying to be dignified.

"How about that second letter?" Sellers asked.

Belder said nervously, "I intended to tell you about that a little later, sergeant. I just wanted time to think it over."

"You've thought it over now," Sellers said.

Belder nodded.

"And what was there you wanted to think over?"

"Nothing. That is, in the sense that you mean."

"Shouldn't have taken you long to think it over, then."

Belder cleared his throat. "A young woman whom I used to know, named Dolly Cornish, called on me. She was glad to see me. I was glad to see her. I hadn't seen her for a long time. She looked me up when she came to town, got my address out of the telephone book. She had no means of knowing I was *still* married."

"What do you mean, 'still'?"

"Well, I went with her for a while, and then—well, then I got married."

"She didn't like that?"

"Oh, she got married herself within a week or two."

"But she didn't like it when you got married?"

"I don't know. I didn't ask her."

Sellers took the cigar from his mouth. His eyes bored into Belder's. "Answer questions and quit beating around the bush."

Belder said, "No. She didn't like it."

"Had you seen her since then?"

"Not until she came here."

"Why did she come?"

"She'd left her husband. She—well, she wanted to see me."

"Okay, you made a play for her?"

"I—I was glad to see her."

"Kiss her?"

"Yes."

"More than once?"

"I—well, perhaps. But that was all of it, just a kiss and— well, hang it, I *was* glad to see her. Just like you'd be glad to run across any old friend whom you hadn't seen for a long time."

"Date her up?"

"No."

"Tell her you were still married?"

"Yes."

"She leave you her address?"

"Yes."

"Where?"

"Locklear Apartments."

"You been there?"

"No."

"Called her?"

"No."

"She ask you to?"

"Well, not exactly. She told me where she was staying."

"Where did she sit?" Sergeant Sellers asked.

Surprise was on Belder's face. "I don't get you."

"When she was here."

"Oh, over in that chair, the one Mrs. Cool's sitting in."

"That's pretty well over at the far end of the office," Sellers said. "Take a look out, Bertha, and tell me what windows you can see across the street."

"I'm afraid I don't understand," Belder said. "What bearing does that have on the case?"

Sergeant Sellers explained patiently. "The person who wrote that second letter must have been able to see what was going on here in the office when Dolly Cornish called. I notice there's an office building across the street. It's not a wide street. Along in the afternoon, the light would be just right so a person standing in an office across the street could see in here."

Belder frowned for a moment, then his face cleared. "By George, *that's* an idea! You think this person was spying on me from an office in the building across the street?"

Bertha Cool said, "Why monkey with that stuff? You have the answer right here in your office."

69

Sellers frowned for her to keep quiet, suddenly switched his point of attack.

"How about the information in this letter? Who do you know who could have known about Dolly being in here on Monday?"

"No one."

"Your secretary?"

"She doesn't know anything at all about Dolly Cornish; thinks she's a business acquaintance."

"What time was this Dolly person in here Monday?"

"I don't know, around—oh, I'd say around the middle of the afternoon."

Sergeant Sellers jerked his fingers toward the telephone. "Get her in here."

"Who?"

"Your secretary."

Belder raised the receiver on the telephone, said, "Can you come in here a moment, please?"

A second later, when Imogene Dearborne opened the door, Sellers said, "Last Monday—a party by the name of Dolly Cornish. What time was she in?"

"Just a moment, I'll consult my daybook."

"She have an appointment?"

"No."

"All right, take a look at your book."

Imogene returned to her desk, secured her daybook, opened it, slid her finger down the page. "Mrs. Cornish came in at two-twenty Monday afternoon. She stayed until three-fifteen."

"She didn't have an appointment?"

"No."

"Stranger to you?"

"Yes."

"Know anything about her business?"

"No. Mr. Belder said not to make any charge."

Sellers tilted back his head, closed his eyes. "What does she look like?"

"A blonde, good figure, fine clothes, attractive, still young but sort of—well, sort of scheming and definitely selfish. If she wants something, she gets it."

Belder said, "I hardly think that's fair, Miss Dearborne, you—"

"I'm running this," Sellers interrupted, his head still tilted back, eyes still closed. "She told you she wanted to see Mr. Belder, is that right?"

"Yes."

"And you asked her if she had an appointment?"

"Yes."

"What did she say?"

"She said Mr. Belder would see her if I'd tell him she was here."

"Belder isn't very busy," Sellers said. "That appointment business is just a stall, isn't it—kind of a racket to impress callers?"

"Yes."

"So you went on in to him and told him a Mrs. Cornish was here?"

"She asked me to announce her as Dolly Cornish; said just to say Dolly Cornish."

"What did Belder do?"

"Why, he said to send her in, said she was a friend of his."

"Any emotion?"

"I didn't notice."

"What happened when they met each other?"

"I don't know. I wasn't there."

"Didn't Belder come to the door?"

"He was part way around the desk as I held the door open for her. I heard him say her name as though he—well, as though he liked the sound of it."

"And then?"

"I closed the door."

"See him kiss her?"

Her cheeks flamed. "No."

"When did you see her next?"

"Three-fifteen—when she came out."

"Anyone else know she was here?"

"Not so far as I know."

"No one waiting in the outer office when she came in here?"

"No."

71

"Anyone shadow her when she left?"

"I can't be certain of that, but I would say probably not. There was no one else in the office all the time she was in here."

Bertha Cool interrupted. "What's the use of beating around the bush. This is the party you want."

Sellers frowned warningly at Bertha Cool. "I'm not so certain you're right on that, Bertha."

"*I'm* certain," Bertha snapped.

Sellers looked through the window at the building across the street. "There's some pretty strong evidence in favor of that office-window theory, Bertha."

Bertha turned to Imogene Dearborne, zipped open her purse, pulled out the typewritten memo she had pilfered from Everett Belder's files. "Who wrote this?" she demanded, thrusting the paper out at Imogene Dearborne.

"Why—why—why, I guess *I* did. That was a note I put on Mr. Belder's—"

Bertha Cool said to Sergeant Sellers, "Let's have those two letters."

Sellers wordlessly passed them over.

Bertha Cool spread them out on the table. "Take a look at these, young woman. All written on the same typewriter, weren't they?"

"I—I don't know. What are you trying to do?"

Bertha said, with cold-blooded callousness, "I'm trying to show you up, you little twirp. You were in love with your boss. You thought he'd marry you if his wife didn't stand in the way. You wrote those letters to Mrs. Belder. You knew your boss was making a play for the maid. You listened at the door and peeked through the keyhole and knew what went on when Dolly Cornish called. You thought you'd get rid of a wife and two rivals all at once. You wrote those letters to Mrs. Belder and then put on your innocent act around the office. A smug, mealymouthed, goddamned hypocrite."

Imogene Dearborne was crying now. "I didn't," she denied wildly. "I don't know what you're talking about."

Bertha said remorselessly, "Oh, yes you do. And now I'm going to prove it. Those letters were written by a skilled typist. She used a beautiful, even-spaced, touch system. She wrote 'em on a portable typewriter. It was a Remington portable, about the first model they put out. You have a portable machine at home. You used it to write these letters. This memo wasn't written on the machine you're using in the office. I tricked you into giving me a specimen of the writing on that machine. You admitted that you have a portable at home. Now, then, you'd better come clean and tell us—"

"Great Scott!" Belder exclaimed, as he stared down at the memorandum on the desk.

Bertha Cool smiled at him with calm assurance. "Hits you with something of a jolt, doesn't it? Finding out that you've had a little twirp in your office who—"

"It isn't that," Belder interrupted. "It's what you said about the Remington portable."

"What about it?" Bertha asked.

"That's my wife's machine."

The door from the outer office opened. Carlotta Goldring, her prominent blue eyes taking in everything and everybody in the room, said, "There was no one in the reception room, so I came on in. I hope I'm not—"

No one paid any attention to her. Bertha Cool pointed her finger at Imogene. "Look at her. You can tell I've called the turn. The twirp may have managed to write these letters on your wife's machine at your house, but *she wrote those letters!* She—"

"It's a lie!" Imogene screamed. "And what's more, the portable I have at home *isn't* a Remington. It's a Corona!"

Carlotta, wide-eyed, moved around to the edge of the room, stopped near the fireplace, her back to the fire, regarding the scene with speechless amazement.

"Try to deny that you're in love with your boss," Bertha accused. "Try to deny that you thought if you could only get rid of his wife, you'd have easy sailing; that you wrote these letters—"

"Wait a minute," Belder interrupted. *"She* couldn't have done it, Mrs. Cool. She wrote that memo one day when I had my wife's machine at the office—taking it home after an overhaul. Imogene tried it out. I remember the whole thing very clearly now."

"Then she wrote both letters that same day," Bertha

charged.

"She couldn't have. That was before either of these women —before Dolly entered the picture."

Sellers said to Belder, "Who else had access to this typewriter?"

"Why—no one, I guess. My wife's family—"

Sellers's eyes were narrowed and hard. "And the maid, of course."

"Sally?"

"Yes. Who else would I be talking about?"

Belder said, "Why—yes—but why should Sally have written a letter to my wife suggesting that she was playing around with me? It's cockeyed. It's crazy."

"But Sally could have had access to that machine," Sellers insisted.

"She could have, yes."

Imogene Dearborne slumped down in a chair, her handkerchief at her eyes. The sound of her sobs filled the room whenever there was a lull in the conversation.

Sellers said to Bertha Cool, "You may be right. You may not be right. There's something screwy about this whole business. . . . Belder, get up and quit stalling around. Put this chair in just about the same position it was when Dolly Cornish was sitting in it. . . . Okay, it was sitting in that position. All right—now let me sit there. Let me see what's visible through the window from this angle."

Sergeant Sellers moved his body back and forth enlarging the angle of his vision as far as possible.

"Imogene, cut out that damn bawling, take your pencil, and make a note of these places: Doctor Cawlburn, physician and surgeon. . . . Doctor Elwood Z. Champlin, dentist. . . . The dentist looks the most promising. We'll take a chance on him first; dental chairs always face the windows. I can look across and see a patient from that chair right now. Get those telephone numbers for me, Imogene. . . . Come on, snap out of it!"

Imogene might not have heard him. She sat in the chair sobbing.

Sergeant Sellers got up out of the chair, reached across, grabbed her shoulder, gave it a quick shake, said, "Snap out of it. Do your bawling after office hours. I'm working on a murder case. Get out there and look up those numbers."

Imogene glanced up at him and, at the expression on his face, suddenly got to her feet, crossed to Belder's desk, picked up a telephone directory and began looking up numbers, dabbing at her eyes with a handkerchief from time to time.

Belder handed her a pencil and a memo pad. He patted her arm awkwardly. "There, there, Miss Dearborne," he said. "Don't feel that way about it."

She jerked her arm away from his touch, wrote out the telephone numbers, tore the sheet off the memo pad, and handed it to Sergeant Sellers.

Sellers picked up the telephone, dialed a number, said, "This is Sergeant Sellers of Police Headquarters. I want to talk with Doctor Elwood Champlin, personally. . . . Okay, put him on. . . . Police Headquarters. Tell him it's important . . ." While he was waiting, Sellers picked up the cigar which he had deposited on the desk, puffed it into renewed activity, and held it tilted at an aggressive upward angle. Abruptly he removed it, said into the mouthpiece, "Hello, this Doctor Champlin? . . . That's right. Yes, Sergeant Sellers from Headquarters. Look on your appointment book and tell me what patient you had in the chair in your office last Monday between two o'clock and three-fifteen. . . . No, just the names of the patients. . . . All right, what's that man's name? H-a-r-w-o-o-d. All right, I've got that. Who's next?"

A slow grin came over Sergeant Sellers's face. "Miss or Mrs.?" he asked.

"I see. All right, thank you very much, doctor, I'll get in touch with you later on. . . . Yes, that's all I wanted to know."

Sellers dropped the receiver back into place and grinned at Bertha Cool.

"The second patient in Doctor Champlin's office," he said, "from two-fifteen to two forty-five was a Miss Sally Brentner."

9

BERTHA GOES FISHING

ELSIE BRAND looked up from her typewriter as Bertha Cool entered the office.

"I'll bet you forgot all about having a ten-thirty appointment with George K. Nunnely," she said.

"I did for a fact," Bertha admitted. "Was he in?"

"He not only was in, but he paced the floor and kept biting his upper lip. He was definitely nervous and annoyed."

Bertha Cool flopped down in a chair, said, "Well, that's what comes of fraternizing with cops. That damned detective barged in on me before breakfast this morning, made me feed him, and then dragged me around as though I'd been an assistant coroner or something. . . . Hell of a note when I can't take care of my own business. That's important, too— a chance to clean up a little dough. . . . Was he sore when he left?"

"I don't know. He was certainly worried. He used the telephone twice while he was here."

"Didn't find out what number he was calling, did you?"

"No. He had me connect him with an outside line, and then dialed the number himself."

"Leave any message?"

"He wanted you to call his office as soon as you came in."

Bertha grinned. "Gone a long way from the poker-faced, high and mighty big shot that slammed up the phone in my ear, hasn't he?"

"Personally, I think he's almost crazy with worry," Elsie said. "Who was the detective who called on you, Sergeant Sellers?"

"Uh huh."

"I think *he's* nice."

"He's all right if you like flatfeet," Bertha said wearily. "I don't. I just wish they'd leave me alone. They get delusions of grandeur. The way he busts in and orders me around! The hell with him."

"What was it all about?" Elsie Brand asked.

"Looks as though Mrs. Belder has committed a murder."

Elsie Brand's eyes widened.

Bertha said, "It could have been an accident, but the cops don't think so—and I don't think so."

"Who was the victim?"

"Sally Brentner, the maid in the house."

"Any motive?"

"Jealousy."

"Her husband?"

"A poison-pen letter indicated her husband was playing around with Sally and that Sally was staying on the job simply to be near him. And the hell of it is, Sally must have written that letter herself."

"For what possible reason?"

"Probably to bring about a showdown. She was in love with Belder. Belder was stringing her along, but wasn't leaving his wife. He couldn't. His wife was holding the purse strings—all of them. Anyway, that's the theory that all of them are playing around with."

"What does Mrs. Belder say?"

"Mrs. Belder remains very much out of the picture. She skipped out. She must have committed the crime before I started shadowing her. Probably while her husband was calling at the office.

"This man, Belder, seems to be rather a complex individual. Women in his life—and lots of women. They seem to go crazy about him and keep coming back for more. The situation may have been precipitated by an old sweetheart who called on him at his office Monday and went into a clinch as soon as the secretary had closed the door. Sally Brentner was having a tooth fixed at the time in a dental office across the street. From the chair in front of the window, she could look across into Belder's office."

"Did Mrs. Belder seem nervous when you were shadowing her?"

"No. She certainly didn't act like a woman who had just committed a murder. . . . Wait a minute! She must have committed it just *after* I shadowed her. . . . That's what happened! Good Lord, why didn't I think of it before?"

Bertha's voice began to show increasing excitement.

"What is it?" Elsie asked.

"I was shadowing her. She had just walked out of the house, casually carrying a pet cat on her arm, climbed into the automobile, and was driving away—going some place to keep an appointment she'd made over the telephone. She didn't have any bag with her, except a small hand purse. Then, all of a sudden, she whizzes past an intersection, beating it through on a closed signal, and gives me the slip; then she doubles back to the house, kills Sally, packs up a few things, and skips out. . . . Why," Bertha went on, her eyes sparkling with interest, "I can tell the exact moment when the idea of killing the woman occurred to her. It was right at that street intersection. Now what in the world could she have seen out there that would have suddenly inspired her to rush home and kill her maid?"

"You think something happened to give her the idea right then?" Elsie asked.

"Almost certain of it. She was driving along at slow speed, apparently just minding her own business, going out to keep a rendezvous with someone who had telephoned. And then all of a sudden she gets dumb and goes through this closed signal, makes a left-hand turn, and then must have made another left-hand turn and doubled back to the boulevard. I played her for a right-hand turn and drew a blank."

"What," Elsie asked, "are you going to do? Are you going to help Mr. Belder try and prove she's innocent. Or is he going to stick by her?"

"Stick by her!" Bertha exclaimed. "He's going to stick to her closer than a brother. Without her, he wouldn't even have carfare. He's got to get her back and get the thing straightened out somehow."

"Then you're going to try and prove she's innocent?"

"I," Bertha Cool declared, "am going fishing."

"I'm afraid I don't get it."

Bertha said, "The big trouble with this partnership when Donald Lam was here was that he never knew when to let go. Nothing seemed impossible to him. No matter how the cards were stacked against him, he'd keep on playing."

"He always came out all right," Elsie pointed out with a quick flare of feeling.

"I know," Bertha conceded. "He always pulled out somehow by the skin of his eyeteeth, but that's too high-pressure stuff for me."

"You mean you're going to walk out on the case?"

"Walk out on the case, nothing," Bertha retorted. "Just what case is there to walk out on? Belder wanted me to compromise a twenty-thousand-dollar judgment for twenty-five hundred dollars. All right, I've done it. What's the result? Belder can't get the money until he gets it out of his wife. He can't find his wife because she's skipped out after—"

"After what?" Elsie asked as Bertha ceased abruptly in midsentence.

"I just had a thought about that," Bertha said. "She *might* have skipped out after killing Sally; then again, she might have skipped out after simply finding Sally's body in the basement. . . . Well, anyway, she skipped out. Belder can't get the money to compromise the judgment until he can get his wife."

"Don't you suppose he'll want you to try and find his wife?"

"Probably. But what chance would *I* stand? The police are going to be looking for his wife, and the police are going to look a hell of a lot faster, and in a hell of a lot more places, than I can. No, I'm going fishing. That was the trouble with Donald—he didn't know when to quit. I know when to quit. I'm going to quit before I lead with my chin and get into a lot of trouble."

Bertha waved her hand vaguely toward the private office. "Any mail in there?"

"Half a dozen letters."

"Important?"

"Nothing urgent."

"All right, I'm going to duck out."

"What'll I tell Mr. Nunnely if he comes back?"

"Tell him I've been called out of town on business. Tell everyone just that—Belder, Sergeant Sellers, and the whole outfit. I'm going to stay away until this thing settles down; then there may be a chance to pick up a little money. In the meantime I'd be sticking my neck out if I tried to do anything. . . . Once you get really involved in a case, you can't quit. Then you've got to ride it through to the finish. To hell with that stuff. I'm taking life easy. No more getting mixed up in a lot of trouble."

"Where can *I* reach you in case anything important turns up?"

"At Balboa."

"Suppose Sergeant Sellers wants you as a witness?"

Bertha's face hardened into an expression of distaste. "Tell Sergeant Sellers to go— Well, tell him I'm out of town."

"He may think you're meeting Mrs. Belder somewhere."

Bertha grinned. "Let him think so. I hope he does. I hope he tries to follow me. Damn him, I hope he chokes."

Bertha gave a quick look around the office, started for the door.

The phone began to ring as Bertha had her hand on the knob.

Elsie Brand reached for the telephone, then held her hand over the receiver, lifting her eyebrows questioningly at Bertha Cool.

Bertha said, "If it's going to bother your conscience to tell him I'm not here, this will fix it so you won't have to lie about it."

She jerked the door open and stepped out into the corridor.

10
THE TWIRP TURNS

BERTHA COOL came marching into the office, a folded newspaper under her arm.

"I was trying to reach you but I couldn't locate you. You'd left the hotel," Elsie Brand said.

"Got up at daylight to catch the tide," Bertha explained.

"Any luck?"

"They weren't biting."

"A man has been in twice," Elsie said, looking at her daybook. "He wouldn't leave his name. He said it was particularly important."

"Look as though he had any money?" Bertha asked.

"Some. Seems to be an ordinary, salaried man."

"Humph," Bertha said.

"He'll be back. He seems very anxious to see you. Says he must see you *personally*."

"I'll see him," Bertha said. "I've got to see everyone, now. What the hell? If Donald is out whooping it up in Europe, I'm going to carry on here and make him a sockful of dough. I thought for a while I'd settle back and take only the easy cases. That stuff's the bunk. I'm going to do *my* share—"

The door opened.

Elsie Brand, looking up quickly, said in a low voice, "Here's the man now."

Bertha put on her best receiving-a-client manner. She walked vigorously across the office, radiating a calm competency.

"*Good* morning! Something I can do for you?" she asked.
"You're Mrs. Cool?"

"That's right."

"Bertha Cool, one of the partners of the firm of Cool and Lam?"

"That's right," Bertha said, smiling. "Just tell me what I can do for you. Lots of agencies only handle certain types of cases. We take anything—that there's money in."

She smiled reassuringly.

The man's hand went to his inside pocket. "Very well, Mrs. Cool," he said, "you can take these."

He shoved some papers into Bertha's hand. She reached for them, looked at the typewriting on the folded backs and said, "What's this?"

The answer came with machine-gun rapidity. "Action filed in the Superior Court of Los Angeles County. Imogene Dearborne, plaintiff, versus Bertha Cool, defendant. You have there copies of summons and complaint as Bertha Cool an individual, and Bertha Cool a co-partner. Here's your original summons calling your attention to the seal of court and—"

Bertha drew back the hand that held the papers, started to throw them at him.

"Don't do it," the man warned, rattling off the words in rapid-fire tempo without even a pause as he switched in his talk from a description of the papers to the recitation of a formula. "It won't get you anywhere. If you're sore, go tell your lawyer about it, don't blame it on me. That's all. Thank you. Good morning."

He whirled around and darted out the door before Bertha could get her vocabulary into action.

Elsie was the first to recover. "What in the world," she asked, "is all *that* about?"

Bertha Cool snapped an elastic off the bundle of papers, unfolded a crisp-looking legal document, started reading aloud:

IN THE SUPERIOR COURT OF THE STATE OF CALIFORNIA, IN AND FOR THE COUNTY OF LOS ANGELES

IMOGENE DEARBORNE,   )

    :

              Plaintiff)

    —*vs*—   :

)

BERTHA COOL, *an individual, and as a*:

co-partner transacting business under)   *COMPLAINT*

the firm name and style of Cool and :

Lam; DONALD LAM, an individual,)

and as a co-partner transacting business:

under the firm name and style of Cool)

and Lam.   :

            Defendants)

Plaintiff complains of defendants, and for cause of action alleges:

I

That the defendants are now, and at all of the times hereinafter mentioned were, co-partners transacting business under the firm name and style of Cool and Lam, and having their offices in the City of Los Angeles aforesaid.

II

That on or about the 8th day of April, 19— within the City of Los Angeles, County of Los Angeles, State of California, the defendants willfully and maliciously uttered false and defamatory statements concerning the said plaintiff and reflecting upon her character, honesty, integrity, and which said statements were then and there well calculated to, and did, damage the reputation of the plaintiff.

III

That at said time and place, the defendants aforesaid stated to one Everett G. Belder, who was then and there the em-

ployer of the plaintiff, that said plaintiff was a twirp, that the plaintiff was in love with her said employer, that in order to induce her said employer to become more susceptible to her affections and advances, the said plaintiff had previously written anonymous letters to the wife of said employer, accusing said employer of being unfaithful and untrue to his said wife, hoping thereby to bring about a severance of the said marital relationship so that said employer would be free to marry plaintiff; that as a result of said letters, one Sally Brentner, employed as a maid in the Belder household, had met her death, either accidentally or by suicide, all of which was intended and planned by the said plaintiff to be a result of writing said letters, and all of which was a natural and logical result therefrom, and reasonably, logically and naturally to be anticipated by a reasonable person.

IV

That said statements, and each of them, were false and untrue, and were then and there uttered by the defendants with knowledge of their falsity, and/or with a recklessness which constituted a complete disregard of the truth.

V

That said statements, and each of them, were made in the presence of the plaintiff, her employer, and other witnesses, and that as a result thereof, the plaintiff sustained great nervous shock and suffered embarrassment, annoyance, and humiliation; that as a further result of said statements, and each of them, jointly and severally, and solely because of same, on or about the eighth day of April, 19— plaintiff's said employer discharged the said plaintiff from his employ.

VI

That all of said statements were not only false, and were then and there known to be false to the said defendants at the time they were made, but each of said statements was then and there uttered with malice toward this plaintiff, and with a reckless disregard of the truth, and with the deliberate intent of defaming the character of the plaintiff.

WHEREFORE, plaintiff prays judgment against the said defendants in the sum of fifty thousand dollars actual damages, and in an additional sum of fifty thousand dollars as punitive or exemplary damages, making a total of one hundred thousand dollars, and plaintiff prays for her costs of suit incurred herein.

> *A. FRANKLINE KOLBER*
> *Attorney for the Plaintiff*

All of the sea-breeze vitality oozed out of Bertha Cool. She sat down in a chair with knee-buckling finality. "Fry me for an oyster!" she exclaimed.

"But how can she sue *you?*" Elsie Brand demanded indignantly. "My heavens! You didn't have her arrested or anything."

Bertha said, "She's crazy! It was all straightened up right there in Belder's office before we left. Sally Brentner had been writing the letters. God only knows why. You can't conceive of her writing poison-pen letters directing Mrs. Belder's attention and suspicion to her, but that's just what she did. No one will ever know why she did it. But Imogene has no beef coming. It was all straightened out before we left."

"Did you apologize to her?" Elsie asked.

"Hell, no. I hadn't done her any damage, except make her spill a few synthetic tears."

"But she says in that complaint that Belder discharged her," Elsie Brand said. "Why would he have fired her if it was all cleared up?"

"I don't know," Bertha said, "but he must have had it in for her over something else. They'd been having a fight before Sellers and I got to his office that morning."

"How do you know?"

"I could tell she'd been crying. Damn it, you don't suppose that fourflusher used what I said just as an excuse to get rid of the girl, do you?"

"He may have."

85

"Well, I'm going to settle that right now," Bertha Cool said.

"How can she sue the partnership on this?" Elsie asked. "Donald didn't have anything to do with it."

Bertha said, "They'll claim that I was acting for myself and also for and on behalf of the partnership. I can stall the case off on account of Donald being in Europe. . . . No. Damned if I will. I'll appear for myself and the partnership. Donald isn't going to have this to worry about. It'll all be over before he knows anything about it."

Bertha glanced at her wrist watch. "I'm going to see Everett Belder and give him something to think about. I'll damn soon find out what's back of this. He can't use me as a stalking-horse and get away with it. That's what comes of trying to lead the simple life. I pick up what I think is an easy case, try to let go of it when it gets tough, and get sued for a hundred thousand dollars worth of damages."

"Did you," Elsie asked as Bertha Cool started for the door, "call her a twirp?"

Bertha Cool jerked the door open, turned and said, "You're goddamned right I called her a twirp," and pounded her way indignantly down the corridor, managing to find a vacant taxi in front of the building.

"Rockaway Building," she said as she hauled herself into the cab, "and make it snappy."

Bertha Cool found a new secretary in the office of Everett G. Belder, a tall, thin woman somewhere in the forties, with a thin face, muddy complexion, a pointed chin, prominent high-bridged nose, and an austere manner. "Good morning."

"Mr. Belder in?"

"Who is calling, please?" The words were articulated with conscious care, making the simple request seem long and formal.

"Bertha Cool."

"Do you have a card, Miss Cool?"

"Mrs. Cool," Bertha said, raising her voice. "I want to see him about business. I don't have an appointment, and I've been here before. Practice your elocution on someone else. And— Oh, the hell with that stuff. I'm going in."

Bertha strode across the room, heedless of the protests

which the tall, angular woman made with a frigid formality. She jerked the door open.

Everett Belder was tilted back in his chair, his feet up on the desk, ankles crossed, an open newspaper held in front of his face.

"It's all right, Miss Horrison," he said. "Just put the letters on the desk. I'll sign them later."

He turned the page of the paper.

Bertha Cool slammed the door shut with a jar that shook the pictures on the wall.

Everett Belder lowered his newspaper in surprised irritation. "Good heavens! It's Mrs. Cool! Why didn't you let Miss Horrison announce you?"

"Because I'm in a hurry," Bertha said, "and she took too goddamned long pronouncing her words. Get that newspaper out of the way, and tell me what in hell you mean by firing Imogene Dearborne."

Belder slowly folded the newspaper, frowned at Bertha.

"She's my employee. I believe I have the right to terminate the employment any time I wish, Mrs. Cool."

Bertha said angrily, "Don't be so damned formal. You must be trying to live up to that new secretary. I don't care when you fire her, or how you fire her, just so you leave *me* out of it. But she's sued me for a hundred thousand bucks, claiming that I defamed her character and you fired her on account of that."

Belder sat forward in his chair, putting his feet down on the floor with a thud. "*What* do you say she did, Mrs. Cool?"

"Sued me for a hundred thousand."

"I can't believe it."

"Well, she did. Papers were served on me this morning."

"Exactly what does she claim?"

"That I called her a twirp, said she was in love with you, and that she sent those letters. She claims you fired her on the strength of it."

"Why, the damned little liar! She knows better than that."

Bertha settled back comfortably in her chair. For the first time the tense lines about her eyes relaxed. "That," she said, "is what I came over here to find out. Why *did* you fire her?"

"There wasn't anything personal about it," Belder said.

"That is, in a way."

Bertha said angrily, "Quit beating around the bush. Why did you fire her?"

"Well, for one reason, she was too good-looking. She carried herself in a provocative manner. It's hard to explain. She was not only good-looking, but conscious of her good looks."

"What's that got to do with it?"

"Well, when you have a sister-in-law who is as observing as Carlotta Goldring, and a mother-in-law as suspicious as Theresa Goldring, it has a lot to do with it."

"Did they tell you to fire her?"

"No, no. Now, don't misunderstand me, Mrs. Cool. They didn't make any definite suggestions. Imogene was a very nice secretary. A very competent young woman, but she had certain habits, certain—"

Bertha leaned forward in her chair, her eyes boring into those of the sales engineer. "Of all the damned wishy-washy excuses," she said. "Now, come on. Out with it. You'd been having an argument with her before Sergeant Sellers and I got here yesterday morning. She'd been crying. That's when you'd told her she was fired, wasn't it?"

"Well, no. Not exactly."

Bertha said, "Now listen, I *know* you'd been having an argument. If you told her she was fired, or that you weren't going to keep her, *before* I arrived on the scene, it would help a lot in showing that this suit is just a trumped-up piece of blackmail. Can't you see? I've got to show that she didn't get fired because of what I said."

"I can assure you she didn't, Mrs. Cool."

Bertha Cool settled back in exasperation. "Oh, you can, can you. Well *isn't* that just perfectly lovely? Are you accustomed to firing secretaries without having any reason whatever?"

"But, Mrs. Cool, I did have a reason. I'm trying to explain."

"And I'm trying to find out," Bertha said with elaborate sarcasm. "I've been listening and listening, and you've been talking and talking, and you still haven't explained, and I still haven't found out. I don't know whether there's anything we can do about it or not."

"Well, Mrs. Cool, to be perfectly frank with you, there were several things which entered into it. I am hesitating somewhat because I can't put my finger upon any one particular thing and say that that was the determining factor. However, the girl was a little too conscious of her good looks. That is, a person walking into an office and seeing her would immediately wonder— Oh, well, you know."

Bertha said, "I don't, and apparently you don't."

"And another thing," Belder went on, "is that she was indiscreet."

"In what way?"

"She gave out information she had no right to give out."

"*Now* we're getting somewhere. What did she give out?"

"Well, of course, Mrs. Cool, I— Hang it, it's nothing I care to talk about."

"It's something *I* care to talk about," Bertha said, "and you've got me into this mess, so it's up to you to do what you can to get me out. Now, what information did she give out?"

"She was indiscreet."

Bertha's face colored. "You talk just like a merry-go-round. And every time we come around to the place where the record starts repeating, damned if I don't grab the brass ring and have to ride all over again. Pardon me for seeming impatient. Just keep right on. She was indiscreet. Why was she indiscreet? She gave out information. What was the information? Well, you see, she was indiscreet. Why was she indiscreet? Well, she's good-looking. What's indiscreet about being good-looking? Well, there was information she gave out. Who did she give out information to? Well, she looks provocative. Anyone coming in the office would think— Go right ahead. When you start running down, perhaps you'll *say* something."

"It was what she told my mother-in-law," Belder blurted.

Bertha's eyes snapped with interest.

"Now we *are* getting somewhere. What did she tell Mrs. Goldring?"

"That I was going to compromise that Nunnely judgment as soon as I could get hold of Mabel, and that I was moving heaven and earth to find her for *that* reason."

"What was wrong with that?" Bertha asked.

"Everything."

"I don't get you."

"In the first place, the minute Mrs. Goldring knew I was trying to compromise that judgment, she'd try throwing monkey wrenches in the machinery just on general principles. In the second place, I'd been telling her how much I loved Mabel and how much it would mean to me if she walked out on me. I thought that perhaps some of that would get back to Mabel and might help ·the situation some. Now, if Mrs. Goldring thinks that my interest was purely financial— Well, you can see the predicament I'm in."

"Why didn't you tell your mother-in-law the stuff I told you to tell her? That you hoped your wife hadn't left you but if she *had*, there were plenty of other women—"

"That may be good advice on general principles, Mrs. Cool, but it wouldn't work in this particular instance. It sounded very logical in your office, but when I got home and faced my mother-in-law— Well, I thought this other way was better, that's all."

"I see. You got my advice but didn't follow it, is that right?"

"In a way, yes."

"All right. Let's get back to this secretary of yours. She spilled that information to your mother-in-law. You found out about it. *How* did you find out about it?"

"Good heavens! *How* did I find out about it? I found out about it because my mother-in-law became hysterical; because she kept yapping at me that my entire interest in the matter was financial, and all I wanted my wife for was to get some money out of her."

"This was before Sally Brentner's body was discovered?"

"Yes, of course."

"When?"

"To be exact it was shortly before the office closed Wednesday afternoon. And after I'd had that dinned in my ears all night, I wasn't in any mood to be charitable with Miss Dearborne."

"Specifically then, you were all on edge when you came up to the office Thursday morning. That was yesterday. You were angry and worried and you hadn't slept. You called Imogene into your office and proceeded to put her on the carpet. Is that right?"

"Yes, in a way."

"Now, you knew that Sergeant Sellers was going to call on you that morning?"

"Yes."

"And you had suggested that the interview should take place at the office rather than at the house?"

"That's right. I wanted to keep my mother-in-law from nagging me about Mrs. Cornish."

"And before we arrived, you called Imogene in and proceeded to tell her off?"

"Well—I'm afraid I rebuked her."

"*What* did you tell her?"

"I told her she'd volunteered information that she had no right to give."

"What did she do?"

"She said she was simply trying to appease Mrs. Goldring; that she thought that was the best way to handle the situation."

"Then what did you say?"

"I told her that I was capable of doing the thinking for the office."

"All right. Go on. Then what happened?"

"Then she made some remark that I thought was a little impertinent and then is when I lost my temper. I told her she'd put me in a bad position because of her indiscretion."

"What were the exact words you used?"

"I'm afraid I was angry."

"What were the words you used?"

"I said she'd been shooting off her big mouth."

"Then what?"

"That started her crying."

"Well, go on. I can't stand here and pump it out of you a word at a time. What happened? She started crying—then you fired her, didn't you?"

"No, I didn't. She got up and left the office without a word and went back to her typewriter."

"Still crying?"

"I guess so. She was when she left the office."

"So you got up and followed her out and—"

"No. To tell the truth, I didn't."

"What did you do?"

"I just sat here waiting—then you came in."

Bertha said angrily, "Damn it, why didn't you go ahead and fire her then and there and get it over with?"

"Because I wasn't certain I was going to discharge her at the time. I'd lost my temper and I wanted to think it over. I—"

"But you *intended* to fire her just as soon as she'd calmed down—just as soon as you could do it without making a scene?"

"I'm not certain that I did. To be frank with you, Mrs. Cool, I didn't know exactly *what* to do."

"You certainly didn't intend to let her keep on working for you," Bertha said.

"Well, I wasn't certain but what I'd been at fault—at least partially."

Bertha said with exasperation, "My God! How many times do I have to lead you up to the trough before you take a drink?"

"I'm afraid I don't understand you, Mrs. Cool."

"All you've got to say," Bertha explained patiently, "is that you intended to fire her because of this indiscretion; that you had your mind made up; that the only reason you didn't have it all over with before Sellers and I got here was that you didn't want to pick on her when she was crying and you didn't want to have a scene. So you decided to wait until after Sergeant Sellers and I had left and then tell her you didn't need her any more. Once you testify to those facts, it's absolutely clear that she wasn't fired on account of anything I said. Do you get the point?"

"I believe I understand the legal point, yes."

"Well, that's all there is to it," Bertha said. "But I keep bringing you up to it, and you keep pulling back on the lead rope like a frightened horse. For God's sake, let's not muff our signals on this thing."

"But," Belder said, "while I appreciate the *legal point*, Mrs. Cool, I'm afraid I can't co-operate with you."

"What do you mean now?"

"Simply that I hadn't actually decided to discharge Miss

Dearborne at that time. I made up my mind afterward."

Bertha sighed. "All right, I can at least depend on you to testify that you'd had words with her over this—"

"Good heavens, no, Mrs. Cool!"

"What?"

"Emphatically not. Then I'd be asked why I was rebuking her—and if it ever came out that I had taken her to task over something she had told my mother-in-law, then Mrs. Goldring would never forgive me. You know, claim I was trying to keep things from her. That, as Mabel's mother— No, Mrs. Cool, I can't help you at all. This is just between you and me. If you ever asked me in court, I'd even deny there had been any trouble at all. I'd have to."

Bertha Cool lurched to her feet, glowered angrily at Everett Belder.

"Nuts!" she said, and stalked out of the office.

11 A QUESTION OF MALICE

ROGER P. DRUMSON, senior partner of Drumson, Holbret, and Drumson, finished reading the complaint, then looked up over his glasses at Bertha Cool. "As I understand it, Mrs. Cool, you were employed to find out who wrote these letters. You had reasonable grounds to believe the plaintiff wrote them?"

"Yes."

"That's good. *Very* good! Now just what were these grounds?"

"I knew they had been written by a first-rate typist on a portable. I knew Imogene Dearborne had actually written a message to her employer on this same typewriter."

"How did you know that?"

"By comparing the typewriting."

"No, no. I mean how did you know *she* had written it on that same typewriter?"

"She admitted she had."

"In the presence of witnesses?"

"Yes."

"Before you made this accusation?"

"Sure. I made certain of my grounds before I exploded my bombshell."

Drumson beamed at Bertha. "Very, very clever, Mrs. Cool. Now, as I understand it, you were giving this information in the highest good faith to interested parties, is that right?"

"That's right."

"Splendid!"

Drumson returned to a perusal of the complaint, frowned,

looked accusingly up at Bertha. "*Did* you call her a twirp, Mrs. Cool?"

"Yes."

"That's bad."

"Why?"

"It implies malice."

"What the hell's that got to do with it?"

Drumson smiled a fatherly, slightly patronizing smile. "You see, Mrs. Cool, the law provides certain immunities to a person who acts in good faith and without malice, as a reasonable person might do. In other words, certain communications are known, in the eyes of the law, as privileged communications; but in order to take advantage of the privileged communication provisions of the law, a person must show that everything he said was said in good faith, and without malice.

"Now, as I understand the situation, you are a private detective. You had been employed by Everett Belder, among other things, to ferret out the person who was responsible for writing certain letters. You had reasonable grounds to make you believe that this secretary was the person in question. It was a mistake, but an honest mistake which any person might have made."

Bertha's nod was eager.

"So," Drumson went on, "your communication was privileged, *provided* it was made without malice, Mrs. Cool."

"Well, it was. I didn't even know the girl."

"Then *why* did you call her a twirp?"

"It's just an expression."

Drumson shook his head in mild rebuke, and said, "Tut tut!"

"Then I had a right to act on that assumption," Bertha said. "She can't stick me. Is that right?"

"Well, now, Mrs. Cool, that also depends. Your assumption of her guilt must have been a *reasonable* assumption, predicated upon an investigation of all the evidence. I believe you stated that a certain Sally Brentner turned out to be the guilty party?"

"Yes."

"How did you discover that?"

95

"The police discovered it," Bertha admitted reluctantly.

"How?"

"The second letter showed that the woman must have been able to see what was going on in Belder's office. Police decided that she must have been in an office across the street looking through the window into Belder's office. The police stood in Belder's office, looked across the street, and found there were only one or two offices the person could possibly have used for such a purpose. They knew the time of day they wanted to cover. She'd been a patient in a dentist chair."

Drumson frowned. "But why didn't *you* do that, Mrs. Cool? It seems to me it was the most logical method of trapping the guilty person."

Bertha said, "I thought I didn't have to."

"Why?"

"I thought I had all the evidence I needed."

"Then you deliberately overlooked this bit of evidence?"

"Well, I don't know that there was anything deliberate about it."

"In other words," Drumson said, "it just hadn't occurred to you at the time, is that it?"

"Well," Bertha said, "it—" She hesitated.

"Come, come," Drumson said, "you must tell your lawyer *all* the facts of the case, Mrs. Cool, or he cannot work to your best advantage."

"Well," Bertha blurted, "Sergeant Sellers kept wanting to go at it that way, but I told him there wasn't any need to."

Drumson's voice held shocked incredulity. "My dear Mrs. Cool! Do you mean to say that the police suggested to you that this logical, this perfectly simple, this very feasible method of locating the person you wanted should be followed, and that you not only refused to conduct such an investigation, but dissuaded *them* from doing so, and *then* made this charge against this Imogene Dearborne?"

Bertha said, "It sounds like hell when you put it that way."

"It's the way the attorney for the other side will put it, Mrs. Cool."

"Well, I guess that's about right."

"That's bad, Mrs. Cool, very bad."

"Why?"

"It means that you refused to make an investigation. It means that you had no *reasonable* grounds for making the accusation you did. That has a tendency to imply malice, and that, in turn, robs you of your privileged-communication immunity."

"Well, you're making it sound as though *you* were the lawyer for the other side."

Drumson smiled. "Just wait until you actually hear the lawyer on the other side. Now that expression of opprobrium— What was it? let's see. . . . Oh, yes, a twirp—a *twirp*, Mrs. Cool. Why on earth did you call her that?"

Bertha flushed. "Because it's the mildest term you could use in describing the mealymouthed little bit—"

"Mrs. Cool!" Drumson exploded.

Bertha lapsed into silence.

"Mrs. Cool, the question of malice is one of the most important in this whole case. If you are to win this case, you'll have to establish that you held no malice toward the plaintiff, none whatever. In the future, refer to the plaintiff in this action as a very estimable young woman of unimpeachable moral character. She is, perhaps, mistaken, but as far as her character is concerned, she is a paragon of virtue. Otherwise, Mrs. Cool, *it—is—going—to—cost—you—money*. Do you understand?'

"Well, when I'm talking to you, can't I tell the truth?"

"When you are talking to me, when you are talking to friends, even when you are thinking, you must refer to this young woman only in words that can be repeated anywhere. Can't you see, Mrs. Cool, that your thoughts as well as your conversation are habit-forming patterns? If you use derogatory expressions in your thoughts, or in some of your conversations, those words will unconsciously slip out at inopportune times. Now, repeat after me, 'This young woman is a very estimable young woman.' "

Bertha Cool said, with evident reluctance, "Goddamn her, she's a very estimable young woman."

"And see that you always so refer to her," Drumson warned.

"I'll try. If it'll save me money, I'll try."

"Now, what is this about witnesses being present?"

"Everett Belder and—"

"Now, just a moment. Mr. Belder was your employer?"

"My client."

"I see. Pardon me, your client. And who else was present?"

"Sergeant Sellers."

"He was from the police?"

"From Headquarters, that's right."

Drumson beamed. "I think that does it very nicely, Mrs. Cool. There were no other persons there except the plaintiff?"

"And this Carlotta Goldring. She's Belder's sister-in-law."

"And was she one of your clients?"

"No."

"What was she doing there?"

"She just opened the door and walked in."

"And do you mean to say that you made this accusation in front of Carlotta Goldring?"

"Well, I don't know just how much I said before she came in, and how much I said afterward."

"But, Mrs. Cool, *why* didn't you wait until this young woman had left the office? If she was virtually a stranger to you, it seems that reasonable prudence would have caused you to withhold any accusation while she was there. We can't possibly claim a privileged communication as far as this Carlotta Goldring is concerned."

Bertha said angrily, "I'll tell you why I didn't do it; because I was trying to carry on my business. That's the trouble with you lawyers. All you think about is lawsuits. If a person tried to carry on business so he'd be within the letter of the law, he'd *never* get anything done."

Drumson shook his head chidingly. "I'm sorry, Mrs. Cool, but you've been indiscreet. You can't minimize that indiscretion by abusing the law or blaming the lawyers. This is going to be a very difficult action to defend. I'll want five hundred dollars as a retainer, then we'll see what can be done. That retainer will carry the case through the pleadings and up to the time of trial. At that time you can make an additional remuneration in case we haven't been able to get the case disposed of before—"

"Five hundred dollars!" Bertha all but screamed.

"That's right, Mrs. Cool."

"Why, fry me for an oyster! *Five—hundred—dollars!*"

"Five hundred dollars, Mrs. Cool."

"What the hell are you talking about? I didn't make but fifty dollars out of the whole case."

"I'm afraid you don't understand, Mrs. Cool. It isn't what you have made out of the employment that counts, it's the fact that right now," and Drumson tapped the papers on his desk with a solemn forefinger, "you have a potential liability of one hundred thousand dollars chalked up against you in a court of justice. My associates and I *may* be able to beat this case. I can't tell, but—"

Bertha got up from her chair, reached over and pulled the papers out from under the lawyer's hand.

"You're crazy. I'm not going to pay any five hundred dollars."

"But my *dear* Mrs. Cool, if you don't do something within ten days of the time this paper was served on you, you'll—"

"How do you go about denying you owe anything like this?" Bertha asked.

"You file what we lawyers call an 'answer,' denying the charges contained in the complaint."

"How much will you charge me to draw me one of these answers?"

"Do you mean just to draw up an answer?"

"Yes."

"Well—I wouldn't advise you to do that, Mrs. Cool."

"Why not?"

"Well, there are certain things about the complaint which impressed me as being rather ambiguous. The document quite evidently was hastily drawn. I think it is subject to a special demurrer, and perhaps to a general demurrer as well."

"What's a demurrer?"

"That's another pleading—a paper filed in court—in which you point out defects in the complaint."

"And what happens after you file that?"

"You argue it."

"Is the other lawyer there?"

"Oh, yes, naturally."

"Then what happens?"

"If your point is well taken, the judge sustains the demurrer."

"And that means you win the lawsuit?"

"Oh, no. Then the other side is given ten days to amend the complaint."

"So that it makes a better complaint?"

"In a way, yes. That's a layman's way of expressing it."

"I suppose all this argument costs money."

"Naturally, I have to be compensated for my time. That was why I told you five hundred dollars as a retainer would take the case through the stage of pleadings and up to—"

"Why in hell," Bertha interrupted, "should I pay a lawyer five hundred dollars to go into court to tell the other lawyer how to make his complaint better?"

"You don't understand, Mrs. Cool. You persist in looking at it as a layman. There is a tactical advantage in having a demurrer sustained."

"What advantage? What does it get you?"

"You gain time."

"What good does it do to gain time?"

"Why, you've postponed the matter. You've gained time."

"And what do you do with this time when you've gained it?"

Drumson's smile tried to be patronizing but there was a vague uneasiness in his manner as he faced Bertha's glittering eyes. "My *dear* Mrs. Cool, you're letting yourself get all worked up. After all, you're merely a layman. These matters—"

"What the hell do you do with the time when you've gained it?" Bertha interrupted in a voice which stridently demanded the conversational right of way.

"Why, we work on your case, study up on it."

"And I pay for all the time you put in?"

"Naturally I have to be compensated—"

"So I pay you to tell the other lawyer how to make a better case so you can gain time to charge me more for putting in more time on *my* case. To hell with that stuff. Don't you know enough law to know how to try this lawsuit right now?"

"Of course. If I—"

"Then what the hell do you want to put in more time on more study for? If you don't know how to handle this case say so, and I'll get someone who does."

"My *dear* Mrs. Cool! You simply——"

"The hell with that stuff," Bertha interrupted. "I don't want any demurrers. I don't want to pay fancy prices to gain time I'm going to have to pay for. I simply want to file an answer telling this goddamned little twirp where she gets off."

"My dear Mrs. Cool! *Please!* I ask you as your attorney, *don't* keep referring to the plaintiff as a twirp."

"She's a damned gold-digging little bitch," Bertha said, angrily raising her voice. "She's a mealymouthed hypocrite."

"Mrs. Cool! Mrs. Cool! You'll ruin your chances of defending this lawsuit."

"You know what she is as well as I do. She——"

"Mrs. Cool! *Please.* Now I am going to tell you something once and for all. If you even *think* of the plaintiff in this action in that way, you're going to lose your temper in court and throw your entire case out the window. Those words show malice. I instruct you as your lawyer, I warn you, that you must studiously make a habit of referring to this young woman as a thoroughly estimable young lady, otherwise you're going to regret it."

"You mean I've got to let her throw this action in my face and still like her?"

"She's misguided. She took offense where none was meant. She's high-strung and her lawyers have taken advantage of an unusual situation to try and collect an excessive amount. But the young woman in the case, the plaintiff herself is, so far as you know, a thoroughly estimable young woman, and you must school yourself to refer to her as such."

Bertha took a deep breath.

"How much?"

"For just drawing an answer?"

"Yes."

"Well, I would say that in order to do that we'd need to have a preliminary discussion as to the facts of the case, and——"

"How much?"

"Oh, say seventy-five dollars."

"For just drawing an answer? Why, I'll bet I could get somebody to just draw an answer for—"

"But we'd have to discuss the facts with you first."

"Facts nothing," Bertha said. "All I want is an answer that will call this—this estimable young woman a goddamned liar. An answer that will claim that she didn't get fired because of anything I said, that whatever I said was what you call a privileged communication, and all that stuff."

"Well," Drumson said with obvious reluctance, "I guess perhaps, under those circumstances, a charge of twenty-five dollars. . . . But you understand, Mrs. Cool, we wouldn't accept any responsibility for anything in connection with the case. We wouldn't want our name to appear on the pleading. It would simply be an answer that we would draw, and you could sign, appearing *in propria persona.*"

"What does that mean?" Bertha asked.

"That's a legal expression that means a person is appearing without a lawyer. That is, that the party filing the pleading is acting as his own lawyer."

Bertha said, "That's what I want. Draw up the answer. I'll sign it myself, and appear myself, representing myself. And I want to get it by Monday morning. I'll file that and have it off my mind."

Drumson watched her leave the office. Then with a sigh he pressed the button which summoned his stenographer.

12

ALL WOOL AND—

SERGEANT SELLERS tilted back a somewhat battered, uncushioned swivel chair at Headquarters and grinned across at Bertha Cool. "You're looking great, Bertha. What's this about that Dearborne girl filing suit against you?"

Bertha said, "The little—" and stopped.

"Go ahead," Sellers remarked, grinning. "I've probably heard all of the words you know. Get them off your chest, you'll feel better."

Bertha said, "I've just come from my lawyer's. Any names I call her might show malice, and that might hurt my lawsuit. So far as I'm concerned, she's a very estimable young lady, mistaken perhaps, misguided certainly; but a very charming young bitch of unquestioned virtue."

Sellers threw back his head and laughed. He pulled a cigar from his pocket, and Bertha took a cigarette from her purse. Sellers leaned across the table to hold a match to her cigarette.

"We're getting polite," Bertha said.

"Oh, hell," Sellers observed cheerfully. "We know the conventional obligations of a host. We just don't pay attention to them most of the time."

He dropped the match into a large-mouthed polished brass cuspidor which sat on a rubber mat by the side of the big table. All over the table and on the floor around the cuspidor, ribbons of black had been burned into the wood, places where cigarettes had been allowed to lie neglected.

Sergeant Sellers followed Bertha's glance, and grinned.

103

"You always see that around Police Headquarters," he said. "A man could write a book about the stories back of those cigarette marks. Sometimes you put a cigarette down to answer the telephone. It's a homicide, and you go busting out and forget all about your cigarette. Sometimes you're pouring questions at a guy and he begins to crack. He starts wanting cigarettes, just a whiff or two, and then tosses them away. He's nervous, he couldn't hit the mouth of the spittoon if it were four feet in diameter. And those short marks— Well, they're caused by the boys getting careless. Toss 'em in the general direction you want 'em to go, and forget 'em. What do you want me to do with this Dearborne girl?"

"What can you do with her?"

"Plenty."

"I don't get you."

Sellers said, "You gave me a break in that case involving the blind man. I'll never forget it, Bertha. We don't forgive our enemies, or forget our friends up here. Now, that girl sues you for slander. She's asking for damages for her reputation. That means she puts her reputation into the issues. We'll go back over her past with a fine-toothed comb. We'll dig up things that will make her squirm. Then your lawyers can let her lawyers know that you have the dope on her, and she'll quit."

Bertha said, "I'm my own lawyer, and don't tell me I've got a fool for a client."

"What's the idea acting as your own lawyer?"

"The lawyer who does my work wanted five hundred bucks for a retainer, then had the crust to tell me I could pay more when trial came up."

Sergeant Sellers whistled.

"That's just the way I felt about it," Bertha said.

"Well, let me talk with him, Bertha. Perhaps I can do something about it."

"I've already talked with him about it," Bertha said. "Something's been done about it."

"Then he's going to represent you?"

"No. He's going to draw an answer. I'm going to file the answer and pay him twenty-five dollars. From then on I'm on my own."

Sellers said, "Well, let me go to work on Imogene. Perhaps I can dig something up. A girl who runs to a law office that way and files suit against you almost before the words are off your lips is apt to have something in her past she won't want dragged out into the open."

Bertha said, "Damn her. If I get my hands on her, I'll slap her to sleep. The goddamned—estimable young lady!"

Sellers grinned. "I know just how you feel."

"What have you found out about the Belder business?" Bertha asked.

"I think it's murder."

"Didn't you think so all along?"

"Not quite as strongly as I do now. An autopsy shows that she died of carbon-monoxide poisoning. She'd been dead for some little time—perhaps an hour or two before the knife was stuck into her."

"Any clues?" Bertha asked, her eyes narrowing watchfully.

Sellers hesitated for a moment as though debating whether to tell Bertha what was on his mind, then he said abruptly, "It's a man's crime."

"What do you mean by that?"

"I mean a man did it."

"Not Mrs. Belder?"

"I'm crossing her out."

"Why?"

"The carving knife."

"What about it?"

"A maid doesn't peel potatoes with a ten-inch knife."

"Naturally."

"A woman would know that. A man wouldn't. Either Sally met her death accidentally, and someone, fearing he'd be blamed, tried to make it look like an accident, or else he was trying to cover up a murder."

"Who could have murdered her?" Bertha asked.

Sellers grinned at her. "Everett Belder, for one."

"Phooey!"

"Don't be too damned certain. . . . By the way, Mrs. Belder's cat came back."

"The deuce it did!"

"That's right."

"When?"

"Last night."

"Early?"

"Around midnight."

"Belder let it in?"

"No. Mrs. Goldring heard it yowling and opened the door. The cat came in. Seemed to be well fed, but kept yowling, kept padding around the house all night and yowling. Wouldn't stay put and settle down."

"Probably misses Mrs. Belder," Bertha said.

"Probably."

The telephone on Sellers's desk tinkled tentatively.

Sergeant Sellers picked up the receiver, said, "Hello," then nodded to Bertha. "For you, Bertha. Your office calling. Says it's important."

Bertha took the telephone, heard Elsie Brand's voice speaking in the low, somewhat muffled tones of one who is trying to be secretive by holding her lips well within the mouthpiece of the telephone. "Mrs. Cool, Mr. Belder keeps telephoning. He says he has to see you right away."

"To hell with him," Bertha announced cheerfully and promptly.

"I think he has another letter."

"And hasn't guts enough to do anything about it, eh?" Bertha asked.

"Something like that."

"Well, you know what he can do," Bertha said, and then with growing impatience, "My God, Elsie, don't chase me around when I'm working on a case just because Belder wants—"

"Another matter," Elsie broke in. "Just hold the phone a moment, Mrs. Cool. I'll go in the other office and see if I can find it among your papers."

Bertha frowned, then, realizing that Elsie was making an excuse to get away from a client in the office, waited until she heard a faint click on the line. Elsie Brand's voice, sounding less muffled, said, "There's a woman here who wants to see you; won't give her name. Says she has to see you at once, that it will be worth a great deal of money to you."

"What's she look like?"

"She's somewhere around forty, but she has a very good figure. She looks a little—well, as though she could be hard on occasion. She has a short veil hanging down from her hat brim and ducks her head so the veil conceals her eyes every time she catches me looking at her. She says she can't wait."

Bertha said, "I'll come up right away."

"And what shall I tell Mr. Belder? He's been calling every few minutes."

"You know what you can tell him," Bertha said, and hung up.

Sergeant Sellers grinned at her. "Business pretty good, Bertha?"

"So-so."

"Glad to see it. You deserve the best there is. You're all wool and—"

Bertha got angrily to her feet. "It wouldn't have been so bad if you hadn't stopped there," she said. "Why the hell didn't you go ahead and say 'a yard wide' and act as though it didn't mean anything. But no, you had to stop and—"

"I was afraid you might take offense. I didn't realize how it was going to sound until—"

"And *why* should I take offense?" Bertha demanded.

Sergeant Sellers coughed apologetically. "I was just trying to pay you a compliment, Bertha."

"I see," Bertha said sarcastically. *"A yard wide!* Phooey!"

Sergeant Sellers's eyes remained fixed on the door after Bertha had slammed it shut. A smile twitched the corners of his mouth. He reached across the desk, picked up the receiver, said into the telephone, "Did you get all of that conversation Bertha had with her office? . . . Okay, write it out and bring it in. I want to look it over. . . . No, let her go. Give her lots of rope. . . . No, I don't want her to hang herself, but when she gets tangled up, she starts moving with rapidity and violence. Someone who's on the other end of the rope is going to get jerked into the limelight so fast it'll scare him to death. . . . No, no. Don't try to intercept that Belder letter; *we* don't want to take the responsibility of opening it. Let Bertha steam it open and then *I'll* take it from Bertha."

107

13

SIMPLE, BUT VERY IMPORTANT

THE WOMAN who rose as Bertha Cool opened the door of her office seemed, at first glance, an attractive woman in the very early thirties, with a figure that could still have fitted into her wedding dress, and perhaps her graduation dress as well. It was only when Bertha Cool's sharp eyes peered through the protection of the veil, past the mask of rouge and mascara, and detected the fine wrinkles about the eyes and the lines of tension about the mouth, that she placed her visitor as being somewhere around forty.

"You're Mrs. Cool, aren't you?"

"Yes."

"I thought so. The way you opened the door. You fit in with what I've heard about you."

Bertha nodded, glanced inquiringly at Elsie Brand. Elsie nodded her head almost imperceptibly.

"Come in," Bertha invited, and ushered her visitor into her private office.

"Did you," Bertha asked casually, "give your name and address to my secretary?"

"No."

"That's required. It's a custom of the office."

"I understand."

"Well?" Bertha asked.

"My name and address will come later. The first question is whether you are free to accept certain employment."

"What sort of employment?"

"You're working for Mr. Belder?"

108

"I *have* done work for him."

"There's an unfinished matter on which you are working?"

Bertha frowned. "I don't think I care to answer that question—not in so many words. Do you want me to do something against Mr. Belder's interest?"

"No. Something that would probably be very much to his best interest."

"Why the questions then?"

"*Mrs*. Belder might not like it."

Bertha said, "Mrs. Belder is nothing in my young life."

"I think, Mrs. Cool, you're the logical person to do what I want."

Bertha simply sat there waiting.

"Mr. Belder has, of course, told you about the family—Mrs. Goldring and Carlotta."

Bertha jerked her head in a quick affirmation which wasted no time.

"Have you met them?"

"Just met them, that's all."

The woman's black eyes were boring into Bertha Cool's now. Even through the fringe of veil, Bertha could see light from the window reflecting from them as though they had been polished black granite.

"Go on," Bertha said.

"I am Carlotta's mother."

"*Oh,* oh!"

"*Now* you see why it is necessary for me to keep myself in the background until I am very, very certain that you can do what I want."

"What do you want?"

"Before I tell you what I want, I want you to understand my position."

"Before you take up any of my time," Bertha stated firmly, "I want you to understand mine."

"What is it?"

"I work for money. Money talks in this business. Sympathy I give outside of office hours. I can't take a hard-luck story down to the bank, write my name across the back of it, shove it through the window and get a deposit entered to my account."

109

"I understand that perfectly."

"If this is a hard-luck story, I'm not interested. I just didn't want to have any misapprehension on your part."

"There is none, Mrs. Cool."

"All right, go ahead."

"It is absolutely imperative that you understand my position and the reasons back of it."

"You said that before."

"I can't overemphasize it."

"I'm listening."

"You're a rather competent, capable woman, Mrs. Cool. One feels a little embarrassed in discussing— Well, the businesslike atmosphere of your office is hardly conducive to a discussion of romantic details."

Bertha said, "By the time romance gets to this shop it's sordid as hell. Wives want evidence, women want damages, men want out."

"I can understand."

"I suppose," Bertha went on, "you want to tell me something about the dashing personality of the gay seducer who was Carlotta's father."

A faint half smile touched the lips of her visitor, a sardonic travesty on mirth. "I was the seducer."

"You interest me."

"I didn't come here to hide behind any falsehoods."

"That's just as well."

"In my youth I was wild. Ever since I can remember I've been an untamed, rebellious soul. I rebelled against schoolrooms. I rebelled against conventions. I called my mother a liar when she tried to tell me things about Santa Claus. She never explained the facts of life to me. By the time she thought I was ready, I could have told her things she never knew. Gradually, she came to a realization of that. I guess it broke her heart."

Bertha made no comment.

"It's important," the woman went on, "that you get just that picture in its proper perspective."

"Okay, I've got it."

"I doubt if you have, Mrs. Cool. I wasn't the boy-struck young adolescent, nor was I an over-sexed, under-disciplined personality. I was simply a young body with the inquiring mind of an adult. I was impatient of hypocrisy and the false modesty which seemed to shroud the actions of older people. I loved to take chances. That made for excitement, and I thrived on excitement. In fact, Mrs. Cool, it was excitement and change that I craved. I was impatient to plunge into all of the life there was to live, and to see what it was like. And then there was Carlotta.

"I wasn't frightened when I realized. I wasn't particularly ashamed. I was curious, and a little startled that such things could happen to *me*. I left home and went to work in another state. Before Carlotta's birth I put myself in touch with an institution. I refused to sign certain waivers and legal papers so that my child could be properly adopted. My baby was mine. I knew that I couldn't keep her but I had a fierce sense of possession. She was mine. She would always be mine, no matter where we were. Remember, Mrs. Cool, this was when jobs weren't easy. There were times when I went hungry."

"I've been hungry," Bertha said simply.

"And now, Mrs. Cool, I'm going to say something on behalf of the conventions. I still think they're founded on hypocrisy and self-deceit, but they are the conventional pattern of life. They represent the rules under which the game is played. Once you violate those rules, you are cheating on civilization, and when you begin to cheat you soon lose your attitude of proud defiance and begin cutting corners here and there. You cheat on one thing, pretty soon you cheat on another. You start covering up. Slowly, imperceptibly, you lose your proud independence. You become an opportunist, you get on the defensive, and, after that, you develop a furtive side to your nature."

Bertha said impatiently, "Listen, if you're trying to justify yourself to me, don't do it. You don't need to. If you've got the money and I've got the time, I'll do anything you want. If you haven't got money, I haven't got the time. You apparently overlooked the fact that I've had my own ups and downs, and I've lived something of a life myself."

"It isn't that, Mrs. Cool. It's the fact that you must realize the situation."

111

"I understand that all right, but how did Mrs. Goldring adopt your daughter if you didn't sign the proper releases?"

"That is the thing I am trying to explain to you."

"Well, for God's sake go ahead and explain it then."

"Mrs. Goldring, even twenty years ago, was a very scheming, persistent person."

"I can understand that."

"She went to the institution where babies were left for adoption. There was more demand than there were babies to fill that demand. Mrs. Goldring had had one child—the woman who is now Mrs. Belder. She couldn't have any more. Later on she wanted a younger sister for that child. She found she would have to wait for some time. Then she saw Carlotta. She became attracted to her. The persons in charge of the institution told her that I had been paying for Carlotta's board, that recently payments had stopped, but that I still wouldn't sign a release. They were very much concerned about the whole situation."

"Go on," Bertha said. "What did Mrs. Goldring do?"

"Mrs. Goldring either got them to violate one of the rules of the institution, or what is more likely, won their confidence and took advantage of it to steal their records concerning Carlotta."

"She would do that," Bertha said.

"And so she came to me and forced me to sign a release!"

"Forced?"

"Yes."

"How did she do that?"

The black eyes stared defiantly at Bertha. "I told you that once a person started defying conventions, there was no telling just where he'd stop. You—"

"Don't bother with all that stuff. Just tell me why you signed."

"And," the woman went on, heedless of Bertha's interruption, "one person can't fight the world. It makes no difference whether public opinion is right or wrong. No character is big enough or strong enough to stand out against public opinion without getting bruised, without— Have you ever struggled with a great big fat man, Mrs. Cool?"

Bertha Cool frowned as she probed her recollection. "No-o-o," she said at length. "Well, if I have, I can't remember it right now."

"I have," her visitor said. "And fighting against public opinion is like fighting with a big fat man who simply puts his weight on you and smothers you. He doesn't need to do anything; you simply can't fight against that oppressing weight."

"All right," Bertha said impatiently, "you couldn't fight against public opinion. You've told me that four or five times."

Her visitor said, "It explains why Mrs. Goldring got me to sign that release. I was in the penitentiary when she found me."

"Oh, oh!"

"You can understand the position in which she put me. She did it very nicely. It was a beautiful form of blackmail. In prison I was without funds. I couldn't support my daughter. Mrs. Goldring was in a position to give her a good home. Whatever dreams I might have had of waiting until my child had grown to a point where she could understand her mother, and then having a reunion with her, or of being able to provide a home for her while she was still so young that she wouldn't remember about the institution—all those dreams had evaporated. I was in for a five-year stretch. I didn't serve it all, but at that time I didn't know I wouldn't have to."

"What," Bertha asked, "were you in for?"

The mouth tightened. "That, Mrs. Cool, to put it bluntly, is none of your business."

"Go ahead and put it bluntly, dearie," Bertha said. "I'm a blunt woman myself."

"That's going to help things."

"Okay," Bertha announced. "What do you want?"

The woman smiled. "Remember that my hands are tied. Mrs. Goldring has a hold over me."

"I don't get it."

"She holds my past as a threat over me to keep me from playing my hand. Carlotta would be terribly shocked if she knew her mother had been in the penitentiary. Otherwise, I might appear on the scene and make a bid for Carlotta's affections. I'm in a position now to do much more for her than Mrs. Goldring is. Mrs. Goldring has spent the insurance money she received at the time of her husband's death. I am relatively wealthy."

Bertha asked curiously, "How could you have emerged from the penitentiary and made enough money to—"

"I'm afraid I'll have to be blunt again, Mrs. Cool."

"Oh, hell," Bertha said. "I know it's none of my business but you interest me—now."

"Yes," her visitor said dryly, "I can see that the financial details interest you more than the romantic."

Bertha thought that over for a few moments and said, "I guess you're right."

"The only way," the woman went on, "that Mrs. Goldring could compete with me financially would be in the event she inherited money. The only chance she stands of inheriting money is if Mrs. Belder should die, leaving a will, leaving all of her property to her mother. I understand such a will has been made, and I further understand that Mrs. Belder has disappeared."

Bertha tugged at the lobe of her left ear, an infallible sign of intense concentration. "What do you mean when you say 'disappeared'?"

"Committed a murder and skipped out. Eventually she's going to be caught. The excitement incident to all of that is apt to make her heart pop—just like that," and the woman snapped her fingers to illustrate the celerity of Mrs. Belder's departure.

Bertha said nothing, kept her thumb and forefinger pulling at her ear.

"You can see the position in which that leaves me," the woman went on. "Mrs. Goldring would inherit Mrs. Belder's money. She would use that to hold Carlotta."

"You mean Carlotta's affections are something that can be bought?" Bertha Cool asked skeptically.

"Don't be silly, Mrs. Cool. Carlotta isn't like that; and, on the other hand, she isn't a fool. Let's look at the situation this way. I am her mother. There are certain black marks, very definite black marks, in my record. Those constitute reasons why she is very apt to repudiate any claim I might have to her affections because of the natural relationship. I think you understand my position there, don't you?"

Bertha nodded.

114

"Very well. Mrs. Goldring has spent all of the money she has received. She has made no provision whatever for carrying on unless she can marry some wealthy man. Carlotta is just at the age when she is begininng to realize how important it is to attract the right sort of man as a husband. In order to do that, a woman must circulate in the environment in which the right sort of men are to be found. Mrs. Goldring is due to have a complete financial smash-up within thirty days. She'll be stripped clean. She won't have a penny.

"The sudden realization of that disaster is going to be a great emotional shock to Carlotta. The necessity of changing her entire mode of life, of going from comparative affluence to complete, utter poverty is going to give Carlotta a terrific jolt. Carlotta knows nothing of the value of money."

"You feel certain Mrs. Goldring's financial position is as bad as that?"

"I know it. I have made it my business to know it, Mrs. Cool. Mrs. Goldring made this trip from San Francisco to see Mabel Belder and to see if it wasn't possible to get her daughter to make a final split with Everett Belder, and have mother, daughter, and Carlotta all live together—Mabel Belder, of course, footing the bills."

"Wouldn't Carlotta go to work?"

"Eventually, Carlotta would go to work. She has been raised in an entirely different atmosphere. She has cultivated people who are more interested in golf, tennis, and horseback riding than work and achievement. She's tried a job now and then, just to go through the motions. She didn't last long."

"If you ask me," Bertha said, "it will be a damned good thing for her to have this jolt."

"Certainly it will be a good thing for her," Bertha's visitor snapped. "That's what I'm hoping for. Do you think it's been any pleasure for me to see my daughter raised in this particular manner? Good God, woman, do you know what it means to a mother who has certain plans, certain ideals, certain aspirations for her daughter, to see another woman ruin that child's entire life? I've been watching it for the last five years, absolutely, utterly helpless. But remember this: once that crash occurs, once Carlotta is jarred into a realization of what has been done to her, what a vain, scatter-brained nincompoop Mrs. Goldring is, then Carlotta's natural mother can appear on the scene offering a home, the advantages of ample money, security, an opportunity to meet the right people—"

"You can give your daughter those advantages?"

"Yes."

"Meeting the right people?"

"Yes."

"These people know of your record?"

"Don't be silly. Of course not."

"Mrs. Goldring does."

"Yes."

"Wouldn't she tell them if you took Carlotta from her?"

"She might."

"But you don't think she would?"

"I think I could take steps to prevent that."

"What steps?"

The visitor smiled. "After all, Mrs. Cool, I came here to employ you, not to submit to a cross-examination concerning my personal affairs."

"Go ahead," Bertha said dryly. "I guess I ask too damned many questions. You're going to pay for the time, so do it your own way—the telling of what you have to tell."

"In many ways," Bertha's visitor continued, "Mrs. Goldring has made Carlotta a good mother. In other ways she has been very, very foolish. She is a vain woman, one who is angling for a husband and trying to use the same bait with which she caught her first husband.

"I've seen a lot of life, Mrs. Cool. Probably you have, too. The women in the forties and fifties, even in the sixties, who get the desirable matrimonial catches—the widowers who have been trained to double-harness and have money—are the ones who are plump, comfortable, contented, and not too anxious to get married. The ones who starve themselves with diet, try to assume the vivacity of a young woman in the twenties, who appear coy and kittenish, never get to first base. Make no mistake, Mrs. Cool, a mature woman has something that appeals to an older man, something that the young filly can never have. On the other hand, the youngster has the freshness of youth, the rounded firmness of body that an older woman doesn't have. In order to get anywhere, the older woman needs to use her own weapons and not try to steal the weapons of the younger woman. Once she does that she's licked."

Bertha said, "Nice philosophy. What does it add up to in this case?"

"It adds up to the fact that Mrs. Goldring is a fool—a frivolous fool. She's deliberately squandered her insurance money, acting on the assumption that she could invest that money in getting another husband. She's had clothes, beauty treatments, expensive apartments and contacts. In case you're interested I can even give you the sordid details."

"Sordid details always interest me," Bertha said.

"Very well. Her insurance was twenty thousand dollars. In place of investing that wisely, Mrs. Goldring decided she would spend four thousand dollars a year for five years, thinking that would be plenty; that sometime during the five years she would land a desirable husband. Having once reached that decision, it was difficult for her to remain within the price limits she set for herself. And I will say one thing, she was generous to Carlotta. Partially for Carlotta's sake, and partially, perhaps, because she had to provide generously for Carlotta in order to keep up her own background.

"She made a mental limit of four thousand dollars a year. She spent over seven thousand dollars the first year. For the most part she traveled extensively, hoping to meet the type of person she wanted in the intimacy of a long voyage. She might have made a go of it if she hadn't made the mistake so many women make."

"What?"

"She fell in love with a man who had no intention of marrying her. He wasted a year of her time and finally got the bulk of her money.

"When Mrs. Goldring awakened to the truth, she redoubled her efforts to capture her lost youth. Ever play golf, Mrs. Cool?"

"Some."

"You'll realize what I mean, then, by trying too hard. When you click out your easy shots down the center of the fairway, you're simply swinging in a perfect rhythm of coordination. When you get too eager, get in too much of a hurry, get too anxious to get distance with your drives, you foozle your shots. Well, Mrs. Goldring got too eager. She foozled her matrimonial shots.

"She is within thirty days of the end of her rope. In fact she'd gone through everything she had more than a month ago. She's been getting by ever since on desperate expedients, and on the strength of the fact that her credit has always been good. She came to Los Angeles in order to persuade her daughter, Mabel, to throw Everett Belder over, get a divorce, and live with Mrs. Goldring and Carlotta—furnishing the entire finances, of course."

"You seem to know a lot about it."

"I've made it my business to know everything that concerns Carlotta's welfare."

"All right, where do I come in? Exactly what do you want *me* to do?"

Her visitor smiled. "It seems such a simple thing," she said, "simple—and yet so terribly, so vitally important."

"Well, come on. What is it?"

"I want some information."

Bertha said, with a touch of sarcasm, "You'd be surprised how many of my clients do."

The woman smiled, opened her purse, took out a flat wallet. She flipped this open and took out a fifty-dollar bill. She tossed it casually over on Bertha's desk. "I'm paying you in advance, you see."

Bertha's eyes caressed the money, then shifted to her visitor. "What's it for?"

"Information."

"What's the information?"

"You'll be surprised when—"

Bertha interrupted impatiently. "Listen, I've got work to do. If I'm to get the information you want, I'll have more to do. Now, let's get it over with. What do you want?"

"I want the name of Everett Belder's barber."

Despite herself, expression showed on Bertha Cool's face. "His *barber!*"

"That's right."

"Good Heavens, why?"

The woman extended a long, pointed, coral-tipped finger

toward the fifty dollars on the desk. "Isn't that reason enough?"

Bertha's eyes narrowed. "I'm not certain that I'm free to get that information for you. I'm doing some work for Mr. Belder. Let me go out and look at the carbon copy of the receipt I gave Belder, and see just what it covers. I—"

The woman laughed. "Come, come, Mrs. Cool. I thought you were smarter than that. You want to arrange for someone to shadow me when I leave the office. I think we understand each other perfectly. There's the money, and I want the name of Everett Belder's barber."

"But why on earth do you want that?"

"Because I'd like to have him cut my hair. And of course, Mrs. Cool, you will treat this visit as absolutely confidential. The minute you touch that fifty dollars I become your client so far as this one matter is concerned. You will not say anything to Mr. Belder or anyone else about my visit. You will get only that one bit of information for me, and if you betray my confidence, you will be guilty of unprofessional conduct. Do I make myself clear?"

"How will I get in touch with you to let you know—?"

"Call me at this number. I'll be there to take the call. Good afternoon."

The telephone rang as the woman got to her feet.

Bertha picked up the receiver, but didn't touch the fifty-dollar bill which lay on the desk.

Elsie Brand's voice said cautiously, "Everett Belder's out here."

Bertha cupped her hand over the mouthpiece, said, "Everett Belder's out there."

The frown of annoyance which flickered across the woman's face was visible even under the black veil. "Mrs. Cool, you really should have an office that has a private exit."

Bertha said angrily, "Well, if you feel that way about it, just rent me the office—even find it for me, and I'll move in. If you don't want him to see you, I can tell the girl to tell him I can't see him for ten minutes, and ask him to come back—"

The woman marched across to the door. "On second thought, Mrs. Cool, I think I prefer it this way. Do you take the money, or do I?"

Bertha hesitated for an instant, then reached across the desk and picked up the fifty-dollar bill.

"Thank you," the woman said, and opened the door.

Bertha Cool managed to get around the desk in time to watch Everett Belder's reactions as the woman walked past him.

He gave her a briefly casual glance, then scrambled hastily to his feet, started at once toward Bertha's private office.

14

NO TEA FOR THE SERGEANT

BELDER, VISIBLY EXCITED, seated himself across from Bertha Cool. "We've got it," he said.

"Got what?"

"You remember my telling you about a young woman I'd helped to land a job in San Francisco?"

Bertha gave the question frowning consideration. "Another woman?"

"Not another one. The one we were talking about. The one whose letter you saw."

"Oh. The one who called you Sindbad?"

"That's the one."

"What about her?"

"She's going to help out."

"In what?"

"In giving me money enough to clean up this judgment. She's been making a good salary, putting it away, and making an investment here and there. She's got twenty-three hundred dollars in the savings bank. I can raise the other two hundred dollars. Go ahead and close the deal with Nunnely."

"How did you get in touch with this woman," Bertha asked, "by telephone?"

"No. She was down here on a trip in connection with her job. She telephoned me and I ran over to her hotel. I've been trying to get you. The money's in San Francisco, and she's arranging to have it sent down here by wire. We'll be able to close the deal by ten o'clock tomorrow morning."

Bertha said, "You certainly have plenty of women in your life!"

121

"What do you mean by that, Mrs. Cool?"

"Exactly what I said."

"I don't know *what* you mean, Mrs. Cool, but this young woman is really not '*in*' my life."

"Twenty-three hundred bucks of her money is going to be."

"That's different."

"You're damned right it is," Bertha said. "Who's your barber?"

"I— What?"

"Who's your barber?"

"Why—I don't understand what you're getting at."

"Neither do I," Bertha said. "I just wanted to know, that's all."

"What difference does it make?"

"It might make a lot. Do you go to one shop regularly?"

"Yes."

"Where?"

Belder hesitated for a moment, then said, "It's the Terminal Tonsorial Parlor near the Pacific Greyhound bus station."

"Go there regularly?"

"Yes."

"Been going there quite a long while?"

"Yes. Really, Mrs. Cool, I don't understand why you're asking this."

"There's nothing secret about it, is there?"

"Good Heavens, no."

"No objection to coming right out and telling anyone where you get your hair cut?"

"Good Heavens, no! What's the idea? Are you crazy, or am I?"

Bertha grinned. "It's all right. I just wanted to make certain there wasn't anything secret about it. You aren't having any business dealings with the proprietor of the shop, are you?"

"No, of course not."

"Own any interest in the shop?"

"No. Mrs. Cool, will you please tell me the reasons for asking these questions?"

"I'm trying to find out the reason why it should make a damned bit of difference where you get your hair cut."

"But it doesn't."

"It shouldn't."

"It doesn't."

"It does."

"I don't understand."

"Neither do I. What's this about another letter?"

Belder's manner showed complete exasperation. He hesitated as though trying to let Bertha see he was debating whether to walk out or let her see the letter. After a few moments he took a sealed envelope from his pocket. Bertha extended her hand. He gave it to her and she turned it over and over in her fingers.

"When did this come?"

"In the mail that's delivered about three o'clock in the afternoon."

"Your mother-in-law see *this* letter?"

"She did, and Carlotta did. Trust Carlotta."

Bertha said musingly, "Same sort of typewriting. Letter addressed to your wife, marked *Personal and confidential!*" She raised her voice, "Oh, Elsie—" Through the door came the muffled sound of a clacking typewriter. Bertha Cool picked up the telephone receiver and said to Elsie Brand, "Put on the kettle again, Elsie. We've got another letter."

Bertha replaced the telephone, kept studying the envelope. "Well," she said, "we'll have to get something to put in this— same sort of an envelope as the other was—a plain, stamped envelope. I'll have to dig up another advertisement from the fur company."

"Couldn't we put something else in this?"

"Don't be silly," Bertha said. "If your mother-in-law sees two envelopes addressed *Personal and confidential,* and one of them contains an ad for the fur company and the other one an invitation to contribute to the Red Cross, she'll smell a rat right then and there. Only thing to do is to make it appear it's a slick advertising stunt on the part of the furrier, and they got her name on the mailing-list twice."

"That's right," Belder admitted. "I hadn't thought of that."

"What's new out at your house?" Bertha asked.

"Nothing new. Just the same old seven and six. Police detectives trooping over the place, messing around and asking questions. Mrs. Goldring crying. Carlotta snooping on me every minute of the time."

"What's she snooping on you for?"

"I don't know."

Bertha lit a cigarette.

"What caused you to ask about my barber?" Belder asked.

"It seems to worry you."

"It doesn't worry me. I'm simply curious, that's all."

"What was the reason you didn't want to tell me who your barber was?"

"Why, there's no reason on earth."

"Then why did you stall around about it?"

"Don't be silly, I didn't stall around. I simply wanted to know what was back of the question. I'm not objecting. I was trying to find out why you asked me."

"I just wanted to know. What's the name of this girl—the one that's going to put up the money?"

"Mamie Rosslyn."

"What does she do?"

"She has complete charge now of the advertising for a big San Francisco department store. She's moved right up to the top."

"What does Dolly Cornish have to say about her?"

"Why, what do you mean?"

"Have you told Dolly this Rosslyn woman is going to put up some money for you?"

"Why, no. Why should I?"

"Why shouldn't you?"

"I fail to see any reason why I should."

"How long is she going to be in town?"

"Who, Dolly Cornish?"

"No. This Rosslyn girl."

"She's taking the train tonight and is sending the money down by telegram tomorrow. That's what I wanted to see you about. I want you to get in touch with Nunnely and make certain the thing doesn't get away from us. It's particularly important that we get that judgment cleaned up before noon tomorrow."

Elsie Brand opened the door. "The water's boiling."

Bertha shoved back her creaking swivel chair, heaved herself to her feet. "Well," she announced, "here's where we violate some more postal regulations."

The teakettle over on Elsie Brand's desk was boiling briskly. Underneath it the electric plate cast a reflected red glow down upon the magazine which Elsie had placed under the plate to protect her desk.

Bertha, holding the envelope in her thumb and forefinger, stalked over to the teakettle, saying to Belder over her shoulder, "Lock the door."

Bertha bent over the teakettle, skillfully applying the flap to the live steam, concentrating on the task at hand.

Elsie Brand hurriedly pushed against her desk, sending her office chair shooting back on well-oiled casters.

"What is it?" Bertha asked without looking up.

"The door," Elsie Brand said, and started running.

Bertha glanced up. A black shadow was blotted against the frosted glass on the outside of the door, the shadow of broad shoulders, the silhouette of a grim profile, a long cigar clamped at a slight upward angle. Belder was standing at Bertha's shoulder intently gazing down at the letter. Elsie Brand had her hand extended to throw the lock on the door.

"Damn it," Bertha blazed at Belder. "I told you to lock that door. I—"

Elsie Brand's hand touched the lock.

The shadow on the frosted glass moved. The knob turned, just as Elsie's fingers touched the lock.

In a panic, Elsie flung her weight against the door in a futile attempt to keep it closed.

Sergeant Sellers shouldered the door and looked through the open segment at the figures over by Elsie's desk, took in the tea kettle, the electric plate, Bertha Cool's indignation, Everett Belder's consternation.

Wordlessly, and without taking his eyes from Bertha and Belder, Sellers slid his hand along the jamb of the door until he came to the spring lock. His forefinger snapped it back and forth. He said to Elsie, without looking at her, "What's the idea? Trying to keep me out?"

"I was just closing the office," Elsie said hastily. "Mrs. Cool was tired and didn't want to see anyone else."

"I see," Sellers observed. "Going to have a pot of tea, I suppose?"

"Yes." Elsie Brand's acquiescence was just a bit too quick

and enthusiastic. "That's right. We were just going to have tea. Quite frequently we have tea. I—"

"That's swell," Sellers observed. "Count me in. Put an extra cup in the pot, Bertha. Go ahead and close the office, Elsie."

Sellers entered the room, and Elsie Brand, glancing helplessly at Mrs. Cool, pushed the door shut.

Bertha said, "My God, you cops are all alike. The smell of food brings you around like flies. It doesn't make any difference what time of day it is—morning, noon, afternoon, or night—"

"That's right," Sellers interpolated. "Only I didn't know there was going to be food. I thought it was just tea. Food makes it that much better. Got some nice assorted cookies, Bertha? The kind with sweet fillings in the center? I love those."

Bertha glared at him.

"Don't let your water boil away," Sellers said. "Go ahead and get your tea, Bertha."

Bertha glanced at Elsie. "Where *is* the tea, Elsie?"

"Why, I—I—gosh, Mrs. Cool, come to think of it, I think we used up the last yesterday. I remember now, you told me to get some more, and I forgot it."

"Damn it," Bertha blazed. "Can't you ever remember anything? That's twice you've forgotten things. I told you positively to get some more tea yesterday afternoon. I remember using up the last and throwing the carton away."

"I remember it now," Elsie admitted shamefacedly. "I forgot it this morning."

Grinning, Sellers sat down. "Oh, well," he said, "get out the cups and saucers and I'll see if I can't promote some tea."

"I suppose you carry a package of it around in your pocket."

"I'll get some," Sellers promised, adjusting himself to a comfortable position in one of the office chairs, and pulling a cigar from his pocket. "Go right ahead, Bertha. Bring out the cups and saucers, Elsie."

Elsie glanced at Bertha.

Bertha said, "On second thought I've changed my mind. If we haven't any tea, I'm not going to wait for you to promote some. I'm sick and tired to death of—"

"Okay, okay," Sellers interrupted. "Let's see the cups and saucers, Bertha. Where do you keep them?"

"I told you I'm not going to use them."

"I know, but I'm interested in them."

"Well, stay interested then. I have other things to do. Come on, Mr. Belder. We'll finish that matter we were going to discuss when we were interrupted."

"Might as well finish it right now," Sellers said.

"Thank you. My clients prefer privacy. Strange of them, I'm certain, but somehow they do. A sort of subconscious clinging to the obsolete rights of an American citizen."

Sellers kept grinning good-naturedly. "No cups and saucers, eh, Bertha? Mrs. Goldring told me there'd been another letter come for Mrs. Belder. Thought I might find you here, Belder. Of course, if you have that letter in your pocket, I'll just take it along. It may be valuable as evidence."

"You and who else?" Bertha blazed. "After all, there are certain Federal regulations that rate just a little higher than you smart-Aleck cops. If a letter's addressed to Mrs. Belder, you can't—"

"Come, come, Bertha. Don't run up a blood pressure over it. If you're so touchy about the Federal regulations, what were *you* about to do?"

"I was about to cook a pot of tea," Bertha all but shouted, "and I guess as yet there's no law says you can't cook a pot of tea in your own office."

"You'd be surprised about that," Sellers told her. "City ordinances concerning cooking—zoning ordinances concerning places where meals or refreshments are habitually furnished, given away, or—"

"I guess I could cook a client a cup of tea without having to take out a restaurant license."

"That 'habitually furnished' covers a lot of ground," Sellers said, still keeping his affable smile. "Elsie works here. Evidently you serve tea at this time every day."

Bertha's angry glare didn't disturb the Sergeant's serene complacency.

"Now then," he went on, turning to Belder, "if you've received another poison-pen letter and were getting ready to

127

steam it open, just cut me in on the party."

"How the hell do you get that way?" Bertha said. "Busting into my office and—"

"Take it easy, Bertha. Don't scream. Your office is open to the public. I dropped in. I'd been out at Belder's house just checking up on a few details. I talked with Mrs. Goldring, who's naturally much concerned over the whole affair, and is trying to convince me there's some reason for her daughter's absence. A reason that isn't connected with the death of Sally Brentner. Trying to think back over recent events in order to see if there wasn't some clue to her daughter's disappearance, Mrs. Goldring remembered that there had been two letters in the mail marked *Personal and confidential*. She suggested that we might go through the mail, find them, and see if they offered a clue. We did it. We found only one of the envelopes.

"I didn't feel like taking the liberty of opening Mrs. Belder's mail, but I saw no reason why we couldn't hold the envelope up to a strong light and see what was inside. I arranged a cardboard funnel, put it over a hundred-and-fifty-watt light, held the envelope over the funnel, and saw that the envelope contained only the advertisement of a furrier. A little closer inspection convinced me that the envelope had been opened. I remembered there had been *two* poison-pen letters; that you tried to hold one out on me; that you didn't have the envelope it came in. Mrs. Goldring was much put out because she couldn't find the letter that had come this afternoon marked *Personal and confidential*. Putting two and two together, I thought I might make a guess as to where the envelope might be, and where Everett Belder might be. I come up here and find you grouped around a teakettle, brewing tea with no tea cups, no tea pot, and no tea leaves.

"Now, Bertha, as one detective to another, what would you think if you were in my position?"

"Oh, hell," Bertha said wearily to Belder. "Let him in on it."

"That's better." Sellers grinned. "After all, Belder, I'm protecting you as far as your mother-in-law is concerned. I haven't told her anything about that second letter. Incidentally, you'll probably be interested to know that your mother-in-law thinks you'd been having an affair with Sally, either got tired of her, or Sally was standing in your way, keeping you from taking on another mistress. She thinks you got rid of her and she's beginning to have a horrible suspicion that you may have made away with your wife."

"Made away with my wife!" Belder shouted. "Made away with Mabel! Good God! I'd give my right hand if I could locate her right now. Bertha can tell you that I'm putting across a deal that—"

"Shut up," Bertha interrupted. "He's just trying to get your goat to make you start talking. That's an old police trick, playing you against your mother-in-law, and your mother-in-law against you."

"Why stop him from talking, Bertha? Is he concealing something?"

"A fat chance anybody stands of concealing things with you opening purses, breaking into offices, and egging his mother-in-law into hysterics. Hell, no! All I'm trying to do is to keep his mouth shut so you can't run back to the mother-in-law and tell her what Belder said about her."

Sellers said affably, "Well, you've got to admit it was a swell try, Bertha. I shouldn't have tried it when you were here. I think I'd have got somewhere with it if you hadn't butted in."

Belder faced Sellers angrily. "I don't know how much of this stuff a citizen has to take from the police department."

"Quite a bit," Sellers told him, "particularly when wives disappear shortly after former sweethearts, who are pretty well heeled, have called on the husband. You'd be surprised, Belder, how many times wives have 'simply disappeared' or gone to visit relatives and haven't returned. Well, no, I won't say it in that way. It sounds as though *I* were accusing you of something. I'm not. I'm only investigating. It's your mother-in-law who's made the accusation."

"There he goes again," Bertha interrupted. "Don't let him get your goat, Belder. Let's get this letter opened and see what it says."

Bertha raised some papers on Elsie's desk, picked up the envelope which she had hastily concealed as Sellers opened the door. Sellers settled back in the chair, puffing cigar smoke contentedly, watching operations.

Bertha loosened the adhesive on the flap with steam, inserted a lead pencil near the upper part of the flap, and rolled it down under the flap.

"Rather neat," Sellers commented. "Shows long practice."

Bertha refused to be baited.

Belder said, nervously, "I think I should be the first to read this. There may be something—"

Sellers came up out of the chair with the smooth, easy motion of an athlete. Belder jerked the letter from Bertha's hand. Sellers's big thick fingers clamped around Belder's wrist.

"Naughty, naughty," Sellers said. "Drop it."

Belder tried to jerk away. Sellers increased his pressure on the man's wrist, suddenly whipped around, throwing his elbow over Belder's arm. His other hand caught the back of Belder's hand, and pressed it down with the leverage of a locked forearm.

Belder's fingers loosened. The letter fluttered to the floor. Sellers beat Bertha to it, his shoulders striking against Bertha as they both grabbed for the letter.

"Damn you," Bertha said.

"Always pick things up for a lady," Sellers observed, and returned to his chair carrying the letter, the cigar still clamped in his mouth.

"Well," Bertha said, "go ahead and read it."

"I'm reading it."

"Read it out loud."

Sellers merely grinned. He read the letter with avid interest, folded it, and put it in his pocket. "Ain't we got fun!" he observed.

Bertha said, "Damn you. You can't bust in my office and pull high-handed stuff like that. You let me see that letter."

Sellers said, "You have the envelope, Bertha. I'd suggest you put in another circular from the furrier and make as good a job of sealing it up again as you did on the other. Not that *I* give a damn. I'm simply trying to fix it so your client's home life won't be quite so disagreeable. Mrs. Goldring was very much interested in that trick of putting the hundred-and-fifty-watt light in the cardboard cone and holding a letter against it. She'll be laying for this envelope, waiting to pounce on it. About the first question she'll ask Belder is whether he has it in his pocket. Well, I've got to be getting on."

Sellers got up, reached across Elsie Brand's desk, and calmly tapped ashes from the end of his cigar with his little finger.

Belder turned to Bertha Cool.

"Can't we do something about this? Doesn't a citizen have *some* right?"

Bertha didn't say anything until the door closed. "He caught us red-handed," Bertha said bitterly. "He had us over a barrel—and how well he knew it. Damn him."

Belder's voice held the dignity of cold rage. "Well, Mrs. Cool. I think that is just about the last straw. You've bungled everything in this case from the time you started on it. If you had used ordinary skill in shadowing my wife, we'd have known exactly where she went. I gave you a letter in strictest confidence, and you let that letter fall into the hands of the police. I come to you with a third letter which may contain some important information, and you let that get whipped out from under your nose. I had misgivings about hiring a woman detective in the first place. Sergeant Sellers wouldn't have imposed on a *man* in this way."

Bertha looked through the man, her forehead furrowed in thought. She gave no indication that she had heard a word Belder said.

Belder marched stiffly to the door and followed Sergeant Sellers out into the corridor.

Elsie Brand looked sympathetically at Bertha Cool. "Tough luck," she said. "But after all, it wasn't your fault."

Bertha might not have heard her.

Her eyes were slitted into level-lidded concentration. "So *that's* it."

"What?" Elsie asked.

"They think Belder murdered his wife, and Belder spent that morning at the barber shop. I remember when he came in. It was cold. A raw wind was just blowing away a heavy fog. Belder was wearing an overcoat and hadn't been shaved. He left me in front of his house. When I arrived at his office, he was shaved, massaged, manicured, and had had his hair

131

trimmed. So *that's* why that woman wanted to know about his barber. That barber shop is his only alibi, and if there's a hole in it—then he has no alibi."

Bertha sailed into her private office and grabbed her hat and purse.

15 THE FORGOTTEN OVERCOAT

THE TERMINAL TONSORIAL PARLOR was a seven-chair shop with only three men working. Bertha, entering, surveyed the filled chairs, the half dozen men who were waiting. "Where's the boss?" she asked.

"Out getting a bite to eat," one of the men said.

"You mean to say he goes to dinner at this hour?"

"Lunch at this hour," the man grinned. "He's been trying to get away ever since two o'clock—that's supposed to be his lunch time. He— Here he comes now."

Bertha turned, surveyed the man who was just opening the street door, ignored the curious glances of the waiting patrons, shoved a card in front of the bewildered barber, and said, "Where can we talk for five minutes?"

The barber wearily looked at the filled chairs. "I don't have time to talk," he said. "I'm so shorthanded I—"

"Five minutes," Bertha insisted. "And you'll like it better if we talk where other people can't hear us."

The man was too utterly tired to argue. "All right," he surrendered. "Come on back here," and led the way toward the back room. "You'll have to talk with me while I'm putting on my shop coat," he warned in a voice loud enough to reach the men who were waiting. "I've got a shopful of customers."

"Okay," Bertha said.

The back room was a small, dimly lit place which had been partitioned off from the main shop. Several coats on hangers were suspended from hooks which had been screwed into a board that ran the length of the room. An old-fash-

133

ioned hat tree held three hats. The barber took off his and made it four.

"All right, what do you want?" he asked.

"Everett Belder," Bertha said, "know him?"

"Yes. I know him. Has an office in the Rockaway Building. I've done his work for years."

"Think back to last Wednesday. Was Belder in here?"

"Wednesday," the barber said, knitting his forehead. "Let's see. Yes, that's right. It was Wednesday. He was in here and got quite a job done—haircut, manicure, shine, massage. Don't do much massage work any more—seems like people are too rushed and too busy. Lord knows we are. I can't get men and—"

"How long was he here?" Bertha asked.

The barber took off his coat and vest, carefully fitted them to a wooden coat hanger, and put the coat hanger back on the hook. "Must have been here an hour and a half in all," he said, taking a white barber's jacket from another hanger and struggling his right arm into it.

"Know the exact time?" Bertha asked.

"Why, yes. Mr. Belder doesn't like to wait. He comes in during the slack time—along about eleven o'clock in the morning. He was a little late Wednesday; got in just before half-past eleven. I remember now. There was a high fog that day with a raw wind. He had his overcoat with him. The sun came out shortly after he got in the chair and we talked about the wind blowing the fog away. When he left, he left his overcoat. That's it hanging on the hook over there. I rang him up and told him I had it, and he said he'd come by and pick it up. Say, why are you checking up on him?"

"I'm not checking up on him," Bertha said. "I'm just trying to help him."

"He hiring you?"

Bertha said, "I told you I'm trying to help him. Has anyone else been in here asking questions about him?"

The man shook his head.

"They probably will," Bertha said.

"I remember seeing in the papers, now, there'd been some trouble up at his house. A maid fell down the cellar stairs and killed herself, didn't she?"

"Something like that."

"This anything to do with that?"

Quite apparently the man had been too tired to give much thought to Bertha's first questions. He had answered them while changing his clothes, anxious to get rid of her so he could finish up with the afternoon rush. Now, as he turned inquisitor, he was beginning to become suspicious.

Bertha glared him into submission. "What possible connection would there be between the time that he came to your shop and a maid falling down the stairs?"

The barber thought that over while he was buttoning the white jacket. "Nothing, I guess. I was just wondering. That's all I know about Belder's last visit here."

Bertha followed him out of the little room with a meek docility which would have aroused Sergeant Sellers's instant suspicions, but the barber had already forgotten her by the time he took up his position back of his chair.

"Who's next?" he asked.

A man got up, started for the barber's chair. Bertha, her hand on the doorknob, said, "I left my purse in there," and started for the back room.

The barber glanced after her, then devoted his attention to whipping a white cloth around the neck of his customer. "Hair trim?" he asked.

Bertha had all the time she needed in the back room. She went over to where Everett Belder's overcoat was hanging and began a methodical search of the pockets.

There was a handkerchief and a half-used paper of matches in the left pocket. The right-hand pocket held a pair of gloves and a spectacle case of the kind that snaps shut.

Bertha casually opened the spectacle case.

There were no glasses on the inside—only a removable gold bridge containing two teeth.

Bertha picked up the purse she had purposely left on the small table, opened it, dropped in the spectacle case and walked out through the barber shop.

"Good day," the man said mechanically. "Come again."

"Thank you," Bertha told him, "I will."

16

A BODY IN A CAR

EARLY EVENING TRAFFIC had brisked up as Bertha Cool cruised down the boulevard, carefully watching her speedometer. She slowed for the intersection where she had lost Mrs. Belder, brought the car to a full stop, then slammed home the gears and pushed the throttle all the way down, keeping in her mind a mental picture of just how the car ahead had proceeded; about how fast, and about how much headstart it had had when it turned the corner.

Bertha swung around the corner, speeded up to the next corner, then brought her car to a stop and surveyed the street ahead, the street to the left, and the street to the right. She then realized something that had not dawned on her before. The blocks to the left and right were double blocks with no streets cut through the boulevard.

Bertha parked her car at the curb and did mental arithmetic.

If Mrs. Belder's machine had stayed on the road straight ahead, Bertha would certainly have seen it as she turned the corner from the boulevard. Bertha had been gaining on the car for the last hundred yards before she lost it. It might have made either a right or a left turn on a single block, but the possibilities that it could have done so on a double block were negligible.

Faced with the knowledge that the car couldn't have evaporated into the thin air, and now realizing the importance of what had originally seemed to be merely a routine shadowing job, Bertha cudgeled her mind, trying to think of some-

136

thing which might furnish a possible clue to what had taken place.

From the depths of her memory came the hazy recollection that someone had been standing at a garage door somewhere in the block as Bertha had swung in from the boulevard. At the time Bertha had been intent only on getting to the corner.

She tried to remember just where the garage had been. Somewhere on the left-hand side of the street.

Bertha swung her car in a U-turn and cruised slowly down the street.

The second house from the corner looked about right— 709 North Harkington Avenue. It was, of course, a forlorn hope—a chance of one in a thousand, but Bertha was gunning for big game now, and one chance in a thousand couldn't be overlooked.

Bertha stopped her car, marched up the cement walk, and pushed the bell button of the house. From the interior she could hear the faint sound of electric chimes.

She waited fifteen seconds, then pushed the bell again. There was no sound of motion from the interior of the house.

Bertha stepped back from the door to make a more careful appraisal of the house. There was about it almost a deserted atmosphere. The shades were pulled about two-thirds of the way down. There was an accumulation of dust in the corner of the threshold where the front door was recessed from the porch.

Disappointed, Bertha jabbed her thumb against the door button once again and turned to appraise the neighborhood.

The sun, shielded by a low-hanging bank of clouds in the west, had given the effect of an early twilight. The day had, however, been warm. In a yard across the street some children were playing—a girl eight or nine, and a boy a couple of years younger.

Bertha walked across to them. "Who lives in that house across the street?" she asked.

It was the girl who answered the question. "Mr. and Mrs. Cuttring."

"They don't seem to be home."

The girl hesitated.

The boy blurted out, "They went away for a ten-day vacation."

The girl said, "Mother told you not to say anything about that. Burglars get in when they know people aren't home."

Bertha smiled reassuringly. "I had heard they wanted to rent their garage; do you know anything about it?"

"Why, no. They have a car. They took it with them."

"Thank you," Bertha told them courteously. "I'll just take a look in the garage. They want to rent it."

She retraced her steps, more confidently this time, crossing the street and walking up the cement driveway to the garage. Behind her, the children watched her for a moment, and then went on with their play. By the time Bertha had reached the garage, they had entirely forgotten her, and the shrill treble of children's voices raised in screaming play reached Bertha's ears.

Bertha tentatively tried the garage door, expecting it to be locked.

It swung smoothly on well-oiled hinges.

Bertha pushed the door back a few cautious inches. She didn't intend to go inside unless—

She saw a car inside the garage.

There was something vaguely familiar about the back of the car. Bertha glanced at the license number.

It was the number of Mrs. Belder's automobile.

Bertha walked around to the right-hand side of the car.

The subdued light of late afternoon, filtering in through the door which opened to the east and through the window on the north, gave sufficient illumination for Bertha to see objects in the garage; but it took a minute or two for her eyes to accustom themselves to the gloomy interior.

At first Bertha thought the car was empty. She opened the door on the right-hand side and started to get in behind the steering-wheel. Her foot hit some obstruction. She glanced down to see what it was, and by that time her eyes had accommodated themselves to the dim light sufficiently to show her the shod foot and stockinged leg of the body that lay half on the seat, half on the floor, sprawled down behind the steering-wheel.

A moment more and the stale stench of death assailed

Bertha's nostrils.

Bertha backed out of the car, started for the garage door, thought better of it, went back, located the light switch and turned on the light in the garage.

The light was high up, and the top of the car threw shadows over the corpse, but Bertha had a job to do and this was the only chance she'd have to do it.

The body was clothed in the distinctive plaid coat Bertha remembered so well; also the dark glasses with glaring white rims which shielded the dead eyes, yet gave the corpse a peculiar owl-like appearance of regarding Bertha Cool from white-rimmed black eyes.

Light from the dangling bulb came through the windshield and illuminated a piece of paper which had evidently fluttered to the floor of the car.

Bertha picked it up and read it.

It was typewritten and, as nearly as Bertha could determine, it had been typed on the same Remington portable that had typed the letters.

I am to drive out Westmore Boulevard. I will appear to be very unsuspicious and not turn my head at any time to look back, but I will watch the rear-view mirror out of the corner of my eye. If I am being followed, then I am to jockey the car so I will hit a changing signal at Dawson Avenue. I am to go through that signal, but at average speed. I am to turn left on North Harkington Avenue—that is the second block beyond Dawson. The second house from the corner is 709. The garage door will be open. I am to drive into that garage, jump out of the car, close the door, get back in my car and wait with the motor running until I hear an automobile horn blow three times. Then I am to open the door and back out. It is imperative that I follow these instructions to the letter.— M. B.

Bertha let the paper drop back to the floor. She leaned across the body, put her thumb against the cold mouth, braced herself, and drew back the lips.

A removable bridge was missing from the lower right-hand side of Mrs. Belder's jaw—the side nearest Bertha. It was a bridge that would have taken two teeth.

Bertha backed out of the car, hastily closed the door. She closed the garage door and, walking almost on tiptoes, so great was her desire for secrecy, was halfway to her automobile before the sound of childish voices made her realize that, having made the mistake of asking questions of the children, she had no alternative but to telephone Sergeant Sellers.

"I do have the damnedest luck!" she muttered under her breath, and jerked open the door of her automobile.

17 DIABOLICAL AND INGENIOUS

BERTHA COOL SAID TO THE OFFICER, "Go in and tell Sergeant Sellers that I can't wait any longer. I've got work to do."

The cop merely grinned.

"I mean it," Bertha stormed. "I've been held here for over two hours while they're doing all their messing around. Sergeant Sellers knows where to find me when he wants me."

"He does for a fact," the officer said.

"That wasn't what I meant."

"It's what *I* meant."

"You go tell Sellers what I said."

"He's busy. I can't keep interrupting him with a lot of trivial messages."

"This isn't trivial. Damn it, I'm going to walk out."

"I was told to keep you here."

"And why should I have to stay here simply because I discovered a body for Sellers?"

"You'll have to take that up with Sellers."

"They let Mrs. Goldring go."

"She was hysterical. They only wanted her to identify the body, anyway."

"Well, what the hell do they want *me* for?"

"I wouldn't know."

"Is Sergeant Sellers finished with his investigation in the garage?"

"I wouldn't know."

"Well, what have they found out about the cause of death?"

"I wouldn't know that either."

"There seems to be a hell of a lot you don't know."

"There is for a fact."

"What *do* you know?"

The officer grinned. "I know I was told to keep you here, and I'm going to keep you here. Right now, Mrs. Cool, I don't hardly know a single thing outside of that."

Bertha lapsed into indignant silence.

Abruptly the door opened. Sergeant Sellers walked in, made a slight signal to the officer, and grinned at Bertha Cool. "Hi, Bertha."

Bertha glowered at him.

"What's the matter, Bertha, you don't seem happy?"

"Happy! If you think that I— Oh hell!"

Sellers settled himself in the chair. "How did you know she was dead?"

Bertha took a deep breath. "I felt her flesh. It was cold. I smelled the odor of decomposition. She didn't move when I touched her. I called to her. She didn't answer, didn't move. I realized she'd been there in that same position for three days. And then it dawned on me, Sergeant, all in a flash— like those brilliant inspirations the police get. I said to myself, 'My God, she's dead!' "

"Nice stuff, Bertha. That isn't what I meant. How did you know she was dead before you went to the garage?"

"I didn't."

"Then why did you go to the garage?"

"I hate to lose anyone I'm shadowing."

"Naturally."

"Well, that's the reason I came here. I wanted to look the place over."

"I see. When you lose a person on Wednesday noon and decide you really shouldn't have done it, you go back Friday night to the same place so you can pick her up and begin where you left off. Something like one of those motion pictures in the shooting-galleries that comes to a dead stop when you pull the trigger on the gun."

"No. Not that."

"Well, what was it then?"

"I was just looking the place over."

"You'll have to do better than that, Bertha."

"The hell I will. I lost her here, and I had a right to come and look for her here."

"How did you know you'd lost her here?"

"She turned this corner and that was the last I saw of her."

"Then why didn't you stop here when you were doing the shadowing job?"

"Because I thought she'd gone on to the next corner, and then turned right."

"And what caused you to change your mind?"

"I drove to the next corner, saw she hadn't turned right and swung my car to the left."

"You say you saw she hadn't turned right?"

"Yes."

"How did you know that?"

"Because when I started to swing my car to the right, the street was vacant. I didn't think she could have gone to the right and got around the block."

"So you changed your mind and swung your car to the left?"

"That's right."

"But the street on the left was also vacant, wasn't it?"

"Yes."

"And, by the same reasoning, if she didn't have time to turn to the right and go a block, she didn't have time to go to the left."

"That's why I came back out here."

Sellers regarded her with an amiable grin. "That's swell, Bertha. Sometimes when you're making sarcastic comments about how long it takes the police to get an idea through their heads, you might remember that even the best of the private detectives require two or three days for simple matters like that to percolate through their skulls. Now, how did you happen to look in this particular garage?"

"Well, I came out to look the situation over to see where she might have gone—to see what might have happened. I discovered the streets were double blocks on the right and on the left; then I *knew* she couldn't have turned the corner and doubled back on me. She must have disappeared before she got to the corner."

"You didn't notice that about the double blocks before?"

"To tell you the truth, I didn't," Bertha admitted somewhat shamefacedly. "I thought it was just a routine shadowing job, one of those things that's particularly unimportant to everyone except the guy who's paying for it. When a man gets to the point that he's hiring a stranger to shadow his wife, he might just as well write his marriage off the books, and it doesn't make much difference whether she's philandering with Tom, Dick, or Harry."

"Nice philosophy," Sellers said. "I'm sorry I haven't time to discuss marital philosophy with you right now, Bertha. Why did you consider the shadowing job unimportant?"

"I thought it was just a routine job."

"Then why didn't you notice they were double blocks?"

"I was just too damned mad. I was mad at myself and mad at the woman. She'd stalled along, driving so steadily and leaving herself so wide open for a trailing job that she had me half day-dreaming. I was following along more or less mechanically, and had my thoughts a thousand miles away. Then all of a sudden she pulled this fast one. Well, I was mad, and it just never occurred to me that she might have ducked into a garage somewhere."

"Until later?"

"Until later," Bertha said.

"You didn't double back and look the garages over on Wednesday?"

"No, I didn't. I looked the driveways over. I thought she might have swung the car into a driveway and gone into one of these houses."

"And if in the driveway, why not in a garage?"

"I don't know. It just didn't occur to me at the time."

"Another idea that took three days to germinate?"

"Yes, if you want to be so damned sarcastic about it."

"Just giving you a taste of how it feels," Sellers said.

"Well it doesn't feel so good."

"Too bad. Did you see the paper that was on the floor of the automobile?"

Bertha hesitated.

"Yes or no?"

"Yes."

"Touch it?"

"Yes."

"Read it?"

"Yes. That is, I just glanced at it—the way one will."

"The way one will," Sergeant Sellers repeated.

"What the hell? You didn't think I was going to find a woman dead and not look around, did you?"

"You know that we don't like to have people messing around, leaving fingerprints when they come on corpses."

"Well, I had to find out she was dead, didn't I?"

"That's what I'm getting at. You lost her here—let's see, when was it—Wednesday?"

"Wednesday about noon."

"I see. You find her just as it's getting dark Friday night. She's slumped over in the automobile and, as you expressed it, you could smell the odor of death. You touched her and she was cold. You spoke to her and she didn't move. And then you picked up this paper and read it in order to convince yourself she was dead."

"Well, I—"

"Go on."

"How the hell did I know what was on it? It might have been something important. Something she wanted done."

"Something that would have brought her back to life?"

"Don't be sarcastic."

"What I'm getting at," Sergeant Sellers said, "is that there are a couple of very excellent fingerprints on this piece of paper—and I suppose," he said, his voice suddenly weary, "they'll turn out to be the fingerprints of Bertha Cool—just when I think I'm really getting somewhere."

"I'm sorry," Bertha said.

"So am I, Bertha."

"Did she die of monoxide poisoning?"

"It looks that way."

"What do you make of it?"

"A very neat little trap," Sergeant Sellers said. "Someone writes the woman poison-pen letters until she gets so interested she's virtually hypnotized. Put yourself in her position. She has every dime there is in the family; perhaps she'd like to keep it. The evidence indicates that as a wife she was useful to her husband more as a depository of property than an object of affection. The chances are, she'd have liked to wash her hands of the whole business. Naturally, she'd like to keep as much of the property as possible. You can't blame her for that. Her husband has his earning capacity. He can go out and make more money. She's thrown out on the world. If she can find another husband who can support her, she can get along. If she can't, she's going to be faced with the old routine of a separated wife, men who play around but don't contemplate matrimony, a slender stock of cash dwindling from day to day—every day finding her that much older, her looks—"

"What are you trying to do," Bertha interpolated sarcastically, "make me cry?"

"Make you think."

"I don't get you."

"I'm looking at it from her standpoint—as her mind was molded by her mother."

"You think her mother was in on it?"

"The records show that Tuesday afternoon she had a long-distance telephone conversation with her mother in San Francisco. Then about six-thirty her mother sent her a telegram saying she was coming down and for her to meet the train."

"What was the conversation about?"

"I asked Mrs. Goldring and she was evasive, but finally I pinned her down. Mabel had rung up to tell her about having received a letter stating that her husband was having an affair with a woman she'd employed as a maid. Mrs. Goldring told her to wash her hands of the whole business, walk out on Everett, and leave him holding the sack. Mabel wasn't entirely certain that was the right thing to do. She mentioned over the telephone to Mrs. Goldring that the property really and truly wasn't hers; it was her husband's, and she thought there should be some settlement. That made Mrs. Goldring furious. She argued with Mabel for a while on the long-distance telephone, then decided to take the night train down and handle the situation personally. She was going to engineer a family smash-up."

"Mabel got the wire?"

"That's right. Carlotta was there when the wire was delivered. The records of the telegraph company show it was delivered over the telephone, and that Mrs. Belder asked to have it repeated to be sure she got the train on which her mother was arriving. Then she told Carlotta, and they arranged to meet the train. Everett Belder was entirely unconscious of the storm that was brewing. His wife asked him that night to take her car to the service station next morning, have the car filled up with gas, and the tires checked, and have it back before eleven."

"Wait a minute," Bertha said. "She didn't leave the house until eleven-twenty-two Wednesday morning. Wasn't the train due before that?"

"It was due at eleven-fifteen, but it was late and didn't get in until considerably after that."

"How did it happen Carlotta and Mrs. Belder didn't go to meet the train together."

"Carlotta had some things she had to do uptown. Mrs. Belder liked to sleep late in the mornings. Carlotta said she'd do her shopping uptown and meet Mrs. Belder at the depot. We can assume Mrs. Belder telephoned to find out if the train was on time. Now, the point is that the train was first reported as being on time, then as being due at twelve-fifteen. If Mrs. Belder didn't leave the house until eleven-twenty-two, she must·have had the twelve-fifteen report, and she couldn't have intended to do very much before meeting the train. Actually, the train didn't get in until after one o'clock.

"Carlotta left the house about nine, did a few errands in town, got down to the depot a little early, right around eleven, and then got the report that the train would be in at twelve-fifteen. She then rang up the Belder house to tell her sister the train was late, and got no answer. She tried to phone twice. Now figure that out. That was around eleven. According to the way we had the case doped out, Mrs. Belder was sitting at the phone waiting for that call from the writer of the poison-pen letter. You know she was there in the house —yet, when Carlotta rang, she didn't answer the phone. Why?"

"Good Lord!" Bertha exclaimed, "there's only one reason."

"Yes? Let's see if you figure it the same way I do."

"At that exact moment she must have been murdering Sally Brentner."

Sellers nodded. "Exactly."

"So what did Carlotta do?" Bertha asked.

"She concluded that Mabel had left early before the twelve-fifteen bulletin on the train was released. Carlotta was already there at the depot. There wasn't time to go back uptown and do anything, so she simply sat around the depot, waiting for Mabel to show up. Then the train didn't get in till after one o'clock. Mabel didn't show up and didn't try, so far as anyone knows, to communicate with Carlotta. Now, you put that together and tell me what the answer is."

"There isn't any," Bertha said. "Only way to dope it out is that murder was being committed there in that house at eleven o'clock."

"That's the way it looks to me," Sellers said moodily. "Mrs. Belder must have rung up and got the report that the train wouldn't be in until twelve-fifteen. She was anxious to get this eleven-o'clock call from the writer of that letter, yet she didn't answer the phone at eleven. Carlotta tried to get her. The other party must have tried calling but didn't actually get her until around eleven-fifteen."

"Why do you place it at eleven-fifteen?"

"I can't place it any *earlier* than eleven-fifteen. The probabilities are that it was just about eleven-twenty-one, and that it didn't take over sixty seconds for Mrs. Belder to get out of the house and into the car. Therefore, you've got to figure that telephone call between eleven-fifteen and eleven-twenty-one."

Bertha said curiously, "That's not giving her much margin for killing Sally Brentner after eleven o'clock and before she got the call."

Sellers said, "She didn't need to *start* her killing at eleven o'clock. She might have been putting on the finishing touches then."

"But her husband came back at eleven," Bertha pointed out.

"And didn't go in, according to your statement, Bertha. He simply pressed the horn button on the car."

"That's right. You're thinking *she* murdered Sally now—

148

that it wasn't Everett Belder?"

"It looks that way."

"Thought you had it all fixed as being a man's job."

"I did, but this makes me change my mind. I'm beginning to think Mrs. Belder found out about Sally when she got that letter and went almost crazy with jealous rage. She was so worked up she didn't even answer the telephone at eleven—and almost saved her own life. She murdered Sally, and then became the victim of a murder trap that had been set for her."

"Then who murdered *her?*" Bertha asked.

Sellers scraped a match into flame and held it to the cigar he had been neglecting while talking with Bertha Cool. Then he answered Bertha's question indirectly.

"Between eleven-fifteen and eleven-twenty-one Wednesday morning the telephone rang. Mrs. Belder was instructed to get in her car, to drive out the boulevard, to go through that last boulevard stop so as to shake off any shadow, and turn abruptly to the left on Harkington Avenue, zip into the garage, close the door, and leave the motor running, waiting for a signal. A perfect setup for carbon-monoxide poisoning. And in order to be certain that it was perfect, the person who planned it went into that garage and sealed up every crack and crevice with oakum."

Bertha's face showed her startled surprise. "You mean that?"

"Absolutely."

Bertha gave a low whistle.

"Technically," Sergeant Sellers said, "we'll have a hell of a time proving it was murder. The woman died by her own hand—by her own carelessness, and—"

"Wait a minute," Bertha interrupted. "There's one other thing you overlooked. After she got the telephone call she went over to the portable typewriter and wrote out the directions so she wouldn't forget them."

Sergeant Sellers's smile was patronizing. "Don't kid yourself," he said. "She wouldn't have left the telephone and gone to the typewriter. In the first place, those directions were indelibly seared on her memory. She was working under such an emotional strain that her mind was working at high speed.

ERLE STANLEY GARDNER

But in case she had wanted to get the directions straight, she would have had a pencil and paper by the telephone. She'd have scribbled down the directions in her own handwriting, in a scrawl which would have shown the emotional tension under which she was laboring. But the murderer wants us to believe she went over to the typewriter, fed in a small sheet of paper, and carefully typed out the directions. Phooey! That stuff is so raw that it smells."

"You mean the murderer wrote out those directions and planted them with the body?"

"He must have."

"Why?"

"Don't you get it? So that it would be perfectly apparent, even to the dumb police the minute they found the body, that she had killed herself by her own carelessness."

"And that's the way it actually happened?" Bertha asked.

"That's the way it actually happened," Sellers said. "The gasoline tank is bone dry. The ignition switch is still on. The battery is dead. She must have asphyxiated herself within the first few minutes and then the motor went on running until it had used up all the gasoline there was in the tank. We know there were at least four gallons because Belder had put that much in Wednesday morning."

"Then the murderer must have gone to the garage afterward and left this note."

"That's right. That's why I felt so pleased when I saw there were two perfect fingerprints on it, and that's why I was so sarcastic when I realized that it was *your* interference that had started me off on a false lead."

Bertha said, "I'm sorry."

"You should be. You've been in the business long enough to know that you're not to touch anything when you come on a body. You're to keep your hands off everything. It was all right finding your fingerprints on the handle of the door. You had to open the car door to see she was in there, dead, but that was as far as you should have gone."

Sergeant Sellers's voice contained patient rebuke. The man was tired, completely weary, dejected and disappointed.

Bertha said once more, "I'm sorry."

"I know."

150

"I realize that doesn't help."

"It doesn't."

"Look here," Bertha said suddenly, "that murder was planned so the death would seem to be accidental."

"That's right."

"Then the murderer must have gone out to the garage to make certain of what had happened and leave the note."

"Correct."

"Then why didn't the murderer at that time pull the oakum out of the cracks that had been so carefully sealed up? That oakum in the cracks is a dead give-away."

"I've thought of that," Sellers said, "and it puzzled me for a while, but you can understand it if you put yourself in the shoes of the murderer."

"How do you mean?"

"He had accomplished his purpose. He'd got the woman out of the way. He sneaked into the garage, probably in the dead of night, long enough to plant this note in the automobile so that the minute the body was discovered the newspapers would list it as death from carelessness rather than murder. The murderer dared to enter the garage long enough to plant that note, but he didn't dare to stay there. He didn't dare to be found there. If anything went wrong, and someone had seen him enter the garage and had telephoned the police that there was a prowler on the premises, and a radio car had come rushing out and caught this man in the garage—well, it was just the same as though he had been caught shooting her or sticking a knife into her. It would have been first-degree murder, and he knew it. Therefore, he didn't dare to wait long enough to remove the calking from the cracks. He perhaps hoped the police wouldn't discover it, but even if they did, he felt perfectly safe, just so long as he wasn't actually caught on the premises."

"You mean if he wasn't caught on the premises he couldn't be convicted?"

"That's right," Sellers said. "Unless we can dig up some evidence that will show the whole thing as part of a consistent, carefully-thought-out, premeditated plan of campaign, we can never convict the murderer even if we put our finger on him, because he actually didn't kill the woman. He could have been, and probably was, a mile away when it happened. It's diabolical in its ingenuity and in its legal efficiency. A man simply gets a woman's mind so preoccupied, gets her so emotionally excited, that she omits the precautions she might otherwise have taken, and brings about her own death by carelessness. Prove all those facts to a jury, and then try and get a conviction, or try and get a Supreme Court to uphold a first-degree verdict. The probabilities are it can't be done."

"Have you," Bertha asked, "some evidence pointing to the murderer?"

"Yes. Everett Belder. Mr. Belder," Sergeant Sellers went on slowly, "the diabolically clever killer, the inventor, the perverted genius; the man who had his business ruined, who had plenty of time to sit in his office and think; who used the imagination he has used in thinking out sales campaigns to think out a way of killing his wife by which he would be legally in the clear. The man who wrote the poison-pen letters accusing himself of affairs with various women, exposing love affairs which would otherwise never have been discovered; the man who hired a detective so as to be absolutely certain that his wife would be shadowed to this garage. Don't you get it, Bertha? If it hadn't been for you tailing her, there might have been some doubt as to what happened, but as it is, we fix the time of death almost to the minute—a time at which Everett Belder was sitting in the barber shop having his face massaged, his nails manicured, his hair trimmed. A very pretty picture, isn't it?"

"In the barber shop?" Bertha asked somewhat lamely.

"In the barber shop, Bertha, and don't be surprised about that, because we've already checked up on his story. In the barber shop, where he was smart enough to walk away and forget his overcoat, so that the barber would be absolutely certain to remember the time. Don't act innocent, sweetheart, because the barber remembers *you* coming in and checking up on the coat."

Bertha for once was at a loss for words.

"Some other woman," Sellers said, "who came in about twenty minutes after you did, said that Mr. Belder had forgotten his overcoat and had asked her to drop in and pick it up for him."

Expression struggled all over Bertha's face.

"Seems to surprise you," Sellers said. "It shouldn't. You should have realized by this time that he had a feminine accomplice."

"What makes you say that?"

"Someone who could run his wife's typewriter with a professional touch; but above all, someone who could put through the telephone call to his wife and lure her out to the garage. No, Bertha, that's the one weak link in his entire scheme. He needed a female accomplice. And if I can find that woman—and I'm going to find her and make her talk— I may be able to convict Everett Belder. This is one case where there isn't any mystery about *who* committed the murder. The only question is whether I can get the evidence that will prove that it is deliberate murder and send the perpetrator of it to the San Quentin gas chamber."

Bertha managed to say, "I see."

"And," Sellers went on, "I just want to tell you, Bertha, that if you get in my way on this thing, that if you tamper with any more evidence, or ball the thing up for me any more, I'm going to flatten you out as though you'd been run over by a steamroller. That's all. You may go now."

153

18

"WHAT'S IN IT FOR ME?"

ELSIE BRAND GLANCED UP from her typewriter as Bertha opened the door. "Good morning, Mrs. Cool."

"Hello," Bertha said, and walked across to drop down in a chair across from Elsie's desk. "I look like the wrath of God—how do I feel?"

Elsie smiled. "I read in the paper that the body was discovered by a female private detective who had been working on the case. I suppose it was quite a strain. Could you sleep?"

"Not a wink."

"Was it that bad?"

Bertha started to say something, checked herself, took a cigarette instead. "I'd give anything if Donald were only back."

"Yes. I can imagine you miss him. But you aren't working on *this* case, are you?"

Bertha lit the cigarette, didn't say anything.

Elsie went on, "I understood Everett Belder had taken things out of your hands."

Bertha said, "Elsie, if I don't have somebody to talk to, I'm going nuts. Not that you can tell me a damn thing," she added hastily, "but the thing has been going round and round in my mind all night—like a dog chasing its own tail. I'm in so deep I can't back out, and I'm afraid to go ahead."

"I don't understand," Elsie said. "You mean you're in deep with Everett Belder?"

"On this damn murder case."

"The police think it's murder? I thought the way the news-

154

paper explained it that it was just carelessness. She left her motor running—"

"The police think it's murder. *I* think it's murder. What's more, it *is* murder. And I tried to cut corners and be smart, and now *I'm* mixed up in it."

"I don't see how it could be murder," Elsie said. "Are the police certain of their facts?"

"They're certain of their facts. What's more, they know who did it. There's no doubt who did it. This isn't like one of those murder cases where you wonder who the guilty party is. This is a case where you know who it is—and he's sitting back and laughing up his sleeve. And there's only one weak link in the whole damned business—and I just happen to hold that weak link. I should go to Sergeant Sellers and put my cards on the table, but I'm afraid to. I held out on the police and that's bad business."

Elsie's face showed sympathy. "Why did you hold out on the police?"

"I'll be damned if I know," Bertha admitted. "It started, of course, when Sergeant Sellers grabbed that third letter out of my hands and wouldn't tell me what was in it. Damn him, he never *has* told me. I thought at the time, 'Well, the hell with you, buddy. The next time I try to help you out on anything, you'll know it!' "

"I can understand exactly how you feel, Mrs. Cool," and there was a half smile in Elsie Brand's eyes. "I thought at the time that Sergeant Sellers was starting something."

"I was sore," Bertha admitted. "Good and sore. I made up my mind I'd see him in hell before I even gave him so much as a pleasant thought in the future. Then something happened, and I put two and two together and got this clue. I suppose I could blame Donald for that if I really tried good and hard."

"Why blame him because you got a clue?"

"Not that," Bertha said, "but the way I got it. The way I went about the whole thing. I used to run just a simple detective agency. I never thought of holding out on the police. Hell, I never had any reason to hold out on them. I never had anything to hold. I tagged along with a little detective agency, doing odd jobs here and there, picking up a little money, pinching every penny until the Indian head yelled for mercy. Then, along comes Donald."

Bertha stopped long enough for a deep drag at the cigarette. "A brainy little devil if there ever was one," she went on. "Money just didn't meant a damn thing to him. He spent it like water, and damned if he didn't have the knack of making it run in like water coming through a leaky roof. I never saw so much money in my life. And he never played anything the way he was supposed to, or the way it looked as though he was playing it. He was always two or three jumps ahead of everybody, playing the cards close to his chest, getting all ready for that final big blow-off when Donald would bob up with the right answer that *he'd* had all along, and a fistful of money that came to us because he had known the right answer long before anyone else had even guessed it.

"Well, I hated to admit that Donald was better at it than I was. So when I had a chance to play them close to my chest in this case, I just kept quiet. I should have talked. Now, it's too late to talk. I've got a bear by the tail. I can't let go, and I don't know what to do."

"If it's going to make you feel any better, tell me about it," Elsie said.

Bertha said, "Her husband killed her, there's no mystery about that. The point is, he did it in such a clever way they can never convict him of murder. Even if they get the goods on him, they probably can't convict him of anything—but he had a woman accomplice. Now then, who was this woman accomplice?"

Elsie Brand smiled. "I'm not guessing. You want to talk, go ahead and talk."

"Talking makes me feel better," Bertha admitted, "and gets the thing more clear in my mind. He had a female accomplice. Who? I thought for a while it was Carlotta's mother, but it couldn't have been, because they must be working at cross purposes."

"She was the one who was in here yesterday?"

"Yes. She wanted to find out who did Belder's barber work. I found out. I got fifty dollars for finding out. After that, all I had to do was to telephone a certain number. When someone answered the phone, I was to mention the name of the barber shop and then hang up."

"You have that phone number?" Elsie asked.

"I have it—I checked it. It's a pay station in a downtown drugstore. Someone was waiting there to pick up the information. Perhaps Carlotta's mother."

Elsie's nod was sympathetic.

"But," Bertha said, "I did a little thinking. I tried to figure it the way Donald Lam would. I said to myself, 'Now why does she want to know Belder's barber? What does Belder's barber have to do with it?' So I thought back about Belder, trying to place the last time I'd noticed him being all slicked up as though he had been to a barber shop, and I remembered it was Wednesday morning.

"I went down to the barber shop and asked a few questions. The barber who ran the place remembered Belder had been in there, had been wearing an overcoat, and had forgotten and left it there when he walked out. It occurred to me Carlotta's mother knew about that and wanted to search the overcoat. I beat her to it. I found something in the overcoat pocket that's a clue."

"What?" Elsie asked.

"I'm not saying," Bertha said. "I'm not telling even you that, Elsie. Not that Bertha doesn't think she can trust you, but it's something she doesn't dare to tell anyone."

"I understand," Elsie said sympathetically.

"It *might* help Sergeant Sellers convict Belder of murder—it might not. I don't know. I do know that Carlotta's mother wanted this thing. I snatched it right out from under her hand. *She* couldn't have been Belder's accomplice, or she wouldn't have needed to have come to me in the first place."

"Unless it suited Belder's purpose to have you get this thing, and you were just walking into a trap," Elsie said.

"That possibility occurred to me about two o'clock this morning," Bertha admitted. "That's why I didn't get *any* sleep."

"Why don't you go to Sergeant Sellers, put all your cards on the table, and—"

"Because that's the logical thing to do," Bertha said. "That's what I should do. That's what the average detective agency would do, and if I do, I'll wind up behind the eight ball with the fee that an average detective agency would make.

"To hell with that stuff. I'm pinch-hitting for Donald. When he comes back he's going to need dough. Damn me, I'm going to have it all ready for him."

"I can understand just how you feel."

"If I tell Sergeant Sellers about this, the sergeant will take over. That will be all there is to it. He'll bawl hell out of me because I didn't tell him sooner; then I'll be a witness in a murder trial and the lawyers will start picking me to pieces, asking me why I didn't do something about this as soon as I got it, intimating that I was first planning blackmail, that I have it in for Belder and am trying to get him convicted of murder on the strength of it— The whole damned line of stuff that lawyers hand out."

"I know," Elsie said. "I was a witness once."

Bertha thought things over for nearly a minute. "Well," she said, "I've started out and I've got to paddle my own canoe. Carlotta's mother knows that I beat her to it, and have the thing she was looking for. I can count on her trying to get it. If Everett Belder knows I've got it, he'll—well, he'll probably try to kill *me*. Somewhere along the line I've got to play both ends against the middle and come out on top. And from where I'm sitting right now, it looks like a hopeless job."

"If there's anything I can do," Elsie said, "you can count on me."

Bertha heaved herself wearily to her feet. "Well," she announced, "there's Dolly Cornish. She's the forgotten woman in this whole business, and somehow I have a hunch—"

"Somebody coming. Damn it, every time I sit down out here somebody catches me before I can—"

The door opened. Mrs. Goldring, her face swollen from weeping, accompanied by a solicitous Carlotta, entered the office.

Mrs. Goldring's face brightened just a bit at sight of Bertha. Carlotta's nod and smile were cheerful greetings. "Good morning, Mrs. Cool. May we see you for a moment? Mother's had this terrible shock, but—well, some things just can't wait. We'd like to talk with you for a few moments."

"Go right on into my private office," Bertha said, "right on in and sit down. I'll be with you in just a moment. I'm finishing some important dictation to my secretary. Just go on in and make yourselves at home. You'll pardon me while I finish dictating."

"Of course," Mrs. Goldring murmured. "We appreciate this."

"It's so nice of you to see us right away," Carlotta said.

Bertha watched them enter her private office, then turned to Elsie. "This," she announced, "is *it!*"

"An opportunity to let go?"

Bertha smiled. "An opportunity to cash in, dearie. Don't ever kid yourself, Mrs. Goldring may be prostrated with grief, but through her tears of sorrow she sees everything that's going on. That woman is no one's damned fool, and she's the slice of bread that has the butter."

"I'm afraid I don't get you."

"Figure it out," Bertha said in a low voice. "There's an estate of God knows how much money. Everett Belder cashed in and put everything in his wife's name. He kills his wife so he can have his freedom, and at the same time get all of that money back. Mrs. Goldring has just about persuaded her daughter to pull out and take the money with her. You can see what a beautiful tug-of-war that was making. And Everett Belder has made it plain that he's finished with me, so I'm perfectly free to take employment from Mrs. Goldring."

"But how could you change the property rights—"

"Don't you get it?" Bertha said. "Under the law, a man can't inherit property from any person whom he has murdered, regardless of a will or anything else. I know that's the law because Donald told me so once. Now, you just sit here and pound away at the typewriter so the office will look busy as hell, and Bertha's going in and cut herself a great big slice of cake."

Bertha straightened her sagging shoulders, got her chin up and the old look of complete self-confidence on her face. "I know what Donald would do, Elsie. He'd manipulate things around in some way so that he'd pick up this job on a percentage basis. Then he'd use this clue that no one else knows about to pin the murder on Everett Belder, dump the estate into Mrs. Goldring's lap, and collect a percentage. Hell's bells, Elsie, we might even get as much as ten percent; and the estate's probably worth seventy-five thousand dollars. That would be seventy-five hundred dollars jangling the bell in our cash register."

"Yes," Elsie agreed, "I think Donald probably would do something just like that and then handle it in such a way that Sergeant Sellers would be very, very grateful instead of angry."

Determination glinted in Bertha's eyes. "And that's what *I'm* going to do."

Elsie seemed just a little dubious.

"First rattle out of the box," Bertha said, "I'm going to do some real salesmanship. I've been studying sales psychology and I'm going to go to work on that woman and get a percentage of the estate. She thinks she can employ me on a per diem basis. I'll be subtle about it, but determined. Watch the way I handle it, Elsie. This is where Bertha crashes into the big time."

Bertha grabbed some letters from Elsie's desk without even bothering to look at them. She held them in her left hand well out in front of her, put on her most businesslike air of weighty importance, cleared her throat, and pounded across the reception room, bustling into her own office, closing the door crisply, and smiling reassuringly at her visitors.

She flung herself into the squeaking swivel chair, cleared a space in front of her on the desk, put down the correspondence she had been holding, and looked past Carlotta to give Mrs. Goldring the benefit of her most sympathetic smile.

"I know how absolutely useless it is to try and assuage grief by words. All I can say is that you have my sincere sympathy."

"Thank you," Mrs. Goldring said in the toneless voice of a woman whose perceptions are dulled by a great shock.

Carlotta, sharply businesslike, intruded upon the brief conversational pause which followed. "Mrs. Cool, something terrible has happened—something that has upset Mother so much I'm really afraid she may have a complete nervous breakdown.

"Coming on top of the shock of Mabel's death, it is almost

too much for her to bear."

"Don't worry about me," Mrs. Goldring said weakly.

Carlotta, as crisp as a cold lettuce leaf, went on. "Now, before we go any further, Mrs. Cool, I understand that Everett has severed all connection with you. You're not employed by him any longer and are not obligated to tell him anything. Is that right?"

"That's the size of it," Bertha said grimly. "He thought I'd bungled things up, and he washed his hands of me, and I'm glad he did."

"Of course," Carlotta went on, "we have to be *very* careful. We can't make any certain direct accusations, not as things stand at the present time; but I think we all understand the situation. And I think we can carry on this conversation in the light of what we might call an unspoken understanding."

Bertha merely nodded.

"After all," Carlotta hurried to add, "we can't afford to jeopardize *our* positions. You understand what I mean. Everett's secretary is suing you over something you said."

"I was just trying to clear up the case," Bertha snorted, "and that damned little—estimable young lady—goes ahead and files suit."

"I know just how you feel, but I don't see anything estimable about her, Mrs. Cool."

"My lawyer says she should be an estimable young lady until after the trial."

"Well, as far as I'm concerned," Carlotta said positively, "she's just a little—"

Mrs. Goldring coughed.

"Well," Carlotta finished lamely, "I'm very glad that she's no longer connected with Everett's office. I always thought she had a certain air of possessive intimacy. Good Heavens, one would have thought she owned the office."

"She always seemed very conscious of her sex," Mrs. Goldring said, in the impersonal manner of one who has been so completely detached from mundane affairs that human relationships have ceased to have any great meaning. "She was very provocative in her manner—I mean sexually provocative."

"Mother's *terribly* upset," Carlotta said. "I'll do the talking."

Bertha half turned so as to face Carlotta.

Carlotta had the manner of a young woman who has been kept somewhat in the background of life, and then, in a time of great emotional stress, comes forward to prove herself capable of accepting responsibilities. She seemed to enjoy the role very much, and quite apparently had definitely accepted full and complete charge of the situation.

"A matter has risen, Mrs. Cool, on which we will want your assistance."

Bertha said, "Well, that *might* be arranged, if I could do you some good. In my business I tell all my clients that I prefer not to accept one penny from them unless I can do them some good. I've found that quite frequently a percentage arrangement works to advantage. You know, get a percentage of what you bring in. In that way I can afford to devote every minute of my time to their work."

Bertha paused hopefully.

Carlotta Goldring said quickly, "Yes indeed, Mrs. Cool, I'm sure that you give your clients the very best that you have in you."

"I do that," Bertha agreed. "And what's more, once I take a case for a person, I stay with it. I'm something of a bulldog. I keep tugging and worrying until I finally shake a result out of the situation—*the result my clients want.* That's the way I work."

"I've heard that you are *very* competent," Carlotta acknowledged.

Mrs. Goldring lowered her handkerchief from her eyes. "Intensely loyal," she supplemented. "You have an excellent reputation, Mrs. Cool, and I should think that your clients would want to see that you were *very* well compensated."

"Some of them do. Sometimes you get hold of one you have to argue with." Bertha beamed across at her visitors. "But do you know," she went on, "I have found that the more intelligent my clients are, the more they appreciate that I have to be well paid."

"Yes, I can see where that would be the case," Carlotta said, glancing quickly at her mother and then going on.

"Well, Mrs. Cool, you're exceedingly busy, so we'll get right down to brass tacks."

"*I'll* tell her," Mrs. Goldring said.

"That's the way I like to do things," Bertha said. "Shoot fast. Of course, in this case, there are complications—but I'm a fast worker at that."

"So I understand."

Bertha oozed smiling approval. "Suppose you explain just what it is you want, if you feel up to it."

Carlotta looked at Mrs. Goldring expectantly.

Mrs. Goldring sighed, dabbed her handkerchief to her nose, lowered it, said, "I believe you understand that my daughter's husband is a sales engineer. It's a business that's *very* speculative. I don't know just what it is that he does, but occasionally he takes complete charge of the distribution of some line of merchandise on a percentage basis."

Bertha wasted no time making comments while the preliminaries were coming in.

"Of course, recently, there haven't been any sales problems. Some time ago there was a problem of getting materials. Manufacturers had more market than they knew what to do with. They couldn't get the stuff to manufacture—and Everett Belder had some rather sharp reverses."

Bertha contented herself with a nod.

"Some time ago he placed all of his property in my daughter's name."

Bertha didn't even nod, simply sat behind her desk, her eyes watching Mrs. Goldring in glittering concentration.

"Of course," Mrs. Goldring went on, "it would be reasonable to suppose that he simply placed the property in Mabel's name so that he would be safe from his creditors, but he took the witness stand and denied upon oath that such was his intention in making the transfer. I don't understand the law very well, Mrs. Cool, but as I understand it, the intention with which the transfer is made has a lot to do with it. If a person *intends* to defraud his creditors, the transfer is void. If he has some other, and legitimate, intent, the transfer stands up."

"And this stood up?" Bertha asked.

"This stood up."

163

"Then upon your daughter's death the property which she held was her sole and separate property?"

"That's right."

"Rather considerable?" Bertha asked, tentatively feeling the way.

"Quite considerable," Mrs. Goldring said in a tone of cold finality which slammed the door of that particular conversational corridor in Bertha Cool's face.

For a moment there was silence, then Carlotta Goldring said quickly, "What actually happened, Mrs. Cool, is that Mabel and Everett Belder hadn't been getting along very well together for the past few months, and when she had reason to believe that Everett was—well, you know, was—I mean that he was—"

"Playing around?" Bertha interjected.

"Yes."

"All right. She thought he was stepping out, so what happened?"

"She made a will leaving all her property to my mother and myself," Carlotta said positively.

"How do you know?"

"She told us so. That is, she told us she *was making* such a will. She told my mother so over the telephone. She said she was drawing it up on her own typewriter. She knew she'd require two witnesses. I feel confident that Sally Brentner was one. We don't know *who* the other witness was."

"Where's that will now?"

"That's just the point, Mrs. Cool," Mrs. Goldring announced. "My son-in-law *burned that will up.*"

"How do you know?"

Mrs. Goldring's smile was triumphantly inclusive. "I think *you* can help us there, Mrs. Cool."

"Perhaps I can," Bertha admitted cautiously.

"If we could *prove* that the will was burned *after* Mabel's death, then we could introduce other evidence to show what was in the will—Mabel's telephone conversation for instance."

"When was it dated?" Bertha asked.

"We have reason to believe it was made the day before her death, April sixth."

A look of pleased anticipation made Bertha Cool seem

positively cherubic. "Yes, Mrs. Goldring, I think I can help you."

"Oh, I'm *so* glad," Mrs. Goldring said.

"It will make *so* much difference to us," Carlotta interjected. "You just can't imagine what a relief this is. I told Mother that you could help us, I said, 'Mother, if there's anyone who can help us, it will be the delightful woman with the strong ·personality who was there in Everett's office when I walked in.' "

Bertha Cool picked up a pencil and toyed with it cautiously. "Well, now," she said, "just what did you have in mind?"

Mrs. Goldring said, "Simply that you tell what you know, fearlessly and accurately. You can go to my lawyer and make a preliminary affidavit and then when you get on the witness stand you can testify to what you saw when you entered the office, because we know that Everett burned up that will just before you and Sergeant Sellers entered the office."

Bertha struggled with sheer incredulity. "You mean that you want me as a *witness,* and that's all?"

Carlotta nodded brightly. "You see, Mrs. Cool, we have found ashes in Everett's little grate there in the office. An expert is testing those ashes, reconstructing them in some way that they have, fitting them together so that he can prove absolutely that it was my sister's will that Everett had been burning. And those ashes *were on top* of all the others, showing that the will was the last thing put on the fire. We feel certain that Imogene Dearborne knows a lot more about this than she's willing to state. I'm afraid she won't help us voluntarily. But we felt certain that *you* could help us, that you'd remember papers were burning in the fireplace when you first entered the office. That's all you need to remember, Mrs. Cool: that papers were burning at that time. I came in later, you'll remember, and I can testify that when I entered the room the fire was—"

"Wait a minute," Bertha said, the smile definitely gone from her face, her eyes cold and hard. *"What's in all this for me?"*

The women looked at each other, then Carlotta said, "Why, the usual witness fee, Mrs. Cool—and we'd pay you something for your time in going to our lawyer's office."

Bertha, struggling to keep her voice level, said, "Then you came here simple to arrange for my testimony as a witness, is that it?"

"That's it *exactly*," Carlotta said, once more turning on the full force of her personality. "We would, of course, be glad to pay you for your time in going up to the lawyer's office and making a statement—whatever it's worth. I suppose five or ten dollars. Of course, it couldn't be anything unusual or it would look as though we were trying to *buy* your testimony, and we couldn't either one of us afford that, *could* we, Mrs. Cool?"

The two women visitors smiled engagingly at Bertha for the space of a second.

Bertha's mouth was hard. "No, we couldn't, and for that reason I'm not going to swear any papers were burning in any grate, I'm not going up to any lawyer, and I'm not going to be any witness."

"Oh, Mrs. Cool! But I thought you said you could help us."

Bertha said, "I said I could help you establish what you wanted to prove. I was referring to my ability as a detective."

"Oh, but we don't need a detective. That's all cut and dried. Our lawyer says that once the testimony of the handwriting expert establishes that it *was* the will that was burned, there's nothing to it."

"And therefore the lawyer's willing to work for a nominal fee, I suppose," Bertha Cool said dryly.

"Well, he gets a percentage."

"And then in addition to that, if you get all the estate, he acts as your attorney in probating the will and gets another chunk out of it, doesn't he?"

"Why—why, I hadn't thought of that. He said that part of it would be handled in the usual manner."

"I see," Bertha said with frigid politeness. "Well, I'm very sorry that I can't help you—unless you feel that you need someone to gather the facts."

"But, Mrs. Cool, we *have* all the facts. All we need is a witness to swear to them."

"You've covered a lot of ground since your daughter's death was discovered," Bertha said. "Lawyers, handwriting experts, and all that."

"We did most of it before Mabel's body was discovered. I felt certain Everett had murdered her. I've been certain ever since yesterday morning. Therefore, I'd already started to take steps to see that Everett didn't get away with anything or profit by his crime—and we're really deeply indebted to you, Mrs. Cool, for your work in discovering the body."

"Nothing at all," Bertha said hastily. "I might be able to uncover more facts for you if—"

"Our lawyer," Mrs. Goldring interrupted smoothly, "says we have all the facts we need, if we can just get the witnesses to swear to them."

"Well, he should know."

"But, Mrs. Cool, can't you testify there was a fire—"

"I'm afraid not. I make a terrible witness and I'm allergic to lawyers."

"Our attorney said we could serve a subpoena on you and then you'd have to come to court. He thought it would be better to have a friendly chat with you first."

"My memory," Bertha apologized, "is terrible. Right now, I can't remember a thing about whether there was a fire in Everett Belder's office. Of course, it *may* come back to me."

Mrs. Goldring arose from her chair, distantly formal. "I'm so sorry, Mrs. Cool. I had hoped that we could get your testimony without having to serve a subpoena on you."

Bertha Cool reached for the correspondence she had placed on her desk. "*Good* morning."

She watched her visitors out of the door, then when they'd had time to cross the entrance office to the corridor, Bertha Cool indulged in a sulphurous monologue which, because she lacked an audience, seemed somehow ineffective.

She jerked open the door.

Elsie Brand looked up. "They seemed a little angry when they left," she said anxiously.

"*They* seemed angry," Bertha all but screamed. "Why, damn their mealymouthed, two-faced, hypocritical hides! Do you know what those two chiselers wanted? Wanted me to go into court and swear that papers were burning in Everett Belder's grate when I went in there with Sergeant Sellers Thursday morning—*and they wanted to pay me witness fees.*

167

Why—why—the—"

Bertha Cool smothered herself into silence.

Elsie Brand seemed sympathetic but curious. "I think it's the first time I've ever seen you at a loss for words, Mrs. Cool."

"Loss for words," Bertha yelled at her. "Goddamn it, I'm not at a *loss* for words! I just can't decide which ones to use first!"

19

JEWELRY-ROCK

THE LOCKLEAR APARTMENT HOTEL managed to surround itself with an atmosphere of quiet luxury, an aloof reserve, well calculated to put outsiders on the defensive.

The clerk who stood behind the counter was somewhere in the early thirties—tall, slender, suave, and well groomed. He watched Bertha Cool approaching his desk, and imperceptibly his demeanor stiffened as he observed Bertha's free-swinging stride, the manner in which she brushed aside all the swank luxury of the lobby.

The clerk's hair was brushed and oiled into sleek luster. His eyebrows, arched and regular, managed to elevate themselves just enough to put Bertha on the defensive, had Bertha been the type to be put on the defensive by anything less than a battleship.

"Good afternoon," the clerk said in the tone he would have used in greeting an interior decorator who had been summoned by the management. Not quite the tone he reserved for tradesmen, yet definitely not the voice which he would use in addressing an honored guest.

Bertha wasted no time in being polite. "You have a Mrs. Cornish staying here—Dolly Cornish?"

"Ah, yes—Mrs. Cornish. And what was *your* name, please?"

"I'm Mrs. Cool."

"I'm very sorry, Mrs. Cool, but Mrs. Cornish gave up her apartment rather suddenly."

"Where did she go?"

"I'm sure I couldn't tell you. I'm sorry."

"Leave any forwarding address?"

"Her mail is being handled."

"Where are you sending it?"

"If you care to write her a letter, Mrs. Cool, it will be handled in the regular manner."

Bertha looked at him with exasperation. "Listen, you, I'm looking for Dolly Cornish on a matter of considerable importance. Now, if you know where she is, pass on the information. If you don't know where she is, tell me how I can go about finding out."

"I'm sorry, Mrs. Cool. I've given out all the information I'm permitted to."

"When did she leave?"

"I'm sorry, I can't tell you that. All that I'm permitted to say is that she gave up her apartment rather suddenly."

"Anybody been on her tail?" Bertha asked.

"I *beg* your pardon, Mrs. Cool."

"Anyone trying to find out where she is?"

"I'm certain I couldn't tell you that."

The clerk looked past Bertha Cool, over her shoulder, to take in a middle-aged, broad-shouldered man wearing baggy tweeds, who carried in his left hand a sheaf of folded papers, held together with an elastic.

"Good afternoon," the clerk said in a voice that was even more distant than that he had used in greeting Bertha Cool.

The man didn't even bother to return the salutation. He ran through the folded papers, moving them with thick, stubby fingers. Midway through the pile he folded back the top segment by clamping his thumb in position. The darkened fingernail on the index finger held down the bill. "Acme Piano Rental Company," he said. "Dolly Cornish. Rent's due on her piano. Want to pay the bill, or do I go up and get the dough?"

The clerk, for the moment, seemed definitely embarrassed. He glanced at Bertha Cool, said to the piano man, "Mrs. Cornish will get in touch with you within the next day or two."

"She's moved," Bertha said.

The piano man looked at her, said, "Huh? How's that?"

"She's moved—gone away."

"She can't move that piano without written consent."

"Well, she's done it. Ask him."

The man turned to the clerk. "She here?"

"Well—she asked me to—"

"She here, or ain't she?"

The clerk said with exasperation, "I'll take care of the bill and will be responsible for the piano."

"Five bucks," the man said, pushing the bill out on the counter. "If she moves it without written consent it's a serious offense."

"We'll guarantee there won't be any damage and that she'll get in touch with you at once."

"She can't move it. Five bucks."

The clerk opened the cash drawer of the safe, pulled out a five-dollar bill, slapped it crisply down on the counter, and said, "A receipt, please." He looked at Bertha Cool and said, "*Good* afternoon, Mrs. Cool."

Bertha didn't move, remaining with her elbows propped on the counter, staring down at the bill. She watched the man sign a receipt, shove the receipted bill across, put the five dollars in his pocket.

"Tell her to look at her lease agreement. She can't move any leased goods."

The clerk started to say something, checked himself, glanced with exasperation at Bertha Cool.

The man swung away from the desk, headed back across the ornate lobby to the street door.

The clerk moved toward a series of pigeonholes with the receipted bill, then detoured when only halfway there to drop it into the cash drawer in the safe.

"Almost forgot," he said.

"Do some more thinking," Bertha said, "and you might remember something."

He was definitely supercilious. "I think that will be all, Mrs. Cool."

Bertha hesitated a moment, then apparently somewhat crushed, crossed the lobby toward the street door.

Bertha walked across the street to the newsstand. "Somebody moved a piano out of that joint across the street," she said, "within the last day or two. I'd like to get the name on the moving-van."

The man shook his head. "I can't help you."

"Didn't you notice the name?"

"I don't remember seeing any van there within the last day or two, but of course, I'm busy over here."

Bertha covered four more stores with the same result. Then she went to the telephone and called her office. When Elsie Brand answered the telephone, she said, "What can you do on the lah-de-dah, Elsie?"

"What do you mean?" Elsie asked.

Bertha said, "Dolly Cornish was in apartment 15B down at the Locklear Hotel Apartments. The place is as stiff as a starched collar. Put on your most grand-dame air. Don't act human; look down your nose at the male impersonator that's behind the counter. Tell him you want to look over his vacancies, if he has any. String him along."

"When do you want me to do it?" Elsie asked.

"As soon as you can get a cab," Bertha said. "I'll be waiting around on the corner. You'll see me, but don't speak to me. After you come out, walk around the corner and I'll tag along."

Bertha hung up the receiver, decided she had five minutes to wait before Elsie could possibly get there. She walked over to the newsstand, looked over some of the magazines, then strolled up to the corner, waiting. She saw Elsie Brand enter the apartment hotel, emerge some fifteen minutes later. Bertha sauntered around the corner and Elsie joined her.

"Well?" Bertha asked.

"Did I hand that clerk a line!" Elsie said. "He mentioned they'd require references for a single woman. I asked him if the Mayor of the city and the Governor of the state would be all right. He called an assistant manager to show me around. They have two vacancies. One of them is 15B."

"It's vacant?" Bertha asked.

Elsie nodded.

Bertha frowned. "What would you do," she asked, "if you were renting a piano, and wanted to move it?"

"I— Why I don't know," Elsie said, laughing.

Bertha said suddenly, "You'd call up the people you'd

rented it from, wouldn't you?"

"I guess I would."

Bertha said with sudden decision, "Go back in there. Tell him that you understood from a friend there was another vacancy. Ask him if he's certain you've seen them all. Try and find out if they've rented an apartment in the last two or three days. Put on the high-and-mighty act for him. He'll fall for that. Otherwise you won't get to first base."

"Leave it to me," Elsie said. "I have him eating out of my hand already. Do you want to wait here?"

"Yes."

Elsie was back with the information in five minutes. "Apartment 12B was vacant until yesterday. A Mrs. Stevens took it then."

Bertha grinned. "Nice chap, that clerk. It's probably his master mind that originated the idea. All right, Elsie, go on back to the office."

Bertha entered a telephone booth, called the Locklear Apartments, said, "A Mrs. Stevens left word that I was to call her in apartment 12B. Know anything about it?"

"Just a moment."

A connection clicked, and a woman's voice said, cautiously, "Hello?"

Bertha said, "This is the piano company. The clerk paid the bill on the piano, said you'd moved it into another apartment."

"Oh, yes. I'm glad you called. I've been intending to call you. Yes, it's quite all right."

"Apartment in the same building?"

"Yes."

Bertha said, "I have to look it over. There's a charge of fifty cents."

"Oh, that will be quite all right."

"I'm in your neighborhood now," Bertha said.

"All right. I'll be expecting you. 12B is the number. I should have notified you sooner."

Bertha walked back to the Locklear Apartments. The clerk looked at her with exasperation, started to say something, but Bertha moved over toward the elevators.

The clerk raised a folding gate and approached Bertha

173

Cool with businesslike authority. "I'm sorry, but we don't permit strangers to enter the elevators, unannounced."

Bertha Cool smiled sweetly at him. "Mrs. Stevens, in apartment 12B, asked me to come right up," she said. "I was just talking with her over the telephone."

As the clerk tried to keep expression from his face, Bertha nodded to the elevator boy. "Let's go," she said.

Someone was talking on the telephone in apartment 12B when Bertha knocked on the door. A few moments later the conversation terminated, and Bertha knocked more loudly.

There was no sound from within the room. Bertha raised her voice. "Going to let me in, Dolly, or do I wait for you to come out?"

The door opened. An angry woman somewhere in the thirties stood glaring belligerently at Bertha Cool. "I have just been advised," she said, "that you—"

"I know," Bertha told her. "The clerk doesn't like me. I don't like him. More over, dearie, and let me in."

Bertha's powerful frame pushed the lighter woman to one side with an easy lack of effort. She moved on into the apartment, nodded approvingly at the piano, selected the most comfortable chair, dropped down in it, and lit a cigarette.

The woman in the doorway said, "There are rules against this sort of thing, you know."

"I know."

"And the clerk tells me that I can have the authorities eject you."

"He *would* say something like that."

"That is correct, I believe."

"I don't think so."

"Why not?"

"Because I have contacts at headquarters. A word to them, and in place of arresting me, they'd drag you down to the D.A.'s office for questioning. The newspapers would get your picture, and—"

"What do you want?"

"Just to talk with you."

"The clerk tells me that you're a Mrs. Cool."

"That's right."

"He thinks you're a detective."

174

"Even a dumbbell gets a good idea once in a while."

"Mrs. Cool, may I ask *exactly* what you want?"

"Sure," Bertha Cool said. "Close the door. Sit down, take a load off your feet. Tell me about Everett Belder."

"I don't care to discuss Mr. Belder."

"Tell me about his wife."

"I understand she was asphyxiated."

"That's right."

"I never met the woman in my life."

"She got a letter about you," Bertha said.

Mrs. Cornish's silence showed her complete lack of interest.

Bertha said, "I suppose the idea germinated in the master mind of that bright clerk downstairs, but you shouldn't have moved out of your apartment, dearie. That puts you in a bad light. You can imagine how your picture will look in the newspapers with some stuff under it, say like this: *Mrs. Dolly Cornish, who, police claim, surreptitiously vacated her apartment and took another under an assumed name, following news of Mrs. Belder's death. Mrs. Cornish was quite friendly with Everett Belder before his marriage.*"

Bertha dropped ashes from her cigarette into the ash tray.

Mrs. Cornish suddenly looked as if she were going to cry. "What—what do you want to know?"

"What have you got to tell?"

"Nothing."

"Good stuff," Bertha agreed enthusiastically. "The newspapers will eat that up. Keep that expression of near-tears on your face, and say nothing, and they'll put a caption under that, *'Nothing,' sobs woman who sent Mrs. Belder to her death.*"

Dolly Cornish straightened suddenly. "What are you talking about? I didn't send Mrs. Belder to her death."

Bertha sucked in a deep drag from the cigarette, said nothing.

"Mrs. Belder threatened to kill *me*," Dolly Cornish went on, sudden indignation wiping the self-pity from her face.

"How long before she died?"

"The same day."

"What had you done to make her want to kill you?"

"Absolutely nothing."

Bertha said, "Pardon me if I don't seem interested, dearie, but we hear that so *many* times."

"This time it's the absolute truth."

"How did you happen to meet her?" Bertha asked.

"I didn't meet her. She called me here at this apartment hotel—and if you're so interested, *that's* why I changed my apartment. I wanted to be under cover so if she did try to do anything violent she couldn't find me."

Bertha kept her eyes averted so Mrs. Cornish couldn't see the glittering, intense interest in them. "Called you on the telephone?"

"Yes."

"What did she say?"

"It was the weirdest, most spine-chilling conversation I ever had with any woman in my life."

"Now, we're getting somewhere. I might be able to help you if you'd really open up."

"How could you help me?"

Bertha turned then to look Mrs. Cornish full in the face. "Let's not misunderstand each other," she said. "I can help you, if I can help myself by doing it. I'm a detective. I've batted around. I know most of the answers. This is what you choose to call a spine-chilling experience. To me it's routine stuff. Now, either go ahead and talk or try to keep quiet. If you talk, I'll talk. If you try to keep quiet, I'll ring headquarters."

"You haven't left me much choice," Mrs. Cornish said with a nervous little laugh.

"I very seldom do," Bertha retorted.

Mrs. Cornish thought things over for a few moments. Bertha gave her plenty of time.

"All right, I'll talk."

Bertha merely reached forward to grind out the stub of her cigarette.

"You're a woman, Mrs. Cool. I can talk to you and say things that one couldn't say to a man. I have a friend who says that twice in every woman's life comes the chance for genuine happiness, that the big majority of women throw both chances away. He's a mining man. He says that the good mines are those that have a big deposit of medium-grade ore. He says happiness is like that. You have to get a big deposit of medium-grade attributes in a man in order to make for happiness. He says most women throw their chances away to chase after the glittering samples of high-grade ore—what they call 'jewelry-rock' in mining circles. My mining friend says that those veins nearly always pinch out. That life just isn't that easy. That when you find a really rich deposit of jewelry-rock, it's a flash in the pan."

"What was Everett Belder?" Bertha asked. "Jewelry-rock?"

"No. Everett was one of my chances for happiness. He was a great big deposit of better-than-average ore."

Bertha lit another cigarette.

"I wanted to see him again," Dolly Cornish said, "and I was glad I did."

"Decide to hang on to him this time?" Bertha asked.

Dolly Cornish shook her head. There was a wistful look in her eyes. "He's changed."

"In what way?"

"I told you he was a deposit of better-than-average ore. Somewhere he'd got it through his head that he was jewelry-rock. He's trying to be something that he isn't, and he's been trying for several years. It's ruined him."

"Perhaps you could bring him back," Bertha said.

Dolly Cornish smiled and the smile spoke more than words.

"All right," Bertha said, "you've got that off your chest. Now we'll talk about Mrs. Belder."

"Wednesday morning Mrs. Belder telephoned me. She didn't give me a chance to say a word. It was as though she had her speech all carefully memorized. She said, 'I know all about you, Mrs. Cornish. Don't start to evade, and don't try to lie. You think you can turn back the hands of the clock. You can't do it. He's mine, now, and I intend to hang on to him. I assure you that I can be very dangerous, and I am afraid you've made it necessary for me to do something about you.' "

"Did you say anything?" Bertha asked as Dolly Cornish paused momentarily.

"I tried to, but I'm afraid I stuttered and stammered. She

wasn't paying any attention to me anyway. She only waited for a moment to get her breath, then she went on with the part that absolutely terrified me. She said, 'I'm not a woman who relies on halfway measures. There was another woman who was living in my house, pretending to be a servant but trying to make eyes at my husband behind my back. Ask *her* what happens to people who think they can pull the wool over *my* eyes.'"

Dolly Cornish's lips quivered, then became tight.

"That all of it?" Bertha asked.

"All except the laughter. It was the laughter that did it, that wild, half-hysterical, malignant laughter. You can have no idea, unless you could have heard—"

"You hang up, or did she?" Bertha interrupted.

"She did."

"Then what?"

"I was too paralyzed to do anything for a while; then I managed to get the receiver back on the hook. I was trembling."

"If you were as innocent as you claim," Bertha said, "you wouldn't have taken it so hard."

"Get this, Mrs. Cool. I'm going to be fair with you. Everett had been one of my chances at happiness. If I'd taken him when I had the chance, I could have kept him from degenerating into a fourflusher. I knew him. I knew his strength. I knew his weakness."

"What's that got to do with it?" Bertha asked.

"Simply this, Mrs. Cool. I'd made up my mind that this was a world where dog eats dog, that I was going to look up Everett again.

"If I found him the same, if I found that he still had the same appeal—well, I knew he was married, but I made up my mind that I was going to get him anyway."

"Guilty conscience, eh?" Bertha asked.

"I suppose so."

After a few moments' silence Bertha said, "Of course, you're not repeating this woman's exact words. You're giving your recollection of them."

"I think I'm giving you almost her exact words. At any rate, I'm giving you the exact idea she conveyed. That was chiseled in my mind."

Bertha Cool calmly selected another cigarette, lit it, took a deep drag, and blew smoke out into the room.

"What did she say happened to this other woman?"

"It was terrible, that awful laughter—"

"Never mind the laughter, what did she *say* happened to her?" Bertha asked.

"She said to ask this other woman what happened to people who thought they could pull the wool over her eyes—and then I read about the body of the servant being found in her cellar."

Bertha said casually, "You've got yourself in a hell of a mess, haven't you?"

"How well I know it," Dolly Cornish admitted ruefully.

"If you tell your story, it looks as if you'd been breaking up the Belder home, and either drove Mrs. Belder to suicide, or—" Bertha broke off to regard Mrs. Cornish with shrewd little eyes in which there was an unspoken accusation.

"Or what?" Dolly Cornish asked.

"Murdered her."

Dolly drew herself up erect in the chair, showing both surprise and indignation. "Mrs. Cool, *what* do you mean?"

Bertha said, "Skip it. If you did murder her, you'd put on an act like that anyway, and if you didn't, there's no use swapping words. Were you relieved when you learned she was dead?"

Dolly Cornish met Bertha Cool's searching gaze frankly. "Yes."

Bertha turned away to watch the smoke eddying up from the cigarette which she held in her fingers. "In some ways I wish I hadn't heard this story."

"Why?"

"I've got to go to Sergeant Sellers, and I hate going to that man right now."

"Why?"

Bertha somewhat wearily got to her feet. "As a mining proposition, he'd run about twenty dollars to the ton, but every once in a while, when things start going his way, *he* thinks he's what you call jewelry-rock."

Bertha started for the door.

179

"After all, Mrs. Cool," Dolly Cornish said, "men are only human, you know. We have to put up with their weaknesses."

Bertha turned in the doorway, surveyed Dolly Cornish appraisingly. "You do the tragic, sensitive-soul-all-bruised-to-hell act very nicely, dearie. I don't mind if it's just practice, but I'd be sore as hell if you really thought I was falling for it."

20

BERTHA IN A BIND

EVERETT BELDER WAS WAITING in the office when Bertha got back. He jumped up as she opened the door from the corridor. He was talking before Bertha Cool had got her eyes into hard focus on him. "Mrs. Cool, I want to apologize. I want to make you the most abject apology I know how to make."

Bertha stood just inside the doorway, her eyes impaling him with a wordless accusation.

"I just didn't know when I had good service," Belder rushed on. "Now I'm in the most terrible predicament. Mrs. Cool, I want to talk with you."

Bertha hesitated.

Belder, good salesman that he was, launched into the only argument which could possibly move her. "I don't care what I have to pay," he said. "I'll pay anything."

Bertha started for the door of the inner office. "Come in."

Elsie Brand asked, "Is there anything else, Mrs. Cool?"

Bertha looked at her watch, said with some surprise, "That's right, it's Saturday afternoon. No, Elsie, I guess that's all." She turned to Belder, "Come in."

Belder, entering the office, dropped wearily into a chair.

"What are your troubles?" Bertha asked.

"The bottom's dropped out."

"How so?"

"I'm going to be accused of murder."

"Have they got any case?"

"Have they got any case!" Belder exclaimed sarcastically. "With my mother-in-law and sweet little Carlotta searching

181

their minds to dig up every fact they can possibly recollect—every single solitary thing that will put me in bad— Well, you can see my position."

Bertha simply sat there, saying nothing.

"And," Belder went on, "there's that mysterious third letter Sergeant Sellers got. I've simply *got* to know what's in there."

"Why?"

"Because it accuses me of intimacy with some other woman."

"Well?"

Belder was silent for a moment, then suddenly blurted out, "I've got to know what woman it was."

"Like that, eh?" Bertha asked.

"Don't misunderstand me, Mrs. Cool."

"I don't think I did."

"Well, I didn't mean it that way."

"How did you mean it?"

"Well—I— Well, I just wanted to know what I'm accused of, that's all."

Bertha thoughtfully lit a cigarette. "Anything else?"

"Anything *else!* Isn't that enough?"

Bertha didn't say anything.

"Anyway," Belder went on, "they're accusing me of having burned up my wife's will. Good Lord, I never even *thought* about a thing like that. When I put all my property in my wife's name, she made a will leaving everything to me. Now they're saying she left a new will. That's news to me. The fact she might have made a new will never even entered my head. I supposed, of course, her will left everything to me."

"That's bad."

"What do you mean?"

"Gives you a motive for murdering her."

There was exasperation on Belder's face. "That's the way they put a man on the spot. If I knew about that other will, I'm supposed to have burned it. If I didn't, I'm supposed to have killed Mabel to get the property."

Bertha said, "Or you might have killed her to get the property, then found the new will and burned it up."

"That's exactly what they say I did."

"Did you?"

"Of course not!"

"How about this judgment Nunnely has against you? What's happened to that?"

"That's why I owe you an apology, Mrs. Cool. If I'd left it in *your* hands we could have had that settled, but I had to get temperamental and put it in the hands of a lawyer."

"What happened?"

"Everything happened. The lawyer got in touch with Nunnely, made an appointment for Nunnely to come to his office this morning. Last night, after Mabel's body was discovered, I tried and tried to get in touch with this lawyer. I couldn't do it. His home reported that he was out of town. I learned afterward that that was what he had told the maid to tell any-one who called up, because his wife was giving a bridge party and he didn't want to be disturbed."

"And this morning?" Bertha asked.

"This morning we met in the lawyer's office. Nunnely had a morning paper under his arm but he hadn't read it—hadn't opened it, even. I was trembling with anxiety to get the thing over with. The lawyer fooled around with so darned many technicalities in getting the release worded just right that Nunnely finally sat back in his chair, lit a cigarette, and opened the newspaper. I tried to signal that damned fool lawyer, but he was looking up some law on the subject of releases, trying to find out just how to 'protect my interests.' "

"What happened?" Bertha asked, her eyes showing interest.

"Nunnely glanced through the news on the first page, turned to the second page, and the headlines about Mabel hit him in the face."

"What did he do?"

"He did exactly what you'd expect him to do. He got to his feet, smiled rather patronizingly at the lawyer, and told him not to bother making out the release; that on second thought he'd decided he would settle only for the full amount of the judgment, together with interest and court costs. It was a cinch. With Mabel's death, he knew I'd inherit the property, and all he had to do was to grab that property out of the estate."

"That's tough," Bertha said.

"I lost about nineteen thousand dollars right then. Perhaps

more by the time the interest is all figured."

"Tough luck," Bertha said without sympathy. She opened her desk drawer, her eyes on Belder's face, took out the spectacle case she had taken from Belder's overcoat pocket, and placed it over on the far side of the desk where it was directly under Belder's eyes.

Apparently Belder gave no heed to what she was doing.

"Look here, Mrs. Cool, I need you. I need your aggressive, dominant personality. I need your brains, your general competency. Now—"

Knuckles pounded on the closed door.

"Good Lord," Bertha said, "I forgot to tell Elsie to lock the door. She's gone home and some client has—"

"Tell him you're busy. Tell him you can't be disturbed," Belder said. "Don't misunderstand me, Mrs. Cool. I want to hire you and this time *I've got the money*. I'm willing to pay you anything—"

Bertha got up from her creaky swivel chair, walked over and said, through the closed door, "I'm busy. The office is closed. It's Saturday afternoon. I can't see anyone today."

The knob twisted. The door pushed open. "Oh, is that so," Sergeant Sellers said.

Bertha flung her weight against the door. "Get out of here and stay out."

But Sergeant Sellers had glimpsed Everett Belder's frightened face through the crack in the open door. He said, "That's different, Bertha. I'm coming in."

Bertha said grimly, "The hell you are," and set her weight against the door.

Sergeant Sellers, on the other side of the door, exerted pressure. Slowly Bertha was pushed back.

"Come on and help me," she panted to Belder.

Belder made no move, but sat there, apparently paralyzed with fear.

Sergeant Sellers pushed the door open.

"You can't come into my private office this way," Bertha blazed.

"I know it, Bertha," he said placatingly, "but now that I'm in here, I can't go away without taking your client with me."

"Well, you just get the hell out of here," Bertha stormed.

"I'm talking business with this man. I have a right to conclude my business transaction. You can wait out in the corridor. You—"

"Sorry, Bertha," Sellers said, "but I'm not waiting anywhere. I have a warrant for the arrest of Everett Belder on the charge of first-degree murder."

Belder tried to get up out of the chair. His knees refused to function. He made a moaning noise which was almost a groan.

Bertha said angrily, "Well, get out of here for five minutes, anyway. Belder is—he wants to employ me. I want to get the financial end of it straightened out."

Sellers didn't move.

"Just five minutes," Bertha pleaded. "Surely I'm entitled to that. I'm entitled to be paid for what I'm doing."

Sellers grinned at Bertha Cool. "Okay, Bertha. You've been a good sport. You—" His eye fell on the spectacle case on Bertha's desk.

"What's this?" he asked curiously.

Bertha made the mistake of grabbing for it. Sergeant Sellers's big hand clamped down on her wrists. He took the spectacle case from her fingers.

In a frenzy of rage and consternation, Bertha Cool came around the desk at him, but before she could reach him Sellers had the spectacle case open.

The removable bridge gleamed white and gold against the spectacle case.

"I'll be damned!" Sergeant Sellers said softly, almost in a whisper.

Belder, staring at the spectacle case, screamed, "By God, you can't do that to me! I'm being framed! I knew that Mrs. Goldring and Carlotta had been to see her, but I didn't know she'd give me that kind of a double-cross. I tell you I don't know anything about that."

"I," Sellers announced again, in a solemn tone, "will be doubly damned." He looked up at Bertha. "Where did this come from, Bertha?"

Bertha started to say something, then changed her mind and clamped her lips tightly together.

"Go on," Sellers said.

Bertha said, "You give me that five minutes and then I'll talk."

Sellers's grin was cold and mirthless. "Not now you don't get any five minutes, Bertha. You're finished."

"And don't leave me alone with her for a minute," Belder all but screamed. "The dirty double-crosser. She's framing me."

Sellers walked over to Bertha Cool's telephone, dialed Police Headquarters, said into the telephone, "Sergeant Sellers. I'm at the offices of Cool & Lam, Private Detectives. Everett Belder is here. I'm taking him into custody. Bertha Cool is here. I'm not taking her into custody—yet. I'm going to take Belder down to headquarters. When I come back I want to talk with Bertha Cool. Rush a man over here to stay with her until I get back. I want to be sure she's here to answer questions when I get ready to ask them."

Sellers dropped the receiver back into place. His hand moved back to his belt, brought out jangling handcuffs.

Belder said in dismay, "You mean you are going to use those?"

Sellers wasn't grinning now. "You're damned right," he said. "And if *you* think you're better than any other murderer, *I* don't."

21

BODYGUARD WITH BOTTLE

Hours circled across the dial of Bertha Cool's electric clock and into oblivion. The bodyguard whom Sergeant Sellers had placed in charge had proved himself to be a singularly taciturn individual, a huge man who spent hours reading the paper, manicuring his nails, and silently smoking, a distinctly non-social individual who seemed utterly bored by the entire affair.

Bertha Cool had tried him out during the afternoon on several lines of attack, and each time the man had an answer which stopped Bertha in her tracks.

First Bertha had demanded the right to consult an attorney. "I don't think you have any right to pull such a high-handed course as this," she said, "and I'm going to telephone my lawyer."

"Go ahead."

"You don't have any objection?"

"The Sergeant says that if you want to make it legal, then we'll make it legal."

"What do you mean?"

"We'll take you down to headquarters, charge you with being an accessory after the fact, and book you. Then you can see all the lawyers you want."

"But you can't hold me in my office this way.".

"That's right."

"I've got a right to leave any time. You can't stop me."

"That's right."

"Then what's to stop me from walking out of that door?"

"Nothing."

"All right, then, I'm going to do it."

"Only," the man said, "the Sarge left definite orders. The minute you stick your foot through that door, I'm to arrest you, take you down to headquarters, and book you."

"What," Bertha demanded indignantly, "is the idea?"

"The Sarge is trying to protect you, that's all. Once he arrests you, your name gets in the newspapers, and your reputation as a detective is smeared. The Sarge is trying to give you a break."

"How long do I have to stay here like this?"

"Until the Sarge says different."

"And when will that be?"

"When he cleans up this angle of the case he's working on now."

Twice Bertha announced truculently that she was going to the washroom. Her bodyguard silently acquiesced, plodded along behind her, took up his station in the corridor from which he could watch the door of the ladies' room, and waited until Bertha Cool emerged. Whereupon he escorted her back to the office.

Bertha did some office work, scribbled a few personal letters, and tried her best to make it appear that she wasn't scared stiff.

About six o'clock the officer telephoned a restaurant in the neighborhood, explained the circumstances, and the restaurant sent up sandwiches and coffee.

"One hell of a way to eat dinner," Bertha growled belligerently as she pushed back the empty plate and drained the last of the lukewarm coffee from the pottery coffee pot.

She couldn't get an argument with her guard over that. He said, "Isn't it? I don't like it either."

At seven o'clock the telephone rang.

"I'll answer it," the officer said. He picked up the receiver and said, "Hello. . . . Yeah. . . . Okay, Sarge, I get you. . . . uh huh. How soon? . . . Okay, good-by."

He hung up the receiver.

Bertha tried to make her expression hopeful but had to fight back panic in her eyes.

"No dice yet," her bodyguard said. "The guy won't confess. The Sarge says I'm to stay on here for an hour or so.

If something doesn't happen by that time, we'll have to take you down to headquarters and book you. Sorry, we tried to give you the breaks."

"The breaks!" Bertha snorted with sarcastic emphasis.

"That's what I said."

"I heard you the first time."

"You just heard the words. You didn't get the idea."

The situation remained static for another half hour and then the man began to grow more communicative. "Saturday afternoon," he said. "I was due to have a half day off. This isn't any treat for me. I been taking a cold all day, too."

"As far as I'm concerned you can go now," Bertha told him.

He grinned, said abruptly. "This man Belder seems to have cut a pretty wide swath."

Bertha didn't say anything.

"That last letter sure gave the Sarge a kick. I'll bet it was a load off *your* mind."

Bertha picked up a pencil and started making aimless lines on a scratch pad, giving her an excuse to lower her eyes so he might not read the expression in them. "You mean that third letter?" she asked.

"Uh huh. The one that dragged Imogene Dearborne into the mess."

Bertha said, "That little—estimable young thing. I only had a chance to glance at the letter before Sergeant Sellers took it."

"Called the turn on her, all right," the officer said.

"She's suing me for a hundred grand. The little twir—estimable young lady."

The officer threw back his head and laughed. "What the hell makes her so estimable?"

"My lawyer says she's estimable."

"I get you."

Bertha said, "As I remember that last letter, it was just a little ambiguous. It didn't offer anything you could use as definite proof."

"Registration at a hotel," the officer said. "I don't know what more you'd want— Say, it's cold here. I'm feeling chilly."

"They shut the heat off Saturday afternoons."

"Cripes, I wish I had a drink."

Bertha made rapid little triangles on the scratch pad. "I've got a bottle in the cloak closet," she observed.

"I'm not supposed to touch the stuff when I'm on duty," he said, and then added in a burst of confidence, "That's my weakness. I can lay off the stuff for months at a time, just take a drink or two and leave it alone, or get along without touching it altogether. Then something snaps. I get started drinking and the more I drink the more I want. I get so I just *have* to have it. That's what's holding me back on a promotion. If it weren't for a couple of binges I've been on, I'd be sitting pretty right today."

Bertha kept her eyes on her moving pencil point. "I never touch the stuff myself unless I'm real tired, or feel that I'm catching cold. I think it's a lot better to have a couple of drinks than to get laid up with a cold. A cold raises hell with me."

"It does with me too. Say, if you've got a bottle here, bring it out. You look like a good scout. I guess I can trust you not to say anything about it."

Bertha brought out the bottle and a couple of glasses. The officer tossed off his drink, licked his chops, and looked hungrily at the bottle. Bertha poured him another one. That went the way of the first.

"That's good hooch," he complimented her.

"The best money can buy," Bertha agreed.

"Lady, you saved my life. I was just beginning to get a chill."

"Probably the flu coming on. Go right ahead, help yourself. That bottle was given to me by a client."

The officer looked longingly at the bottle. "Nope," he said ruefully, "I don't drink alone. I haven't got that low yet."

"I'm drinking with you."

"You're still nursing that first drink."

Bertha tossed off the whisky, poured two more glasses.

Under the influence of the liquor her bodyguard became loquacious and human. His name, it appeared, was Jack. He felt certain that the Sarge was trying to give Bertha the breaks; that Bertha was in bad, but that the Sarge was working, trying to get her out. She'd helped him on that Bat murder case, and the Sarge wasn't one to forget favors. But Bertha certainly was in bad. Everything depended upon what happened when Belder came clean. If he exonerated Bertha that would be good enough for the Sarge.

Bertha wanted to know if Belder was softening up any.

"I think he is," Jack told her. "The Sarge couldn't tell me much over the telephone, but he said that he was making headway. He said he was hoping he could turn you loose before midnight."

"Midnight's a hell of a long ways off," Bertha said.

"If he has to book you, it'll be a lot of midnights before you're back on the job," Jack warned, and then added hastily, "There, there, now, don't get worked up over it, Bertha. I didn't mean it exactly that way. Don't worry. The Sarge will get you out all right. The Sarge is strong for you. You know that."

Bertha poured another drink.

Another twenty minutes and Jack had gravitated into the position of custodian of the whisky bottle. He had apparently forgotten his earlier compunctions about having Bertha keep up with him on the drinks. He would fill her glass, and then splash liquor into his own. By taking only a few sips at a time, Bertha managed to consume about one-third of the whisky the plain-clothes officer was drinking.

"Wish I could sit and sip it that way," he confided. "I can't. I have to toss it off—down the old hatch—that's me! Can't do anything in moderation. You know, Bertha, you're a good egg. No wonder the Sarge likes you. Guess they must have turned the heat back on, didn't they? I thought it was cold here, but it's warm now, getting hot. Kinda close here, don't you think?"

"Just about right for me," Bertha said, her eyes out from behind her mask now, watching the flushed face, the watery eyes, of the officer in the chair across the desk from her. Jack pushed his big hands down into his trousers pockets, slid down in the chair, stretched his long legs out in front of him, and crossed his ankles.

"You have to work nights?" Bertha asked.

"Uh huh."

"Don't you have a hard time sleeping when you're working nights?"

"Oh, you get used to it." Jack lowered his eyelids. "Worst of it is that it gets your eyes after a while—the lights hurt. Close 'em once in a while and rest 'em—does 'em good. Doctor says there's nothing like giving your eyes a rest once'n while."

Bertha watched him with the intent speculation of a cat concealed in the shadows watching a bird hopping around in the near-by sunlight.

Jack's head nodded a couple of times, jerked forward, then snapped back and his eyes popped open with instant wakefulness.

Bertha picked up the pencil and started on her triangles. She was, she realized, having some trouble getting the lines of the triangles to meet. There was a roaring in her ears, and when she turned her head quickly, the room had a tendency to keep on spinning for a moment after she brought her head to a rest; but her mind was perfectly clear.

"Did Sellers arrest Imogene Dearborne?" she asked.

"I don't think so. Why?"

"In order to pull the job, Belder needed some feminine accomplice. He needed someone to telephone his wife and get her to go down to that garage. If he was playing around with that Dearborne girl, my best guess is she's the one we want."

"Say!" Jack exclaimed with alcoholic enthusiasm, "thaa'sh a hell of a swell idea!"

"And I bet that little bitch wrote the—that estimable little bitch wrote the letters after all."

Jack peered at her owlishly. "Why should she write a letter acushing herself?" he asked.

Bertha had a flash of inspiration. "To divert suspicion from herself, of course. She knew that Mrs. Belder was dead before that letter was mailed. She also knew that things hadn't worked quite as smoothly as she had anticipated, and she was smart enough to know that a letter of that sort would divert suspicion of the murder from her. She'd rather be Everett Belder's mistress than his accomplice—in the eyes of the police."

"Shay, you've got sump'n there." Jack lumbered over to the telephone. "Going to call the Sarge on that. Let'sh shee—what'sh his number? Gotta think."

Jack placed his head on his hand, his elbow on the desk, closed his eyes the better to concentrate.

A few seconds later Bertha saw the big shoulders sag, the arm stretch out flat on the desk. Jack brushed the telephone to one side as though it had been an annoying obstacle. His head sagged to his arm, then after several anxious seconds, a gentle snore sounded through the whisky-steeped atmosphere of the office.

Bertha eased gently back in the swivel chair so that it wouldn't creak. She got to her feet, swaying slightly. She gripped the edge of the desk to steady herself, and tiptoeing cautiously, reached the door to the entrance office. Jack moved restlessly, muttering something unintelligible under his breath, his tongue thick with alcohol.

Bertha noiselessly opened the door, inched her way through, and then carefully turned back the knob so that there would be no telltale click of the latch.

It was dark now, but there was enough light to enable Bertha to walk across the length of the reception room without stumbling over anything. She groped for the knob of the outer door, found it, and made certain that the night latch was on before tiptoeing out into the corridor.

22

THE PERILS OF HOUSEBREAKING

EVERETT BELDER'S HOUSE was a typical southern California Monterey bungalow with a built-in garage. There were grounds which in a less outlying district would have been considered unusually spacious.

Bertha slowed her car to a crawl and sized up the situation. Back of her was a hectic half hour of wild driving, an attempt to shake any shadows who might have been trying to trail her. Not that she had any reason to believe she was being followed, but she simply proposed to make certain no one could "put the finger" on her.

Belder's house was dark, but Bertha couldn't be certain it was unoccupied at the moment. She drove her car halfway to the corner, switched out the lights, locked both the ignition and the doors, and dropped the keys into her purse. She walked slowly back along the sidewalk, climbed the stairs to the cement stoop of the Belder house, and pressed the bell button. She waited fifteen seconds, pressed again—this time longer.

When she heard no sound of motion from the interior of the house, she tried the front door, found it locked, and walked around toward the back of the house. The built-in garage, set back some twenty feet, was on the west side of the house. The walk which led around to the back door skirted the house to the east.

Bertha followed this walk, noticing the half windows which gave light and ventilation to the basement where the body of Sally Brentner had been found. Circling the house, Bertha tried windows and doors, finding that everything was locked.

She returned to the front of the house and tried the garage door. It too was locked.

Bertha, far from the end of her resources, climbed the stoop once more and opened the lacquered mailbox, probing inside with eager fingers.

Her fingertips encountered a key.

Bertha removed the key and inserted it in the lock of the front door. It clicked back the nightlatch. She dropped the key back into the mailbox, snapped the box shut, and entered the house, closing the door behind her, listening to the spring lock click shut.

Mindful of the rule of the housebreaking profession, that the most essential thing in entering a house is to arrange for a getaway, Bertha took a small fountain-pen flashlight from her purse, and, using it to guide her, padded her way through a living-room, dining-room, serving-pantry, and kitchen. She found a key on the inside of the back door. Unlocking the back door with this key, Bertha started an appraisal of the premises.

A disquieting aura hung over the entire house. Bertha Cool always claimed that she could tell something about the people who had lived in a house simply from entering a place and walking through it. Now she couldn't tell whether she was feeling vibrations which, by some unexplained physical laws, were thrown out from the walls of the house as psychic echoes of the personalities that tenanted the place, or whether a knowledge of the discord which had existed between Belder and his wife, of the hatred which Carlotta and Mrs. Goldring held for Belder, plus the knowledge that Sally Brentner had been murdered somewhere on the premises, had excited her imagination so that she saw her surroundings in the light of what had happened.

She was only conscious of the feeling that here was a house of jangling personalities, a house which had lent itself to murder, and which seemed now to be brooding and expectant—waiting only for another murder to be committed.

Big and strong as she was, Bertha had a hard time shaking off the presentiment of impending evil. *Snap out of it, you big boob,* she muttered angrily to herself. *Nothing's going to happen here. You're in bad. If you don't turn up some evi-*

dence that will square things with Sergeant Sellers, you're going to jail.

She completed her tour of inspection of the east rooms of the house, opened a door and found herself in a long corridor from which several doors opened. The one on the right led down another passage, a back bedroom on one side—on the other, a door leading into the rear of the garage. Bertha sniffed the musty odor of the dank interior. The beam of her flashlight was swallowed up in the dark loneliness of the big double garage. A workbench ran along one wall. There was the usual assortment of discarded junk; also an overflow of objects to which the house could apparently give no adequate room—an old wardrobe trunk, a man's wool coat, a pair of grease-stained overalls, a couple of boxes, a litter of old spark plugs, odds and ends of wires, a dilapidated tire cover.

Bertha backed out, closing the door to the garage, and started exploring other doors in the corridor. The next door opened into a bedroom which Bertha assumed was Carlotta's. Pictures of three or four young men adorned the dresser. There was a smell of cosmetics about the room. The adjoining bath held bathroom floor scales, a glass shelf devoted to bath salts and toilet accessories.

Bertha tried the next door and found what she wanted. Here were two bedrooms at the front of the house, finished in knotty pine, connected by a bathroom. The front room was evidently Everett Belder's. The one in back undoubtedly had been used by his wife.

Bertha gave the room itself only a hasty inspection, going almost at once to the closet, taking an inventory of the clothing, searching for some significant clue which would loom large in the eyes of a woman, but would escape the masculine analysis of the detectives.

As Sergeant Sellers had so aptly pointed out the first time, everything about the case pointed to a man: Sally Brentner apparently peeling potatoes with a ten-inch carving-knife. Mabel Belder presumably fleeing from the scene of a murder she had just committed, yet leaving behind a whole closetful of fine clothes, taking only a small assortment of plain garments with her, even leaving her cosmetics behind. Whoever had removed the things which had been taken, however, must have left some clue somewhere. Perhaps in the house itself was concealed the suitcase in which Mabel Belder's things had been packed, stored, and concealed.

Bertha prowled into the back recess of the closet, the beam of her flashlight penetrating the dark corners. She frowned down at several small particles on the floor, then bent down and picked up some of these in her thumb and forefinger. Bits of wood twisted into tight spirals which had broken and left little curved segments of that yellowish appearance which is typical of freshly cut wood.

Beyond doubt these bits of wood had been turned out by an auger from a pine board. Bertha could almost tell the diameter of that auger from the shape of the tightly compressed bits of wood.

But there was no hole.

Bertha made it a point to cover every inch of that closet with her flashlight; no slightest sign of a hole anywhere in the walls, floors, or ceiling.

Forgetful for the moment of her surroundings, Bertha deliberated over her discovery.

"Damn it," she muttered, "if Donald were only here, he'd find a way out of this mess. Brainy little devil! I'm in awfully bad. Only way to get out is to find something. What the hell are these shavings doing in the corner of the closet? Somebody bored a hole and then made the hole disappear. No chance that the hole's been cunningly plugged up—or is there?"

Bertha once more brought her flashlight into action. On her hands and knees she again studied every inch of the closet floor and walls.

So engrossed was she in her task that she forgot her surroundings, so that the sudden slamming of a door somewhere in the house was as terrifying as the repercussion of a revolver shot.

Snatched back to the circumstances of the moment and the peculiar position in which she had placed herself, Bertha crouched on the closet floor listening.

Plainly she could hear steps, the distant subdued sound of feminine voices—then silence.

Bertha debated the possibilities of escaping through the

back door. She tiptoed out of the closet, stood in the bedroom, listening. She could hear the voices more plainly now. The person who had entered the house had gone out to the kitchen. She heard the sound of a plate being scraped along the edge of another plate and the slamming of a cupboard door.

In all probability Carlotta and Mrs. Goldring had returned to the house and were getting a snack in the kitchen.

Bertha, forced to dismiss the back door as a means of escape, thought of the possibilities of the front door, but realized the dangers of moving the length of the corridor. Then she thought of the garage and the passageway on the side of the maid's bedroom that led to the garage. She decided to try it.

Bertha slipped her shoes off, put them under her arm, cautiously crossed the bedroom, stepped out into the corridor. She could hear the dishes and voices much more plainly now, and heard, equally plainly, the impatient "meow" of a cat.

So that was it. They were feeding the cat.

Bertha heard the sound of an icebox door opening and closing, then Carlotta's voice, sounding very plain, saying, "I tell you, Mother, they're going to convict Everett Belder of those murders. And I'm glad of it. They can count on my help. Hanging is too good for that man."

Bertha listened for a reply and could hear none.

She was feeling her way along close to the wall now, trying to avoid any creaking boards. To be caught in that corridor would add a fatal complication to the predicament in which Bertha found herself—a predicament in which all avenues of escape were being closed to her.

Carlotta said, "I'm not too keen about cats myself. I'm going to get rid of this one. He always did hate me. I'm going to get some hand lotion. I get smelly handling him."

Abruptly, and before Bertha realized the full impact of the remark, the knob on the door turned and a wedge of light from the kitchen shot into the back corridor.

Bertha shifted her flashlight over to the left hand which held her shoes, doubled her right into a business-like fist. But Carlotta didn't go after the hand lotion immediately. She apparently changed her mind, and Bertha heard her move back away from the door. Through the half-opened door, Bertha could hear the steady lap-lap-lap of the cat's tongue as it drank up the milk Carlotta had poured into its saucer.

There was no time for caution now. Bertha moved swiftly along the corridor, heedless of creaking boards, down the passage to the garage. She opened the door and heaved a sigh of relief as the musty darkness enveloped her.

She sat down on a tool chest to put on her shoes. Sheer nervousness made her hand tremble slightly. She switched out the flashlight and put on her shoes in the dark, angry with herself because of that nervous tremor which shook her hands.

Bertha got her shoes on, took a couple of steps across the cement toward the garage door, and suddenly halted. The front corner of the garage showed a peculiarly weird illlumination. A light seemed to be coming from behind a copper-covered gasket which hung from the wall on a nail. Bertha gently removed this gasket and found a neat hole approximately an inch in diameter.

Through this hole light was coming, but Bertha, applying her eye, could see nothing save a vague obstacle in front of the hole.

For the moment, Bertha forgot all risk of discovery. The detective in her came to the forefront. Evidently someone had used the garage for the purpose of spying on the interior of the house. That light would be at just about Mabel Belder's bedroom. Bertha picked up a screwdriver from the workbench, inserted it through the hole. The bit of the screwdriver encountered an obstacle on the other side. Bertha pushed against it tentatively and realized that it was a picture hung on the wall of Mrs. Belder's bedroom so that it effectively concealed the hole from that side. If she could push that picture to one side, she would have an unobstructed view of the bedroom. Someone must have utilized this as a means of spying on Mrs. Belder. Therefore, it should be possible to move the picture easily to one side and then in case there was any danger of discovery, let it drop back into position.

Bertha tentatively pushed at the picture and shoved the

long bit of the screwdriver gently to one side. The picture moved, then slid back across the edge of the screwdriver. Bertha heard the sound of a door opening and closing, low voices, a surreptitious whispering.

Bertha's curiosity could stand it no longer. She boldly twisted the screwdriver, put it in the hole at as sharp an angle as she could manage, and using the side of the hole as a fulcrum, pried the picture back and to one side.

She could see a portion of the interior of Mrs. Belder's bedroom, could see Carlotta sitting in front of a dressing-table, rubbing lotion on her hands, regarding herself in the mirror with the critical appraisal which a woman reserves for her more intimate and cynical moments.

Fascinated, Bertha watched as Carlotta opened a drawer in the dressing-table, groped inside. The mirror reflected the expression on her face. Her eyes held the glittering triumph of one who is about to execute a clever coup.

Carlotta reached for the telephone, twisted the dial three quick times and said, "Information, will you give me the number of George K. Nunnely's residence. I don't know the address." There was a pause. "Thank you."

She hung up. Bertha saw her fingers flying over the dial of the telephone with the quick precision of one whose hands have developed smooth dexterity, heard her say, "Hello . . . Hello, is this Mr. Nunnely? . . . Mr. Nunnely, I have never met you, but this is Carlotta Goldring. I'm Mrs. Belder's sister. . . . That's right. . . . I've uncovered some very peculiar evidence, Mr. Nunnely. I thought you might like to talk it over with me. It's about Mabel's murder. I said *murder*, Mr. Nunnely. . . . You, who were desperately in need of money, seem to be in a position to profit very handsomely from my sister's death. You—"

Bertha saw Carlotta's eyes in the mirror, saw them raise slightly as Carlotta, seeming very certain of herself now, shifted into a more comfortable position. Bertha saw the widening horror in those eyes, and for a moment couldn't imagine what was causing it. Then suddenly, in a flash of sickening realization, she understood. In the mirror Carlotta could see that the picture was held far off to one side by Bertha's screwdriver. Bertha cursed herself for a fool for failing to realize how quickly a picture hung on a long wire, and being pushed to one side of the perpendicular, would attract attention.

"Mother!" Carlotta screamed.

Bertha hastily let go of the screwdriver, heard it clatter to the floor of the bedroom. The picture slid along the wall on the other side into a perpendicular position. Bertha turned—

It seemed that a shower of meteors struck her on the head with a terrific blow, then the meteors exploded in all directions, sending out blinding streamers of light. Something cold smacked Bertha on the cheek and stayed there. Vaguely, from some distant and detached part of Bertha's mind, came the realization that this cold surface was the garage floor.

23 THE HOLE IN THE WALL

BERTHA BECAME CONSCIOUS of voices, voices making sounds which her tortured brain laboriously tried to interpret into something with meaning. Lying back with her eyes closed and an interminable aching in her head, Bertha wondered, in a detached way, why a series of *r* sounds such as *murderer* should mean someone had killed someone else.

And abruptly, as though her cogitation had removed an obstruction somewhere in her mind, consciousness came pouring back in a flood.

Bertha's eyes popped open, and as quickly snapped shut. Sergeant Sellers, looking exceedingly grave, was talking with Carlotta and Mrs. Goldring. Evidently he had just arrived on the scene, and Bertha, fully conscious despite the aching in her head, decided to hide behind her injuries, stalling off the evil hour when she would have to make an explanation to the officer.

Carlotta's voice was rapid with excitement, ". . . fixing my hair and I saw this picture all skewgee on the wall. It had been pushed way over to one side. Well, Sergeant, you know how anything like that will attract your attention. I raised my eyes to it and then saw this thing sticking through the wall. I thought at first it was a gun, and I could see a gleam of someone's eye. I screamed for Mother. And almost at the exact moment I screamed, this screwdriver thudded to the floor. I saw it was a screwdriver then, and the picture swung back into position.

"Mother was in the kitchen feeding Mabel's cat. She came

running in to see what was the matter and she thought I'd gone crazy. Of course the picture had swung back into position just as soon as the screwdriver had been dropped."

Mrs. Goldring interjected, "No, darling, not crazy, but I thought something terrible had happened. You have no idea how you looked. Your face was as white as a sheet and you were staring at that screwdriver that had fallen to the floor. You looked as though it were a poisonous snake about to bite you."

"Well, anyway," Carlotta resumed, "I screamed to Mother to run to the garage quick; that someone was out there. And we both of us ran through the passageway. Mother was first. She was the one who saw this man. He was bending over Mrs. Cool—only, of course, we didn't know at the time it was Mrs. Cool. He had a club in his hand—something white. It looked like a piece of pipe wrapped in some heavy paper. But at first I thought it was a long knife wrapped up in the paper."

"And what did he do?" Sergeant Sellers asked. *"Exactly* what did he do?"

"He looked up, saw us, and came running at us brandishing this weapon."

"Did you get a look at his face?"

"No. It was dark in the garage. You know, sort of half dark. You could see only figures. I could tell you the way he was built, but I didn't get to see his face, and Mother didn't either."

"Tall and slender or—"

"No. He was of medium height, and somehow I had the impression that he was very well dressed, and a gentleman, although I don't know what made me think so. Perhaps it was just the way his clothes fitted him, or perhaps the way he moved, the sort of easy grace that men have when they're customarily well dressed and know it. That sounds terribly silly when I hear myself saying it."

"No," Sellers said thoughtfully. "You may have something there. Go ahead, what happened?"

"Well, that's about all. He ran past us. Mother tried to stop him and he hit her."

"Right in the stomach," Mrs. Goldring said indignantly.

"*I* don't agree with Carlotta. I don't think he was a gentleman. A gentleman wouldn't hit a woman."

"With his fist?" Sellers asked.

"No," Mrs. Goldring said indignantly. "He poked me with the end of the piece of pipe, or whatever it was."

"And then what?"

Carlotta said, "Then he ran through the passageway into the house. I was afraid Mother was badly hurt. I thought he'd stabbed her. You see, I thought it was a knife. I kept asking Mother if she was badly hurt, and then we heard the slam of the back door."

"Did you run to the back of the house?"

"I'm afraid," Mrs. Goldring said, "we were more angry than prudent. We dashed to the back of the house. He'd gone through the kitchen, all right. Whiskers, the cat, was up on the table, his eyes big and round, and his tail fluffed out so it looked as big as a toy balloon."

"The cat usually act that way with strangers?"

"No. The cat is usually very affectionate," Mrs. Goldring said. "I know that I told Carlotta afterward that it was just as if this cat knew this man—or had had some disagreeable experience. Perhaps this man had tried to catch it or something, and the cat was afraid of him. You could see the cat was definitely afraid, terrified. It was big-eyed with fright."

"Just as though the man had been a big dog chasing him," Carlotta said.

"Now, let's get this straight," Sellers said. "You called out 'Mother,' and immediately Mrs. Cool dropped the screwdriver and the picture slid back into place. Is that right?"

"That's right. And almost at once I heard a sound from the garage as though something had fallen. I didn't pay any particular attention to that at the moment because I was so thoroughly terrified thinking that it was a revolver that was being poked through the garage at me. It was terrible of her to frighten me that way."

"I see. And then after you had chased this man through the back door, you came back and found that Mrs. Cool wasn't dead, only unconscious, and then is when you telephoned for the police. Is that right?"

"That's right."

"And told them there was a prowler about the place?"

"Yes."

"You should have reported it as an assault case and you'd have got quicker action," Sellers rebuked mildly.

"I'm afraid we were terribly excited—and helpless. It's an all-gone feeling when two women are alone in a house."

"I know how you must have felt," Sellers said.

Bertha, lying on the bed with her eyes closed, reflected that Carlotta had very carefully avoided making any reference whatever to her telephone conversation with Nunnely.

Mrs. Goldring said, "I suppose that detectives all work that way, going around boring holes through people's walls so they can see what's going on, but I think it's—"

Sergeant Sellers interjected, "I'm not too certain she bored that hole."

"She must have. It was just at the right height for her eyes. She could look right in and see what was happening."

Sellers said, "It took time and tools to bore that hole. There's an insulated fire wall between the garage and the house. Of course, the height of the hole might tell us something about the height of the person who bored it, but then the height of the hole may have been determined by the necessity of boring it behind that picture. I think that's the real explanation for the position."

"How interesting! Well, anyway, that's what happened. Now how about Mrs. Cool? Do you think we should undress her? Carlotta and I could get her clothes off. And how about a doctor?"

"I'm going to telephone for a doctor," Sellers said, "but I want to make a superficial examination first. Can she stay here for a day or two if the doctor thinks she shouldn't be moved?"

"Why certainly. Of course, it would be a little inconvenient now that we have no maid, but we'd be glad to have her. We like her, but we're afraid she doesn't like us. The last time we talked with her we wanted her to be a witness for us and she was rather crusty about it. She seemed to think we should pay her."

"She would," Sellers said. "All right, you folks go talk to the officer who's in the garage and tell him to look for fingerprints on the back door, and don't touch that back doorknob. Don't go near the back door. In fact, don't touch anything in that part of the house."

Bertha, lying with her eyes closed, heard the rustle of motion, the gentle closing of a door. Sellers said, "How you feeling, Bertha, the head aching?"

Bertha, sensing the trap, kept her features motionless, lay perfectly still. Sellers sat down on the edge of the bed. "Come on, Bertha, snap out of it! You've got to face it sometime, you may as well do it now."

Bertha made no motion.

"I'm not a damned fool," Sergeant Sellers went on, a trace of irritation in his voice. "I kept watching your face in the mirror. I saw when your eyelids fluttered and then snapped open, saw you take in the situation and promptly close your eyes again."

Bertha said, "Damn it. Doesn't a woman have *any* privacy?"

She opened her eyes, raised her hand to her head, felt something sticky on her hair. "Blood?" she asked.

Sellers grinned. "Oil and grease off the garage floor. You're a mess."

Bertha looked around. She was in the maid's bedroom, stretched out on the top of the bed. She struggled to a sitting position. For a moment the room spun around in a complete circle, then straightened itself.

"How do you feel?" Sellers asked.

"Like hell. How do I look?"

Sellers pointed to a bureau mirror. By turning her head, Bertha was able to catch a glimpse of herself. Her hair, sticky with oil, was plastered down on her head. There was a smear of grease along her right cheek. Her eyes were dead and dopey. "My God!" Bertha said.

"Exactly."

Bertha faced him. "All right, what's the score?"

Sellers became grave. "I'm sorry, Bertha, this is the end of the road as far as you're concerned."

"How come?"

"I knew you were holding out on me," Sellers said. "I didn't know just what or just how much. I couldn't crack

Belder; that meant I had to turn my attention to you. I thought I might have some difficulty giving you a third degree so I rang up the officer I'd left in charge, told him to promote a drink or two from you, tell you he was a habitual drunkard, get properly stewed, and see what you did. I made arrangements to have you followed when you left the office."

"Damn you," Bertha said, "do you mean to say that I poured my good whisky down that cop's throat and—" Bertha sputtered herself into indignant silence.

A smile twitched Sergeant Sellers's mouth, "Exactly, Bertha."

"Why damn you. That was customers' whisky. I keep it for my best clients."

"That's what Jack said. Said it was the first break I'd ever given him in ten years."

Bertha sought for words. While she was groping for the proper epithets, Sellers went on. "I had a couple of men out in front of the place so they could follow you when you left." His face darkened. "Damned if you didn't lose them. Those are a couple of boys that are going back to pavement-pounding."

Bertha said, "They were damned slick. I didn't know they were on my trail. I just took precautions."

"I'll say you took precautions! They said you went around like a flea on a hot stove until you finally ditched them. All right, then you came here. What happened?"

Bertha said, "You won't believe me if I tell you."

"I think I will," Sellers said. "*I* don't think you bored that hole. And what's more, *I* think the hole was bored from the bedroom through to the garage. If you'd bored it, you'd have bored it from the garage through to the bedroom—"

Sergeant Sellers broke off as a doorbell sounded, listened to the faint sounds of excited feminine voices, then he went on patiently, "Now, Bertha, you've got to give me the lowdown about Mrs. Belder's removable bridge—and how it came into your possession. That was one of the things we couldn't understand. When we made a post-mortem on the body we found a removable bridge was missing. That wasn't a particularly significant fact, it was simply a pertinent fact. But when we find that bridge in your office in Mrs. Belder's spectacle case, that's something else. Now we want to know *where you got that bridge*."

"Suppose I don't tell you?"

"That's going to be tough on you, Bertha. You're mixed up in a murder case. If you get some significant evidence and don't tell us, you're out of luck."

"And suppose I do tell you?"

Sellers said, "That's the tough part of it; you're out of luck anyway, Bertha. You can't go around holding out evidence on the police. You've been doing that too much lately. Donald Lam does it and manages to get away with it, but he's crowding his luck all the time. Eventually he'll come a cropper. But when you tried to use his tactics you stubbed your toe and fell flat on your face. And that's where you are right now."

Bertha said grimly, "All right, if I'm going to lose my license whether I keep my mouth shut or whether I talk, I'll keep my mouth shut."

"The point I didn't explain," Sellers went on dryly, "is that if you tell us, you'll lose your license, but if the explanation is okay, you'll keep your freedom. If you don't tell us you'll go to jail as an accomplice."

Bertha said, "I think I may have something on that bridge, and I want to play it my way."

Sellers said, "*I* think you have something, Bertha, and *I* want to play it *my* way."

Abruptly the door to the bedroom opened. Mrs. Goldring, on the threshold, said to Sergeant Sellers, "I hope we're not interrupting, and I hope the patient is all right, but we're *so* happy—Carlotta has found her *real* mother. I want to present her. Mrs. Croftus, this is Sergeant Sellers—and," she added hastily, "Mrs. Cool."

"How do you do, Sergeant Sellers. And Mrs. Cool I think I've met before. I'm sorry to learn that you're indisposed, Mrs. Cool."

Mrs. Croftus seemed very poised, very certain of herself. Bertha, sitting on the edge of the bed, her oily hair plastered to one side of her face, blinked at Mrs. Croftus. "Do I understand *you* located her?" she asked Carlotta.

"No," Mrs. Goldring said, "Mrs. Croftus has been trying

to find her daughter for some time. She had released her for adoption years ago, then when this case came up, she read about it in the newspaper and certain things that the newspaper said convinced her that Carlotta was her daughter. She came to the door and rang the bell. *I* recognized her instantly. You see, I had met her years ago. Well, after all, there's no reason why Carlotta shouldn't have *two* mothers—" And Mrs. Goldring beamed at Bertha Cool and Sergeant Sellers inclusively.

Bertha suddenly whirled to Carlotta. "Why didn't you tell Sergeant Sellers about your telephone conversation to Mr. Nunnely?" she demanded.

"Because it has nothing to do with the case," Carlotta said with dignity. "I merely wanted to get in touch with Mr. Nunnely and see if his judgment against Everett Belder couldn't be settled on a reasonable basis. I don't know what *that* has to do with what happened in the garage, Mrs. Cool."

Mrs. Croftus said, "Dear me! I seem to have picked a most inopportune time for my visit! I'm so sorry to intrude, but—"

"I thought Sergeant Sellers would like to be advised of the latest development," Mrs. Goldring said, and simpered at the Sergeant.

Sellers nodded. "Not that I see that it makes much difference, but—"

"Fry me for an oyster!" Bertha ejaculated suddenly, heaving herself up off the bed and getting to her feet.

"What is it?" Mrs. Goldring asked solicitously.

"What is it!" Bertha said. "I'll show you what it is."

She walked over to the door, slammed it shut, turned the key in the lock.

"May I ask the meaning of this?" Mrs. Croftus demanded.

"You're damned right you can ask the meaning of this," Bertha said, "and I hope you do something about it, dearie. You can sneak up behind me and bang me on the head with a club and get away with it, but you make a move now, and I'll show you what being tough really is. I'll take you apart and see what makes you tick."

Mrs. Goldring said indignantly to Sergeant Sellers, "You represent the law. Are you going to stand by and permit anything like that?"

209

Sergeant Sellers grinned. "I'm certainly not going to do anything to stop it," he announced gleefully.

Carlotta said meaningly, "That blow on her head must have affected her reasoning. You'd think she'd be in enough trouble because of careless statements she's made about people without inviting more trouble for herself."

Bertha Cool glared at Carlotta. "Shut up! You saw that picture moving on the wall a long time before you claimed you did. I heard you having a whispered conversation before I could see into the room. That was when you told your mother to go out and crack my head open; then you were going to concoct this story about the mysterious assailant. And that telephone conversation you had with Nunnely was all faked—just to keep my eyes and ears glued to what was going on in the bedroom. That's why you asked information what his number was—so I'd know whom you were calling and wait right there while your mother—"

Mrs. Goldring said, "I'm going to sue you for that, Mrs. Cool. I have never been so insulted in my life. I—"

"Keep your shirt on," Bertha told her. "Don't start yelling before your toes get stepped on. I said Carlotta's *mother*."

Mrs. Croftus threw back her head and laughed. "Up until five minutes ago," she said, "I haven't seen Carlotta for years and years—not since she was a baby."

Bertha said, "I'm not a whiz at this stuff like Donald Lam, but I don't have to have a ton of bricks fall on me to knock an idea into my head. Mrs. Goldring knew all about you. You knew all about Mrs. Goldring. Mrs. Goldring didn't want Carlotta to have anything to do with you, and she held a club over you that was big enough and heavy enough to keep you in your place. Then all of a sudden everything gets patched up. You wanted it to appear that you just came tripping up the steps and rang the doorbell without any preliminaries. Bah! That's a lousy story. It won't hold water. I don't know whether you approached Carlotta, or whether Carlotta found out about you. Probably Carlotta took the initiative, because *you* were afraid to contact her—on account of the club Mrs. Goldring was holding over you. If I had to make a guess, I'd say that Mrs. Goldring was keeping documentary proof that she could show Carlotta in case she had to. The probabilities are those documents were kept locked in a lock box concealed somewhere in the house, and dear little snooping Carlotta, anxious to find out who her mother was, managed to find that box, then snooped around until she got hold of Mabel's keys and made a wax impression of them. Once she got the box open, she knew who her mother was and went to look her up. A term in the pen wouldn't bother Carlotta as much as her mother was afraid it might, because dear little Carlotta had found out Mrs. Goldring was going broke and that Mabel Belder had made a will leaving all of the property to Everett in case anything should happen to her. Carlotta, the sniveling, hypocritical, spoiled brat, didn't intend to be thrown into the discard quite that easily."

"How you talk," Carlotta said sneeringly. "But don't let me stop you. Get it all out of your system, and *then* we'll see how much of this you can prove."

Bertha glanced at Sergeant Sellers. "How am I doing?"

"Go right ahead, Bertha. You're sticking your neck way out, but keep right on. By the time you get done with *this* session, you'll have enough slander suits to enable you to hire a staff of lawyers by the year. But I'd be a damned liar if I tried to tell you I wasn't enjoying it."

Bertha said, "Carlotta burned up that will."

"In Everett Belder's office grate?" Mrs. Goldring asked sarcastically.

"In Everett Belder's grate," Bertha said. "And I was right there when she did it. And what's more, Frank Sellers, you were standing right there at the time.

"There was a fire burning in the grate. Some other papers were being burned and I had just gone ahead and made my accusation against Imogene Dearborne. It was a hell of a dramatic moment. Everyone was looking at Imogene, and Carlotta came in with this sweet little innocent statement about not being able to find anyone in the outer office so she came right on in. And you remember she sidled around so she was standing with her back to the fireplace. And in the back of my mind there's a memory of the fire in that little grate flaring up just as she stood there."

"By George! You're right on that!" Sellers exclaimed.

"It's a lie!" Carlotta screamed.

ERLE STANLEY GARDNER

Bertha said, "I've got it now. When she found those other papers, she found Mabel's will. It left all the property to her husband. If Mabel died without a will, the property, as her separate property, would go half to the husband and half to her mother. With that will it would *all* go to her husband, and it was, of course, reasonable to suppose Everett Belder knew all about that will. So what does sweet little Carlotta do—although she must have had her mother's help on this little job; she takes the will, tears out the parts that contain the name of Everett Belder so just in case some of the ashes can be reconstructed by a handwriting expert, she won't fall on her face. Then she looks for a chance to plant the will where she can burn it and put the blame on Belder. That's what she's looking for when she walks into the office. And things couldn't have worked out better for her. There was a fire going in the grate and everybody in the room was concentrating on Imogene Dearborne. So dear little Carlotta sidles around with her back to the fire, drops the will in, and then at the proper moment talks about Mabel having made a will leaving everything to her mother, accuses Everett Belder of having burned it up, and calls in a handwriting expert to photograph the ashes in the fireplace. The expert manages to get enough evidence to show that Mabel Belder's will had been the last paper burned in the fireplace. He couldn't get all of the terms of that will. Even if he had, the name of the beneficiary would have been missing, because you can gamble Carlotta didn't take any chances on that.

"Now then, what's wrong with that picture?"

"I am not going to stand here and submit to all of these insults," Carlotta said.

"You don't have to, dear," Mrs. Croftus announced with dignity. "Personally, I think the woman is crazy."

Sergeant Sellers pulled a cigar from his pocket with an air of preoccupation, bit off the top of the cigar, fished a match from his pocket. "I thought she was a little goofy myself," he admitted, "until she pulled that stuff about Carlotta dropping papers in the fireplace. By George, she did! I remember definitely the little fresh puff of flame which came out from behind her. I thought perhaps her skirt was going to catch afire and was thinking what a bad break that would

212

be because it would make a diversion and I wanted to have the cards put on the table while everyone was in the mood for a showdown. What did you drop in the fireplace, Carlotta?"

"Nothing. You're crazy."

Sellers said, "That clinches it. I know you dropped *something*. If you'd had some logical explanation of what it was, it would have been all right, but to swear that you didn't drop a thing is—"

"Oh, I remember now," Carlotta said. "I was reading a letter. A circular I'd received. I had it in my hand when I came in the office and saw the fire going in the fireplace. I'd almost forgotten about it."

Sergeant Sellers grinned at her through the first puffs of the blue cigar smoke. "You walked right into that trap, didn't you, sister? So you *did* drop papers into the fireplace?"

"Yes. But it was this letter. I—"

"Then how do you account for the fact that your handwriting expert says the will was the *last thing burned?* Those ashes were on the very top of the heap."

"I—" Carlotta turned in frantic appeal, not to Mrs. Goldring, but to her mother, Mrs. Croftus.

Mrs. Croftus said with quiet dignity, "I don't think I'd argue the matter with him, darling. It's very plain that he's trying to take the side of this woman, so that we can't sue her for defamation of character. Don't you think we'd all better wait until we've seen a lawyer about suing Mrs. Cool? I know a lawyer who will be glad to handle the case. Let's go and see him right now. He'll file suit against her."

Sergeant Sellers looked at Mrs. Croftus with respect. "That's a damned slick way of smothering an idea with words," he said. "It sounds very nice the way you say it; but, when you strip the verbiage off, what you're actually doing is telling the girl not to say anything more until she's seen a lawyer."

"About bringing a suit for defamation of character," Mrs. Croftus said icily.

"But seeing a lawyer just the same," Sellers insisted.

"Well, what do you want us to do—sit here and take all of these insults?"

"No," Sergeant Sellers announced with slow deliberation. "I want you to go up to the D.A.'s office and make written statements—and I want you to start right now. Is there any objection?"

"Certainly there's an objection. I never heard of such high-handed procedure in my life."

"Well, I should say so!" Mrs. Goldring snapped. "We'll see a lawyer before we——"

Sergeant Sellers frowned at Bertha Cool. "A hell of a way to solve a murder case," he said. "Haven't you anything besides that?"

"The hole in the wall," Bertha said, "was bored from the bedroom into the garage. The picture was hung over the hole from the inside. I took it for granted it was used as a peephole, but there's one other thing it might have been used for."

"What," Sellers asked.

"I'm not like Donald," Bertha apologized, "but——"

"I know, but you're just as inimitable in your sweet way. Go ahead, Bertha, and tell me about the hole in the bedroom wall."

Bertha grinned at him. "I'm not a mechanic, and I'm not built right to get down on my hands and knees, but *you* might take a look at the exhaust pipe on Mrs. Belder's automobile and see if there are any fresh-looking scratches around the end of the exhaust pipe.

"And that cat was switching its tail when the woman I followed came out of the house. Cats don't do that when they're going riding with someone they like. Cats do that when they're angry. And if that was Mrs. Belder I followed, why wasn't the cat asphyxiated too? It would have been shut up in the garage just the same as the woman in the car.

"I tell you she was dead before I ever came out to this house on that shadowing job—and *that's* where the hole in the wall becomes significant. Now, think *that* over!"

Sellers frowned with annoyance. "Damn it, Bertha, you said just enough so *I've* got to start pulling your chestnuts out of the fire for you."

Bertha heaved a sigh. "If you think *that* isn't music to my ears, you're nuts!"

214

24

A LETTER TO DONALD

BERTHA COOL PLUMPED HERSELF triumphantly in the chair across from Elsie Brand's desk. "Well," she announced cheerfully, "here it is Monday morning. The start of a brand-new week."

Elsie Brand nodded.

Bertha said, "Get your notebook, Elsie. Take a letter to Donald. . . . Dear Donald: Bertha has just been mixed up in the *damnedest* case! I certainly did wish you were here to help me. It almost got Bertha down, but she managed to kick through with the winning ticket just when it looked as though the cards were all stacked against her.

"Sergeant Sellers took over after I gave him the key clue to the situation. Well, I guess I may as well begin at the beginning and tell you all about it—

"How am I dictating, Elsie, too fast?"

"No, it's all right," Elsie said. "Go right ahead. Are you going to give him all the details?"

"Yes. I think he'd like them, don't you?"

"I'm certain he would."

"All right. Let's see, where was I? Oh yes, I was telling him about the case. Well, take this down, Elsie. A man by the name of Everett Belder put all of his property in his wife's name. His mother-in-law had an adopted daughter, Carlotta. And Mrs. Belder and the mother-in-law were trying to keep the daughter from finding out who her mother was. Then the mother-in-law, Mrs. Goldring, went broke. She rang up Mabel to get Mabel to help her, and Mabel turned her down cold. Carlotta was a shrewd, scheming little bitch who was

215

book. "I'm up with you on the dictation, Mrs. Cool. Go ahead."

Bertha started to say something, then suddenly checked herself. "And that's enough," she snapped. "We'll leave him something to wonder about so he'll want to come home before his vacation dough runs out. You might put a P.S. on there, that we're sharing in the Belder estate on a percentage basis. . . . No, the hell with it. Just tell him that we're doing all right if the income tax doesn't break us."

And Bertha heaved herself to her feet and started for her private office.

"If any clients come in," she called over her shoulder, "be sure that I see them."

>>> If you've enjoyed this book and would like to discover more great vintage crime and thriller titles, as well as the most exciting crime and thriller authors writing today, visit: >>>

The Murder Room
Where Criminal Minds Meet

themurderroom.com

9 781471 908903